The Paper

A Jewish Jou

A novel by Carole Malkin

1

Albany, California, 1982

"You'll soon forget all the trouble," Lisa said brightly, driving past the mud flats on the Oakland shoreline towards the Bay Bridge.

"Sure, Mom," Karl mumbled without conviction.

Crumpled in the passenger seat, he was grateful she was as reluctant as he to name what he'd done, or to spell out that they'd be separated for the next two years. Nor did she mention--he didn't expect her to--that he was leaving home on what happened to be his sixteenth birthday. August 15, 1982 was the landmark date on which he was old enough to acquire a driver's license. But that wasn't going to happen, not with his mother speeding to the San Francisco airport.

Every mile took him further away from home. Up until now he'd taken for granted his Albany home. Today, longing to be there, he imagined parting the shimmering string of beads strung across the living room doorway and stepping inside. He asked no more than to sink into one of the large pillows strewn on the floor, to gaze up at Lisa's hanging ferns and spider plants, to see her overflowing plank-and-brick bookcases.

Instead, he saw a road sign that announced the airport turnout. An airplane roared overhead. Karl clutched the door handle, wanting to jump out, dodge the trucks and cars on the freeway, and escape home. But he couldn't. Everything had to proceed as the judge had ordered two weeks ago.

In the dim catacombs of the airport's parking lot, Lisa found a space and parked the

Ford. Zombie-like, Karl walked at her side, weighed down by a backpack, and lugging a suitcase of clothes. After a fifteen-minute walk to the international terminal, they joined a long line at the check-in counter.

"Ticket...passport," the airline clerk requested when Karl's turn came. Lisa handed them over. After a cursory study of Karl's documents, the clerk returned them to Lisa, who handed them to Karl. Reluctantly, he plunged them into his backpack. He slid his suitcase onto the scale. There was scarcely time for Karl to note it weighed forty pounds before the clerk thrust it onto a conveyor belt that took it away. In an hour and a half, he'd board his plane and disappear too.

Lisa took his arm and led him away. On the way to the boarding area, she stopped at a coffee shop where she bought coffee and a muffin. After they were seated, she took a tiny candle from her purse, stuck it in the muffin, and lit the wick with a match. Karl was surprised. His absent-minded mother usually didn't remember birthdays. The previous summer, he'd used a mix to bake his own cake and invited three friends to celebrate with him. When Lisa came home and saw the lit candles, she'd asked, "Whose birthday is it?" The other boys burst out laughing, assuming she knew and was joking. The following day, Lisa made it up to him. She bought a giant kite and took him to a windy hill near the Bay where they flew the kite. How could Karl stay angry with her? She was like the things he couldn't touch, wind, sunshine, seagulls, or a blue kite drifting high in the sky.

"Happy Birthday," Lisa sang, looking pretty and animated. The other coffee shop customers stopped their conversations, or set aside newspapers and magazines. Karl was accustomed to people staring at her. She'd majored in drama in college, had always taken pride and pleasure in her mellifluous voice, in declaiming her thoughts in carefully articulated speeches, in gesturing as she spoke them—always gracefully. Many times he'd been with her at a restaurant, store, or on the street when a man approached to introduce himself, ask for her phone number, or hand her a slip of paper with his. When he was small, he hadn't minded. But once he understood about sex, these casual encounters between Lisa and strange men upset him. He wanted his mother to be chaste. His father hadn't been present since he was five. But wasn't she still married to him?

"Blow the candle out," Lisa cried, her blue eyes alight. After Karl did, she cut the muffin in half, and handed him his share. He took a big bite, and a sweet taste filled his mouth. Lisa took tiny bites. Her tongue darted out like a cat's, licking crumbs off her lips. When she finished, she squinted at a delicate gold wristwatch, a gift from her parents. The watch was the only hint she'd grown up a wealthy girl on Park Avenue. Today, she looked like a hippie, her long, dark hair loose, her dress patterned with swirling tie-dyed purples and blues.

"Time to go," Lisa said. They walked to the gate, Karl's knees nearly buckling when a crackling announcement told them his flight was boarding. Lisa whipped out an envelope from her purse and handed it to him, mumbling, "Spending money." Her eyes were glassy.

"Mom," Karl said, his voice cracking. When he was a small boy, he'd hated when she'd left him. He'd throw his arms about her legs and scream, 'Don't go.' As if afraid he'd do it now, Lisa rushed off without even a goodbye hug. "Mom," he called after her. "Wait! Please, wait!"

She turned. Shaken by sobs, she cried, "I'll write," then vanished into a crowd of passengers.

Karl's jaw clenched. Lisa should have stayed until he was on board. She should have pulled herself together for his sake. He was the person being sent away! He dragged himself to the queue to his plane. Everyone else seemed to have companions and was chattering excitedly.

"Welcome aboard," a smiling stewardess said.

Karl squeezed down the aisle and found his seat next to a window. As the plane rolled down the runway, another stewardess demonstrated how to attach a seat belt, employ a seat cushion for a floatation device, and use an oxygen mask. The airplane gathered speed and rose into the air. Looking out, Karl saw receding houses and cars, then San Francisco's pink and green salt flats, then nothing, only a disorienting fog.

He felt trapped in his cramped seat and, more than ever, wished he could escape. His teeth chattered the way they had two months ago, the night he was arrested. Once again, he was being taken against his will to an unknown and frightening destination.

The plane no longer existed for Karl. He was riding in the police van, on his way to Oakland's Juvenile Hall.

As if he were a vicious animal, Karl's wrists were cuffed behind his back and attached to a waist-ankle shackle. Whenever the police van swerved, he jerked in one direction or another, nearly falling over. Through the van's grimy windows, he saw downtown Oakland's run-down streets, the billboards screaming the horrors of drug addiction. He heard the noisy swish of cars from the freeway. Pulling into an alley beside a brown stucco building on Broadway, the van parked beside a door. The guard signaled Karl to get out.

Karl refused to move.

"Come on!"

"You can't make me. My mom doesn't know where I am."

"She'll know soon enough. Come on, now! Don't make me go in there...Steady, now."

Grabbing the waist shackle, the muscular guard jerked Karl up like a puppet and guided him out of the van. 'Boys Receiving' was written in large red letters above the entrance. The door led directly into an elevator with a thick metal door with bars. Humming eerily, the elevator brought them to the second floor. Karl stepped from the elevator into an adjoining cage where another guard waited. Beneath a single light, his shaven scalp looked yellow as he bent to unshackle Karl. "Undress," he barked.

Trembling, Karl took off his shoes and socks, his pants. He stopped when he came to his underpants. The guard reached out, jerked them down so they fell to Karl's ankles. Ashamed and shivering, Karl stepped out of them while covering his genitals with his hands.

The guard snapped a rubber glove and put it on. "Bend over. Cavity search."

"Do you have to? I don't have any weapon. You won't find..."

The man grabbed the back of Karl's neck, pushed him down so he was bent over. Karl struggled to get away, but the guard held him tightly and jabbed a finger up his anus. Feeling a searing pain, Karl moaned. He gasped and coughed, tried to catch his breath. The guard was done. The pants and shirt he shoved at Karl looked like blue hospital scrubs. Karl put them on. He felt raped. He couldn't meet the guard's gaze, or utter a word as he was led to a cell.

An hour later, he was taken to a small courtroom for a detention hearing. A bronze State of California seal was mounted on the wall behind the judge. The other walls had photographs of California scenes, mountains, desert, fields of poppies, the Golden Gate

Bridge. An American flag stood below the judge's dais. To the rear of the court was a spectator gallery with two rows of folding seats connected like seats in a movie theater.

Karl barely understood what the judge said. The word 'accomplice' made him think about Reynaldo. After hours at the Berkeley police station, he'd spewed out everything about his 'accomplice' to his interrogators. Later, as he was led out of the station and about to step into the transport van, he saw a police car drive up with Reynaldo inside. If only he hadn't let Reynaldo talk him into doing the robbery. If only he'd never met Reynaldo.

After the detention hearing, Karl was back in the cell again. A social worker came to see him, an Asian woman who spoke with an accent. Interviewing him in a small room with a desk between them, she informed him she'd checked his record and knew that he'd been caught shoplifting a toy car when he was seven.

"I was only a little kid," Karl said, incredulously. "Why are you bringing it up? Is it supposed to prove I'm a hardened criminal?"

"It shows you have a history. It would be better if you didn't. I'd like to be able to tell the judge you cooperated and answered my questions. Will you?"

He nodded meekly.

The social worker filled in a form with information about the schools he'd attended.

Until he was twelve, he'd gone to public schools. Then an incident occurred, one he didn't mention to the social worker, and that she wouldn't find recorded in his 'record.' Karl was caught high on marijuana and sent to the principal. He hadn't revealed that the marijuana he'd smoked belonged to Lisa. Neither had she when she'd breezed into the principal's office to collect him. She was subjected to a lecture about her son's failings, short attention span, and his disruptions in class.

Over the summer, she'd worked hard to secure him a full scholarship to a small private school, a place Karl started attending and much preferred to the public school. But last December he ruined everything by getting into a fight with three other boys in the gym locker room. All he remembered about the fight was that he'd felt breathless, that he'd shut his eyes, and struck out with both fists. The other kids swore that Karl had hit them first. He was expelled.

Lisa was unable to find another private school that would give him a scholarship. He had to go back into the public school system, and was supposed to go to the public high school in Albany. Lisa considered Berkeley High academically better. It offered more advanced courses. Somehow, she finagled him a spot there.

The social worker inquired, "Why did you switch schools?"

Karl shrugged. "I don't know. My mom wanted me different places."

"Does your mother work?"

"No."

"Tell me about your father."

"He doesn't live with us."

"Are your parents divorced?"

"No."

"I'd like your father's address and phone number."

"I don't know where he is."

The last time Karl had seen his father was twelve years ago. He couldn't even remember what Fritz looked like, except that he was blond and blue-eyed like himself. They'd lived on a commune in Vermont until Lisa took off, leaving his father behind.

Later, she made up a story that he now knew was a fairy tale to stop him from asking when his father would be with them again. The gist of Lisa's story was that a penniless, hungry Fritz had stolen a loaf of bread. The police caught him and sent him back to Austria, where he'd been born. They told him he couldn't ever leave there. At five years old, Karl had believed Lisa. Now that he was in jail, the only parts of her story he considered true were that his father had been a thief and he'd been deported. That meant both he and his father were criminals.

The social worker concluded the interview. Karl was returned to his cell. Restless, he paced back and forth until a guard came for him. He and three other shackled boys were transported by van to San Leandro's Juvenile Hall. When they arrived, Karl was separated from the others, unshackled and searched in the same manner as before. Leaving the main building with a guard, he shuffled through the twilight to a long low building called C-section.

"You gotta use the toilet?" the guard growled.

"No."

"There ain't no toilets in the cell. You sure you don't wanna go first?"

"I don't," Karl said. After the humiliating cavity search, he didn't want to be shamed further by having the guard observe him pee.

The guard took him down a hall with rows of doors with small windows. They stopped before one. Peering inside, Karl saw a tiny cell that contained nothing but a cot.

"Okay, take off your shoes and leave them outside the door."

Karl didn't understand why he must remove his sneakers, but too miserable to object, he bent down to untie the laces. His hands shook as he tried to untangle a knot. Giving up, he jerked the shoes off by force, and stood in his stocking feet on the cold concrete floor.

The guard said, "You gotta call 'Guard' when you need to use the toilet. Or you can wait until we let everybody out for a toilet break. Step into the cell."

Karl froze as he had in the van.

"Get in."

The guard's shove wasn't a hard one, but sufficient to thrust Karl inside. The door slammed. Gray concrete walls seemed to close in on him. He threw himself face down onto the cot. It had iron springs, a thin pad, and a frayed blanket that he drew over his head. It was early, only about eight, but he fell asleep.

A lawyer whom Lisa had hired came to see Karl the day after his transfer to the San Leandro jail. The meeting was held in a room as small as Karl's cell. He and the lawyer sat across from each other at a table. Seymour Huff sounded like a mathematician as he spat out significant numbers: statute 459 about burglary; statute 245 about assault with a deadly weapon; the number of years in prison Karl might receive; Karl's birthday which wasn't until August. The date of his birthday turned out to be significant because he was a month and a half short of sixteen.

"If you'd done the robbery after you turned sixteen, you'd be prosecuted as an adult and get big-time jail-time," Mr. Huff said. "See, if the man you shot died and you were sixteen, you'd get thirteen years to life with a five-year enhancement for use of a firearm. That's no juvenile court slap on the wrist. One thing in your favor is the guy is out of critical care. It looks like he's going to be all right."

Karl felt his body unclench. "I'm not a murderer!"

"You're still in serious trouble. It makes things worse that you broke into the house during nighttime. Worse, you were in possession of a deadly weapon. The D.A. will want to charge you with attempted robbery and attempted murder."

"But I never meant to hurt him. The gun went off accidentally. It's true!"

"That doesn't count if it goes off during a robbery. The way the D.A. thinks is: 'Use a gun; go to jail.' Plus—Karl, this is bad—there were dum-dum bullets in that gun."

Karl winced, remembering the night Reynaldo had set up shop on Lisa's kitchen table. "Like this, Karl," he'd said. "You cut an x on the bullet tip. A cut bullet causes more shit to happen than a regular bullet. The insides swoosh out the cut like a popped zit, and spread." Karl had helped prepare those deadly bullets. Later, he loaded Reynaldo's brother's gun with them.

Mr. Huff shuffled his papers, snapped his briefcase shut, and concluded, "Your crime is serious. The prosecutor will press for a maximum sentence. I'll do my best. The situation isn't hopeless. They won't be so hard on you as they'd be if you were tried as an adult. But don't expect a miracle."

Five days later, Mr. Huff was back, accompanied by the prosecutor from the Oakland District Attorney's office. The District Attorney was a soft-spoken, stocky black man in his forties. The meeting was held in the same small room. The morning was overcast, the light coming through the window dismal.

Whenever Karl was addressed, he answered briefly. Otherwise, he let the two lawyers decide his fate. Expecting the worst, he was surprised when the prosecutor agreed to give him a break. The charges against him were going to be reduced from attempted murder to assault with a deadly weapon because of 'mitigating circumstances:' Karl had performed first-aid to his victim; had phoned 911; had cooperated with the police by confessing and revealing the name of his accomplice, Reynaldo Munez. Most importantly, he'd withheld the gun from Reynaldo when he'd wanted to take it from Karl and shoot the victim again.

The lawyers went out in the hallway to discuss sentencing. Karl nearly stopped breathing. Fellow inmates at Juvenile Hall had informed him that he could be sent to the California Youth Authority, or Y.A. as they called it, until he was twenty-six. They'd said Y.A. had high walls with barbed wire, guards with guns, and that within days of stepping through the doors he'd be beaten and raped. Beyond all this, Karl had a special reason for dreading Y.A. Malakas, Reynaldo's older brother, belonged to a gang. Two *Pinoyz Boyz* gang members were serving time at Y.A. Malakas would make sure they knew Karl was a stool pigeon.

The voices of the two lawyers were audible. Karl heard the D.A. say, "I'm willing to cut a deal about the sentence."

"How much?" Mr. Huff asked.

"Six years at the Youth Authority."

"That's harsh."

"What he did to Mr. Zeiger was harsh."

"Bring it down to four years."

"He shot somebody."

"Can he serve at a different facility?"

"No."

"We don't have anything to talk about," Mr. Huff said. "The judge will decide."

"All right. See you in court."

The prosecutor left, but Mr. Huff returned to the room where Karl waited.

"What difference does it make that charges were reduced?" Karl asked.

"Makes a big difference."

"I'm going to Y.A. anyway, aren't I?"

"Oh, you've heard about Y.A? You might go there, but not necessarily. You're under sixteen. That's really important. I want you to understand that there are no rulings of guilt or innocence in juvenile cases. There's just a 'yes' or 'no' to the prosecutor's allegations. Whatever happens to you will be based on whether the judge believes you have the potential for rehabilitation. I'll make a case that you can be rehabilitated, and that the needs of society are better served in a different set-up than Y.A. It's up to the judge to choose where you go, whether Y.A., or to an unlocked facility like Los Cerros. With a sympathetic judge, kids are sent to group homes instead of jail. If the family can pay for one, there are private facilities with dormitories, on-site schools, even horseback riding and swimming pools."

"Do I have a chance for one of those?"

"You did something serious. Your judge might think places like that are too posh. But he might go for a very, very tough private wilderness camp in Provo, Utah where you'd be forced to learn survival skills. I'd tell the judge that it would be more demanding for you than jail. I'd argue that it would change you, that you'd come out a better person."

"I'd rather go there than Y.A."

"First, I have to talk it over with your mother and see if she goes for it."

"She'll go for it."

"I'll phone her when I get back to my office. Before I leave, I want to prep you for the trial."

"When is it?"

"In two weeks."

After talking for another ten minutes, Mr. Huff signaled a guard to return Karl to his cell.

The cell window was covered with iron mesh that distorted the little view Karl had. He stared out the dirty glass at the concrete path and the next building's gray stucco wall. The sight of a bird gladdened him. He was miserable when it flew off, and he had nothing to think about but his own worthlessness. As much blame as he heaped on Reynaldo, Karl heaped more on himself.

Karl looked forward to Sunday, the visiting day. Breakfast took place in the long, narrow cafeteria with two rows of round tables with wooden chairs. The walls were decorated with artwork done by previous inmates, drawings and plaster bas-relief fish with little bubbles rising from their mouths. A woman in a white apron ladled oatmeal into bowls. Kids jostled each other on the serving line. One boy complained loudly he'd been given a smaller portion of oatmeal.

Once seated, Karl asked a kid sitting beside him, "What time do they let visitors in this afternoon?" He thought he knew, but he wanted to make sure.

"Two o'clock. Who's coming to see you? Your Mama and Daddy?"

"Only my mom," Karl said.

Another kid at their table put down the plastic spoon with which he'd been eating oatmeal, and started laughing. "You think your mamma's gonna come? You land up here and you garbage. My mama don't come. She be glad to forget me. Yours gonna forget you too."

At a nearby table, the boy who'd complained about his serving of oatmeal grabbed another kid's bowl for himself. A fight started. Alarms went off and a guard shouted, "Control." More guards came running to help drag the fighting boys off to solitary confinement cells. The boys not involved in the fight like Karl, continued to calmly eat. Nearly every meal, there was a disturbance.

Instead of returning to his cell after breakfast, Karl chose to attend a religious service. It was the first time in his life he'd done so. He had a vague notion of praying with the hope it would improve the chances that Lisa would visit later. The service was Catholic—the next Sunday it would be Protestant, and the time after that, Jewish. Different kids read from the missal, and as each one finished, everybody clapped. Karl read the twenty-third psalm. 'As I walk through the valley of the shadow of death...' The gravity and beauty of the words moved him. He read with a quaver, on the verge of tears. It was hard to hold them back, but he managed, not wanting to be ridiculed.

Despite the silent prayer he'd said, he dreaded that Lisa wouldn't visit. But that afternoon the guard unlocked his cell and took him to the cafeteria. As the boy at breakfast had predicted, few parents had bothered to come. There were only four mothers, but Lisa was one of them! Karl flung himself into her arms with a jolt that almost knocked her down. She pressed him to her for a moment, and then pulled away. Her lips were stretched in the fixed 'brave smile' she put on whenever he was in trouble. "Here," she said, handing him a bag of cherries, a horror comic, *Popular Mechanics*, and *Mad Magazine*. Visitors were only permitted to give fruit, and no more than three magazines. He'd heard from other boys that the guards searched the fruit beforehand for razor blades and needles.

"You didn't have to bring anything, Mom," Karl said, overcome with guilt for the trouble he'd caused her.

"But I wanted to do something for you. I picked magazines I thought would be popular with the other boys. Pass them around. Remember the visiting day at YMCA camp? My friend, Les, drove me up to see you. I brought you comic books and candy bars to share with the other kids."

"This isn't summer camp, Mom."

"I know," she said, blinking the way she did when she was nervous.

They sat down at a round table. Sunlight burned through the side glass wall. A fan near the steam table whirred away noisily without relieving the heat. Two of the boys in the cafeteria were kids he'd encountered in the transport van from the Oakland jail. One was arguing with his mother.

Karl said, "Mom, did the lawyer talk to you about the wilderness camp?"

She nodded. "It sounds wonderful. But..."

"But what?" he asked, anxiously.

"Well, it's expensive. There's not going to be enough left from the college fund to cover it."

"What college fund?" he asked, astounded.

Lisa explained that her parents, Grandma Bernice and Grandpa Al, had created a college fund for him. Karl was surprised. Because of tensions between Lisa and his grandparents, he'd had little contact with them. On occasion, they'd phoned, but he could barely remember the last time he'd visited them in New York. Nonetheless, they'd set aside a college fund for him. The money was being used to pay his legal fees.

"Ask Grandpa for more money!" Karl pleaded.

She shook her head. "He won't pay for wilderness camp."

At lunch, Karl had eaten French fries and hot dogs. A sour taste from the meal rose in his mouth. He slumped down in his chair, feeling doomed. He was going to end up at

Y.A. with black eyes, broken bones, and bleeding from his ass. Even here at Juvenile Hall, he was afraid. He'd heard that kids made weapons. They'd break off part of a cot's steel springs, pull out a piece of tile from the floor, or sharpen the end of a toothbrush against a stone wall in the yard. He chose to stay locked in his cell for the after-lunch voluntary recreation hour on the basketball court.

"Don't worry," Lisa said. "I'm working on something else. Grandpa Al made a suggestion...one that could work for you."

Karl felt a flicker of hope. His grandfather was a lawyer. He understood the legal system. "What did Grandpa suggest?"

"That I talk to a rabbi. I went to see Rabbi Levy two days ago."

"A rabbi!" Karl exclaimed. "How can a rabbi help?"

"Grandpa Al knows of a case like yours where a boy was sent to a Yeshiva in Israel instead of jail. The Yeshiva gave him a scholarship. I hope that's possible for you. The judge would have to agree, of course."

"What's a Yeshiva?" Karl asked in a daze.

"It's a special Jewish school for boys. Maybe they have some schools like that for girls too. I don't know."

"Why would a Yeshiva want to help me?"

Lisa flushed. "To...to save a Jewish soul," she said, averting her face.

"But I'm not Jewish or Catholic or anything," he said, recalling how strange he'd felt at the morning's services.

"Of course you're Jewish," Lisa said. "I'm Jewish. My parents are Jewish. You were born in Israel! You lived on a *kibbutz* for three years."

"My father isn't Jewish."

Lisa's eyebrows shot up. Karl had crossed a line. They never discussed Fritz. There weren't even any photos of him left.

"You're Jewish when you have a Jewish mother," Lisa said. "That's Jewish law. You don't need a Jewish father."

"What would I do at a Yeshiva in Israel?"

"You could study Jewish law. It's a wonderful opportunity."

"Jewish law...an opportunity," he echoed. "I don't speak Hebrew. I wouldn't know anyone there. I don't think the judge would agree..."

Lisa reproached him in a slow, tired voice, so different from her usual enthusiasm. "This week hasn't been easy for me. I've had to phone your grandparents and tell them what's happened. I had to run from your lawyer, to the high school, to the rabbi, and here to Juvenile Hall. The neighbors ask questions. They want to know where you are... Please, don't make this even harder. I've run out of options..."

"All right. I don't care. I'll go to a Yeshiva," Karl cried with exasperation. What did it matter what he did, a worthless boy like him? He'd always wanted Lisa to be proud of him. Instead, he'd done terrible things. She was ashamed in front of the neighbors.

"That's good." Smiling and in control again, she ruffled his hair. "I asked Rabbi Levy to visit you. It's a little complicated because they say only parents or grandparents are allowed. But surely a clergyman will receive permission. I'll ask the warden before I leave today."

"If the rabbi comes, I'll talk to him," Karl said dully. He couldn't stop himself from adding, "But the judge? Will he let me go to a Yeshiva?"

"Don't worry. I have faith in your lawyer. I was told he's the best criminal lawyer in the Bay Area. You'll see—he'll fix things. He'll make the judge okay the Yeshiva. I know, he will." Rising to leave, she bent and buzzed his cheek with a kiss. "We always manage, don't we?"

He didn't turn to watch her go, but listened to the click of her heels across the cafeteria and down the hall until he couldn't hear the sound any more. Then, escorted by a guard and carrying Lisa's gifts of fruit and magazines, Karl returned to his cell and pondered her plan. Maybe going to a Yeshiva wasn't a hopeless cause. Hadn't Lisa always had a way of making impossible things happen?

He soon witnessed her magic. The warden agreed to give Rabbi Levy a special dispensation to visit. On Tuesday morning Karl was excused from the mandatory high school level English and Math classes. The rabbi was waiting for him in the cafeteria. It smelled from the French toast with syrup served at breakfast.

Rabbi Levy, the head of an orthodox synagogue in Oakland, was a stoop-shouldered, middle-aged man. Stroking his beard, he asked Karl questions. "How do you get along with your mother?... What do you know about Judaism?... How do you like school?..."

After a week in jail, Karl was ready and eager to talk to a sympathetic person. Alone in his cell afternoons and evenings, he did endless sit-ups, or made up silly games like seeing how long he could hold his breath. He jerked off, pretending to have sex with a girl from his high school. He'd never spoken to her, didn't even know her real name, only that other boys called her 'The Bosom,' and wolf whistled whenever she passed in the high school's hallways.

Rabbi Levy asked, "How did you feel about switching from the private school to Berkeley High? Were you able to make friends?"

Berkeley High was bigger and tougher than his old school. Most of the kids had been together since kindergarten and weren't interested in someone new. "There were cliques," Karl said. He related how the rich, popular kids from the hills hung out on the front steps; blacks from the flats clustered on the track near the scoreboard; Hispanics took over the bleachers; jocks ran back and forth on the basketball court; the smart super-achievers and violinist-types hid out in the library.

"Weren't there any kids who weren't in cliques?"

"There were a few," Karl admitted, recalling the other lonely boys drifting about the high school, the fat kid, the midget, the faggot, the brainy guy obsessed with space travel. The homo kid once stopped him to ask about an assignment. Instantly, jeering boys surrounded them, and shouted, "Cock sucking fairies." After that, Karl made sure to avoid kids he thought were seen as losers.

"I didn't connect with them," he replied, looking away. He was ashamed of his cowardice.

"You met this boy, Reynaldo. Why did you connect with him?"

"We had stuff in common."

"Like what?"

"Our mothers are both on their own. Me and Reynaldo were company for each other."

The nights Lisa went off to sleep at a boyfriend's place, he'd call Reynaldo to ask him to come over. Reynaldo's mom took a sleeping pill and went to bed at eight o'clock after a hard day's work as a nurse's aide at Herrick Hospital. Without her waking, Reynaldo slipped her car key from her purse and took off for Karl's.

"Your fathers…?"

"His father's in the Philippines and mine's in Austria."

"Who wanted to do the robbery? You or him?"

"He had the idea." Karl looked away, not completely satisfied with his answer. He'd had qualms about the robbery had resisted doing it—but, in the end, he'd agreed.

The rabbi glanced at his watch. "I'm sorry I have to leave. When's your trial?"

"In about two weeks."

"I'll come back in a day or two. We can talk more before you go to court."

The day of his trial Karl woke with a full bladder. Nervously he hopped about, afraid he'd pee in his pants before the guards unlocked his cell. When they did, he quickly stepped out and slipped into his sneakers. As usual, he lined up in a corridor with the other kids. Everyone stood stock still on small imaginary squares until the order was given to march off to the bathroom.

After breakfast, he was given clothes from home that Lisa had dropped off at the jail. During the last two and a half weeks, he'd lost weight. His pants were loose. He needed to look his best for the trial. It wasn't until he was in the transport van that he thought about wetting his fingers with spit and smoothing down his hair. He couldn't. He was handcuffed.

At Oakland's Juvenile Hall, he was unshackled, taken to the same small courtroom as before, and seated beside Mr. Huff at a front table. A few feet away, the prosecutor he'd met at the prison sat at a second table. The gallery was full. Karl flushed, glimpsing faces of neighbors and teachers. Lisa sat in the first row, barely recognizable in a dark tailored suit, stockings and black pumps. Her long brown hair was drawn back into a severe bun. She wore a hideous, large-brimmed hat.

A plump woman bailiff stepped forward. People quieted and stood at her orders. Judge Thorn appeared in his black robes. He was tall, silver-haired. "Take your seats," he said. Everyone sat down with a whoosh.

"The matter of Karl Graf," the bailiff called out loudly.

The prosecutor rose and spoke, painting a picture of Karl as a misbehaving kid who'd taken a path of rebelliousness, leading up to his current disregard for life and property. Witnesses were called. The Asian cop, the one who'd arrested Karl, testified. After him, a bent-over Sam Zeiger limped to the witness box. He was nothing like the aggressive individual he'd been the night of the robbery. In a trembling voice, he said, "My house was broken into. I was shot. Ever since, I've been in pain."

Mr. Huff's turn to defend Karl came. He called a variety of character witnesses, teachers and neighbors, and read aloud a letter from Grandma Bernice. Lisa approached the witness box with downcast eyes and was sworn in. Replying with a quaver to Mr. Huff's questions, she said Karl was a dutiful boy who helped with chores, read constantly, acted respectfully. She began to sob. The judge offered to let her take a break.

Lisa shook her head. "I'd rather go on...Your Honor, I come before you to plead for my son. He made a bad contact at his high school and did something wrong. He deeply regrets his mistakes. Right now, he's at a vulnerable age, an idealistic age. Please, look to his future when you make your ruling. I beg you to allow him to attend a Yeshiva in Israel.

"The Yeshiva I'm suggesting is in the desert, far from corrupting influences, far from distractions. Every moment will be devoted to prayer, learning, and reading the Bible. The rabbis will teach Karl self-discipline. Not only will he overcome his past mistakes, he will do more. He will become a morally outstanding individual. Your Honor,

I trust to your wisdom. Please allow him to attend the Yeshiva."

At a nod from Mr. Huff, Lisa stepped down from the witness box. There was silence in the courtroom.

Mr. Huff called his final witness. Rabbi Levy was asked to give his impressions of Karl.

"I don't know him well. I visited Karl twice at Juvenile Hall. The visits were the only contact we've had."

Karl shrank inwardly. What good would Rabbi Levy's testimony be?

"Even so," Rabbi Levy continued, "I feel qualified to testify about Karl because I've counseled many troubled kids. He's done something terrible. But I don't think it's his true nature to be a criminal. The point is how can we help him to do better? The teachers who spoke before me praised his academic potential. They said he needs support, intellectual challenge, and individual attention. He'd receive none of these in jail. It would be a mistake to send him there.

"Karl's mother believes that he'd benefit from the instruction in ethics and basic values that's part of every Yeshiva curriculum. I want to argue that the *Beit Sholom* Yeshiva, where Karl would go, has a disciplined, demanding program that instills morality. I say this with confidence because I was a student there. I completed their two-year program for foreigners, the one for which Karl would be eligible.

"I know Rabbi Tubol, *Beit Sholom's* director. I tell you, Rabbi Tubol will help Karl become what we call a *mensch*, a good human being. The director keeps close track of the students, as do the teachers. Karl will have a spiritual advisor who'll meet with him regularly, and who'll be available at any time he has a problem. The other boys will watch after Karl too.

"It will be enriching for him to associate with students from England, Canada, South Africa, Australia, and from other parts of the United States, boys who've attended Jewish schools. They'll be excellent role models and friends.

"When I talked to Karl, he said he'd been lonely when he transferred to Berkeley High from a smaller school last December. Karl clung to the first boy who befriended him. This kid was a regrettable influence. Reynaldo Munez proposed a robbery. Karl was desperate to hold on to this friendship, and agreed.

"At *Beit Sholom*, Karl will learn how to resist bad influences. Days at the Yeshiva begin at five --and except for a rest time during the hottest part of the day--are filled with study. As a member of an Orthodox community, Karl will have to say prayers when he wakes, before he eats, during twice-a-day services, and before going to sleep at midnight."

A smile flickered across the rabbi's lips. "I hope I'm not out of turn for mentioning that there's even a required prayer after returning from the bathroom." A few people laughed.

"Our Sabbath lasts from sunset Friday night to Saturday night when at least three stars are visible in the sky. Even on our day of rest, there are services to attend and rituals to perform. The rabbis will teach Karl that the strict discipline our religion requires is 'a fence around a fence around a fence.' This means that observance creates barriers against evil doing."

Rabbi Levy stepped down. The judge's expression had softened as the rabbi spoke. Karl hoped it meant he'd be spared Y.A.

Mr. Huff poked Karl to stand up and said, "Karl has a few remarks."

Karl swallowed hard. His mouth was dry. Despite earlier coaching by Mr. Huff, he found it hard to get out the words he'd been told to say. "I'm sorry for what I d-d-did.

Please, give me a chance to change. I'll do my best not to let anybody d-d-down. I don't want to hurt anybody ever again." His face burning, he sank back into his chair.

The prosecutor rose for his concluding remarks. Gazing sternly at Karl, he counted off Karl's crimes on his fingers. "Number One. You forced your way into a home in an attempted robbery. Number two. You possessed deadly bullets that enhanced your ability to kill. Number three. You were prepared to, and did in fact use a gun with these deadly bullets. In conclusion, you acted with an abandoned and malignant heart. You deserve to go to prison. Your Honor, I recommend the full term the law allows to be served by this young man at the California Youth Authority."

From the moment the prosecutor had said that he had 'an abandoned and malignant heart,' Karl became certain the judge wouldn't, and couldn't be lenient. Beside him Mr. Huff stood to argue for him. Karl listened to Mr. Huff go on and on, certain the lawyer's efforts were pointless.

"Karl tried to help Mr. Zeiger after he was shot. He made a 911 call. His teachers have praised his intelligence today. A neighbor described him as good-hearted in her testimony. Rabbi Levy said it wasn't in Karl's nature to be a criminal. His grandmother's letter said the same thing..."

Judge Thorn declared a half-hour break while he withdrew to deliberate.

Panicked, Karl reached over and pulled at Mr. Huff's sleeve. "I want the D.A.'s deal. Can I still take it?"

"Let's go," a guard insisted.

Karl had to follow him to a cell. Mr. Huff came along. Once they were in the tiny cell—and the guard outside the door in the hall—Karl rasped, "Take the deal."

"We can do better than the prosecutor's offer."

"I don't believe it. Tell the D.A."

"Let me explain why I don't want you to take the deal."

Karl interrupted. "I don't want to hear. Hurry. Tell him before it's too late."

"The judge is a born-again, Karl."

"So what's that got to do with anything?" Karl cried. Did Mr. Huff think anyone, born-again or not, would take pity on him? Not after the prosecutor had convinced everyone that he was garbage.

"I'm betting he'll go for your mother's idea about the Yeshiva. He's one of those kooks who believe that if all Jews go to Israel, Christ will rise again. The way he'll justify letting you off easy is that you're under sixteen, and the court's supposed to show leniency in these cases." Mr. Huff lit a cigarette, inhaled.

Karl slumped down. Maybe there was hope. Or maybe there wasn't. What difference did it matter what happened to him? He felt his strength floating away like the cigarette smoke drifting through the air. "All right, I'll do what you say."

Mr. Huff went off, leaving Karl alone. Karl wondered whether Reynaldo was in jail. He probably was, but he might have gotten off somehow. He might be home. Or maybe he was in the Philippines with his father, or grandparents, or some aunt or uncle. Karl was glad for him if that was the case.

After a while, Karl called to the guard and asked the time. Judge Thorn was taking more than the half hour break he'd specified. Karl assumed the judge was having trouble deciding on the number of years to send him to jail. What did it matter whether he was sentenced to one, two, or ten years? By tonight, he'd be beat-up, raped, and dead--or wishing he was dead. He felt as if all these things had already happened.

The guard opened the door. "Time to go back." Karl tried to take a step, but his knees buckled. The guard caught him, placed a firm arm around his waist. "Come on, Karl. You can do it," he urged as they walked back to the courtroom. Once again Karl sat down beside Mr. Huff. The lawyer nudged him, a signal to stand. Karl's head swam. He held onto the table with both hands.

Judge Thorn peered down at Karl from his platform. "Karl Graf, you've committed an assault with a deadly weapon. You've attempted a robbery. Before that, you've been truant at school, taken drugs, and gotten in fights. Your lawyer has emphasized the mitigating circumstances of your case. Many people spoke eloquently on your behalf. Even so, I believe most judges would give you the maximum sentence.

"Frankly, I was torn. The two-year Yeshiva program described by Rabbi Levy sounds like it could benefit many boys who come before me. Take note, I will not send a juvenile to an Israeli Yeshiva without conditions. The boy must understand that his freedom is contingent on his completing the program. He must stay at the Yeshiva the full two years. He must agree to mail me a progress report every three months signed by the head of the Yeshiva."

"I'll do it," Karl blurted. His lawyer laid a restraining hand on his shoulder.

After a moment of silence—a moment that seemed to last forever—Judge Thorn said, "I'm going to send you to Israel."

Karl glanced at the prosecutor. The D.A.'s lips pursed as if he'd tasted a sour lemon.

From the back of the courtroom, Sam Zeiger called, "Shame!"

"You'll have to restrain yourself if you want to remain in my courtroom, Mr. Zeiger," the judge said sharply.

"I'll spare you the trouble. I'm leaving."

Sam Zeiger limped out.

The judge continued, "Karl, you are released into your mother's custody with the understanding that she'll send you to the Yeshiva in Israel within the coming month. I assume you can obtain a passport during that time, if you don't already have one. It is because you are leaving this country that I'm not hampering you with probation requirements. As I understand it, as a Jew, you have what is called 'the right of return.' If you adjust to life in Israel, you will be able to remain as a citizen. I want to hear that you are a good one. You have a chance to change your life. I sincerely hope you'll use this opportunity to rehabilitate yourself. On the other hand, if you return to this country and engage in criminal activity again, I guarantee that you will be dealt with harshly."

The judge rapped his gavel. The trial was over. Miracle   Karl could go home. The wall clock showed it was almost noon. He wanted to run to Lisa, but there were procedures to follow before he was released. A guard took him to a storage room where he signed a receipt and retrieved his wristwatch, wallet, keys, and a black plastic bag with the clothes he'd worn on the night of the robbery. When he'd taken them off they'd been soaked with sweat. After three weeks of moldering, they stank. He twisted the bag shut and knotted it. With a wallet in his back pocket and a watch on his wrist, Karl felt almost like his long ago self. He stepped into the hall where Lisa met him.

"Congratulations!" she cried, hugged him, and took the black plastic bag. Once on the street, she threw the bag into a trash bin, along with the hat she'd worn to the trial. "Thank God, that's over," she said.

"It's not over for me. I have to go to Israel," Karl reminded her.

After a twenty-hour trip, Karl arrived at Ben Gurion airport. He collected his suitcase, and went through passport control and customs. Outside the restricted area, people waited to pick up passengers. Karl scanned the crowd, looking for someone holding a sign with his name. What if no one from the Yeshiva came for him? He was exhausted, had no Israeli money, and didn't know Hebrew.

Nearby, a woman caught his attention because she was speaking English. "At last, I'm in Israel. I'm so happy!" she cried rapturously. Karl stared at her, surprised to hear feelings expressed that were so different from his.

He spotted a middle-aged man in a *yarmulka* who held a sign that said 'Karl Graf.' Afraid the man would disappear, Karl hurried over as fast as he could. His backpack was on his back. He lugged his heavy suitcase.

"I'm Karl," he said.

The man shook his hand. "I'm Shloime, Rabbi Tubol's assistant."

As they squeezed through the crowd, Karl noticed that Shloime had white strings dangling from beneath his shirt to halfway down his chino pants. He longed to ask what they meant but didn't dare. The strip in front of the terminal building was filled with people too. Several men were dressed in black suits and homburg hats, and they had weird dangling strings like Shloime's. It was hot and muggy and they looked uncomfortable in their suits. Karl was glad Shloime wore a checked shirt and chinos. That probably meant the Yeshiva wouldn't require students to dress in suits.

Shloime took Karl to the parking lot to a small, rusted Renault. There was scarcely room for Karl's suitcase and backpack in the back. After he drove off to the highway, Shloime concentrated on his driving, while Karl sagged in his seat and leaned his head against the side-window. Hills rose on every side of the winding road. Signs that said 'Tel

Aviv' flashed by. On the plane, Karl had been too anxious to doze off, but now he fell into a deep sleep.

Shloime's voice woke him. "We're almost there." The brightly lit highway was gone. They drove along a road with no cars or buildings in sight. Moonlight illuminated stony fields that gave way to sand, distant brown hills, and, further off, jagged mountains. Karl saw there'd be no way to run away from the Yeshiva. The empty desert would take him nowhere except to danger. An Arab sniper might shoot him; or he'd be captured and tortured by a band of Bedouins; or he'd become dehydrated and disoriented, and attacked by jackals.

As if out of a dream, three two-story white stucco buildings appeared. All the windows were darkened. Shloime parked the Renault inside the iron-slat fence that circled the Yeshiva. Karl felt the same fear he'd experienced when he first glimpsed the San Leandro Juvenile Hall, looming above the freeway. He retrieved his luggage, lugged it over a paved courtyard. Shloime said the two buildings on either side of the central building were the dorm and staff housing. The central building was the heart of the Yeshiva, had classrooms, offices, a cafeteria and synagogue.

Once inside it, they walked down a deserted hallway. Unlocking a door, Shloime flicked on a light and revealed a large room with old, scratched and rickety-looking desks, file cabinets, cupboards, a Xerox machine, and rows of mailbox cubbies.

Nodding at a closed door, he said in a reverential tone, "Through there is Rabbi Tubol's office." He led Karl over to a cluttered desk right outside the head of the Yeshiva's sanctum, saying, "This is where I work. I'm here where I can help Rabbi Tubol whenever he needs me."

Dipping into a big cardboard box under his desk, Shloime took out a black skullcap he called a *keepah,* and also a *tzitzis*, a kind of undershirt with long strings like the ones that dangled over his pants. "You must put this on. Take off your shirt, and put the *tzitzis* on next to your skin."

Karl shuddered. He recalled stripping at 'Boys' Receiving,' and putting on a uniform. Here, it was the same. "Do I have to?"

Clucking his tongue, Shloime chided, "All orthodox Jewish men wear *tzitzis. "*

"Why?"

"Your *tzitzis* has six hundred and thirteen strings to remind you of different *mitzvahs*, good deeds you should perform. That's why you must wear it."

With trembling hands, Karl took off his backpack, then stripped off his shirt and put on the *tzitzis*.

"Wear the *keepah* too. That's right. Now, I'm going to recite the prayer in Hebrew for putting on the *tzitzis*. You follow along."

"I don't know Hebrew."

"Saying the prayer has merit even if you don't understand the words." Shloime spoke the prayer in a monotone not unlike the way the blank-faced guard at the jail had recited, "I have to advise you of the rules of the facility..."

Karl made a half-hearted attempt to repeat the Hebrew words. After the prayer, he pulled his shirt back on over the *tzitzis*. He didn't mind wearing the little skullcap, but the undershirt looked peculiar with its hanging strings. He began pushing them into his pants.

Shloime gasped as if Karl had committed a sacrilege. "Stop! Not like that."

Karl let the strings dangle.

Shloime calmed down. "There are other boys entering the school who've never worn *tzitzis*. In every class we have a few *ba'al tshuvahs*.

"Ba'al tshuvah?" Karl's head was spinning. Here was another word to learn. The necessity of learning a new language was part of his punishment. In jail he'd had to learn new expressions too. 'Zoom-zoom-wham-wham,' was what you said when you wanted a sweet treat. The jail talk still rolled about in his mind, might never go away.

"A *ba'al tshuvah*," Shloime explained, "is someone who is returning to the Jewish religion, like you. The other *ba'al tshuvah* won't know much about Jewish customs and practices either."

"Do I have a roommate?" Locked in his jail cell, he'd resorted to talking aloud to himself in order to feel less alone.

"Yes."

"Will he be one of these kids who never wore the undershirt with the strings?" Karl hoped he'd have one of these 'bal blah-blahs', someone to hang onto who was like himself.

"Rabbi Tubol wanted the experienced boys to be paired with the less experienced, so they could assist them in their studies and guide them in observance. I made the assignments myself. You'll live with Jakob Finkel, a boy from an orthodox South African family. I've told him a little about you. He's agreed to help you."

Shloime opened a cupboard and took out a silk shawl, a book-size velvet bag and two small boxes with leather straps.

"Here is a prayer shawl, and here are your phylacteries and case for carrying them. We call the prayer shawl a *tallis*. The phylacteries are what we call *tefillin*. The boxes have papers rolled up inside them with written prayers that say, 'There is only one God.'

You must pray with *tefillin* twice a day. Jakob will show you how to attach the *tefillin*. One box is strapped a special way to your left arm, the other to your forehead because we are commanded, 'You shall love *HaShem*, your God, with all your heart and with all your soul. Bind it as a sign upon your arm and let it be *tefillin* between your eyes.'"

Shloime handed over these objects, and said, "Now, I'll take you to the dorm." He picked up Karl's suitcase and backpack. Karl's hands were filled with the objects he'd received.

On the way out, Karl paused at the mail cubbies, wondering when he'd get a letter from Lisa. He planned on writing her immediately to say he'd arrived safely. He hoped she'd write soon and tell him, 'I miss you terribly.' She wasn't the perfect mother. Sometimes, he'd felt jealous of other kids and wished he had their parents. Yet he loved her, and knew Lisa loved him.

"Come, you're tired," Shloime said kindly. "The other students are new to the Yeshiva too. They're all a little homesick. The Yeshiva can be strange at first. It's a different experience. The methods of instruction are unique. But don't worry. You'll get used to them in time. You're like 'a stranger in a strange land,' but not for long."

They crossed the courtyard to the dorm, and climbed up a flight of steps, quietly so as not to disturb the sleeping boys. Karl wondered what his room would be like. Not that he was accustomed to luxury. At home, he slept on a mattress on the floor. His cell at Juvenile Hall had had only a cot. The guards claimed that the less a boy had in his cell, the less trouble.

"Your room's number thirteen, a lucky number for Jews because that's how old a boy is when he is *bar mitzvah*," Shloime whispered. He placed Karl's suitcase and backpack in front of the door. After he left, Karl tiptoed inside.

Moonlight streamed through the window. He saw a small room with duplicate twin beds, desks and dressers. Karl's roommate was asleep. Jakob looked handsome with his pale skin and dark hair. Thick lashes ringed his closed eyes. He had a wide, full mouth. As if sensing a stranger's presence, he moaned, then turned over and was still.

After placing the objects Shloime had given him on a desk, Karl went for his backpack and suitcase. Quietly, he unpacked those few things he needed to prepare for bed, his toiletries and pajamas. The bathroom was located between his and the next room. Through a half-open door, he glimpsed two boys asleep in the adjoining room. 'I'll make friends,' he tried to reassure himself.

He climbed into the unoccupied bed, and stretched out. The mattress sagged in the center. The pad he'd slept on at jail had been lumpy too. He wished the dorm mattress were new, a fresh start.

Still tired from his trip, Karl turned over on his side and fell asleep.

2

Albany, California, 1982

After dropping Karl off at the airport, Lisa drove home. The drive across the Bay Bridge with its views of water, bobbing sailboats and distant hills usually exhilarated her. Today, she felt distracted, barely able to steer. She'd promised her parents she'd let them know when Karl was safely on his way. In light of the way they'd acted since his arrest, she wished she didn't have to speak with them today. She wasn't up to hearing Bernice and Al, blaming her for the way Karl had acted. They went on and on about her unstable existence, bohemian wanderings, and living on a commune. Didn't they know there was no accusation they hurled that she hadn't thought of herself? In a telephone conversation two weeks ago, she'd told them, "It sounds as if you think I'm the one who should be in jail." The ensuing silence had made clear that was exactly what they thought.

Back at her flat, Lisa went down the hall to Karl's room, as if she could find him there. She gazed at the rumpled bedding, dusty Beatles posters plastering the walls, airplane model they'd built together, dangling from the ceiling. In a week or two when she was more accustomed to Karl's absence, she'd strip the room and turn it into her study. The thought of clearing away his things, made her cry. With him around, there was always somebody to greet her when she came home. Her meals were never solitary. Even if Karl had already eaten, he'd sit with her, telling stories about the teachers and kids at school. She'd miss his raucous laugh, his stomping around the flat. He'd been a constant in her life.

In the kitchen, Lisa solaced herself with drinking jasmine tea from a cup she'd made, one with a crumpled hand-made look that she liked. With every sip, her reluctance to call her parents increased. Over the years, they'd frequently offered to raise Karl. Now, they claimed that the upbringing they'd have provided would have prevented him from becoming a criminal. More than anything else, she couldn't bear to hear them bemoaning the fact that she hadn't handed him over.

How could she have? Her own childhood had been marked by unhappiness, starting when she was four. At that time, her father suffered a stroke, and her mother whisked him to a rehabilitation clinic in Vallejo, California, leaving Lisa behind with her grandparents.

Too young to grasp what was happening, she'd felt abandoned. Six months later when her parents returned, they seemed like strangers, absorbed in each other, forgetful of her needs. The year before her mother's sister had died, a loss that made Bernice all the more determined to protect Al. "I lost Elaine, but I'm not going to lose your dad...don't stress him," Bernice kept warning. The words frightened Lisa. She supposed her father would disappear back to California unless she kept quiet.

Children who lived in her apartment building knocked on the door and asked to play with Lisa, normal boisterous kids who ran up and down the hall, laughing and shouting. One afternoon, Bernice rushed from the kitchen, grabbed Lisa by the arm and rebuked her for the commotion. After the children left, she said, "You make more than enough noise on your own, Lisa. From now on, no more children can visit." Al protested that he didn't mind the noise. But Bernice prevailed.

Even this precaution to shield Al wasn't enough for her. A few weeks later, Lisa overheard her mother on the phone, saying in a voice as tremulous as when she spoke of Elaine's melanoma, "Lisa had one of her tantrums. I've told her over and over that Al needs peace and quiet. But she can't control herself. I might have to send her away."

Remembering how terrifying the threat had been, Lisa felt all the more badly about Karl having been sent away today. He must be suffering. She must write the letter she'd promised at once, try to comfort him! She put her cup in the sink, got a thin sheet of onionskin typewriter paper, and began a letter.

"Dear Karl, I said I'd write immediately. We were together only two hours ago; so I have no new news except that it's lonely without you...The words aren't flowing. I pause, and look out the window. I see the cherry tree in the next yard. Ah, inspiration! I'll draw the tree for you."

She sketched a cherry tree branch in brown ink. Beneath, she wrote a poem --

The promise of sweetness

In the fog, sun, and dark night

A wine red

Secret

The ringing phone startled Lisa. It wasn't until the fifth ring that she relented, rushed to the living room and picked up the receiver.

Her mother gave no greeting, just blurted, "Has he left?"

Forcing herself to speak cheerily, Lisa said, "Yes. He's on his way."

On another line, Al growled, "Let's hope he doesn't get into trouble over there."

Lisa gripped the receiver tightly. Her father had often said how much he loved Karl. Yet not once during the past six weeks had he phoned him, not even to say goodbye before his trip to Israel. She said, "Dad. It's all over. He's not going to be in trouble again."

After conversing stiffly with her for a minute or two more, Bernice and Al said 'goodbye.' The call wearied Lisa. She didn't have the energy to mail her letter. Instead, she sank down on the couch and curled up in a ball. She'd told her father, 'It's all over.' But even so she worried and felt panicked about Karl as if he were still in jail…how empty the rooms were without him.

After a while, she rose and glanced over the bookshelves, hoping to find a book that would redirect her racing thoughts to a calmer channel. Pulling out *Jane Eyre*, she read a sentence, sighed and put it back. She went on to another volume. Nothing engaged her for more than a sentence or two.

A spiral-bound notebook on the bottom shelf stuck out from beneath a pile of books. Pulling it out, she blew dust off the cover, and flipped through yellowed pages covered with her small handwriting. She'd begun her journal while she was in high school, a time when she viewed her home as a dreary mausoleum, and herself as an unwelcome nuisance. She couldn't wait to go to college.

Her heart had been set on an experimental school that emphasized the arts, but her parents insisted she attend a proper women's college in a remote corner of Massachusetts. In many ways, the cloistered college turned out to be the same as the private girls' schools she'd previously attended. Except in high school, the teachers had given her automatic A's, while the college professors, mostly middle-aged single women, were far stricter. Fortunately, the college policy was to report grades only to students.

At the end of four years, Al and Bernice collected Lisa, taking her back to the Park Avenue apartment with its Oriental rugs, velvet drapes, and heavy gleaming furniture. Everything was the same, including her parents' desire to run her life. They'd chosen another school for her to attend, the Columbia School of Journalism, close enough so she could live at home.

Somehow, Lisa broke free of them that summer. She wanted to remember the weeks that led up to that leave-taking because of Karl's going away today. Only now did it occur to her she should have told him that, no matter what the preceding circumstances had been, he was starting on a great adventure.

New York, 1964

Her first morning at home after returning from college, Lisa slept late. The apartment was empty when she awoke. Her parents had left for work hours earlier. She went to the kitchen to make breakfast. A newspaper lay on the counter, folded to the 'help wanted' advertisements. Receptionist, file clerk, and sales jobs were circled in red ink. At last night's supper, her mother had said, "What are you doing this summer? Not moping around, I hope. Maybe you could get a summer job." The suggestion had surprised Lisa. Her previous summers were spent at camp, or at art or music workshops. When she was seventeen, she'd longed to get a job at a summer camp for disabled kids, but her mother had said 'no,' without giving any justification. Now, though, Bernice wanted her to find work.

Lisa tossed the newspaper aside. She ate a breakfast of tea and toast, then showered, dressed, and left the apartment. Stepping out into a bright, hot June day, she walked over to Central Park. She liked to walk, particularly when she felt distressed as she did now. There was something important she must tell her parents. Procrastinator that she was, she'd put it off for months. At the park, she distracted herself by watching a baseball game. She talked to two French boys who were sailing miniature boats on a lake, patted a Great Dane, bought popcorn. Half the carton she devoured hungrily, and fed the rest to blue-pink-gray pigeons who gathered about her ankles, fluttering and cooing.

On the way home on a street of small shops, Lisa noticed a stationer with a 'help wanted' sign in the window. If she were to get a summer job this one might be ideal. The store was walking distance to her home. Peering in its window, she saw there were no customers. A middle-aged woman sat a desk reading a book. Lisa supposed the job that was available would involve little more than sitting at that desk, reading and daydreaming. She was tempted to step in and inquire about the duties, salary and hours required, but stopped herself. There was not going to be any temporary summer job for her!

Walking the remaining blocks home, she felt more burdened than when she'd left that morning. She had to confront her mother and father, tonight. Everything would come out; how she'd spent her time at college, swept up by acting in the all-women theater productions; or hanging out at the coffee shop talking about avant-garde poetry, sex, visionary drugs, all of which she scarcely knew a thing about. The last place she'd wanted to be was alone at a desk, writing endless papers, or reading the mountains of books assigned to an English major. Not that she couldn't be a hard worker--but the one thing she couldn't bear was feeling alone, the way she had while she was growing up.

Her parents had assumed she was an A student in college the way she'd been in high school. She didn't disabuse them of their false assumptions. At the start of her senior year, they insisted she apply to the Columbia School of Journalism. In March, they began to press her about whether she'd heard back. Lisa wanted to tell them about the rejection letter. She would have, but belatedly, she realized that her father was fully capable of stopping by the Columbia admissions department to ask why they'd refused her. Panicked, she blurted, "I've been accepted." The words just popped out. A deliberate lie upset her. The following day, she resolved to phone and confess the truth. The trouble was she had no plausible alternative plan to put forward for her future. If she had, she might have spoken up. As it was, she put off rectifying her falsehood. 'I'll do it after graduation,' was her thought.

Now, the time had come! At home, she sat propped up in bed, writing down in a notebook what she intended to say that evening, then memorized it. Pacing about her room as if she was on a stage, she recited, "You never asked me whether I wanted to go to graduate school. You make me feel it's a crime for me to have personal desires. The truth is, I don't know what I'm going to do, where I'm going, only that it won't be to journalism school. To take a summer job would only prolong the pretense that I will be going there. It's pointless to look for a temporary summer job. I need to launch my real life."

Her stomach churned at the sound of a key clicking in the front door that night. Her parents had returned from work. It was one thing to practice her speech in her room, another to actually say it to their faces. Her father was busy glancing through the mail he'd brought up. Her mother kicked off her high heels, and changed out of her tailored suit into a bathrobe. Striding swiftly about the kitchen, she prepared rice, grilled chops, assembled a salad. "Lisa, go set the table," she ordered. Obviously, she wasn't receptive to having a serious talk.

As Lisa set plates, silver, glasses and napkins on the dining room table, her father peered at a wine bottle label with his slightly protuberant, nearsighted blue eyes. Responding to more of her mother's orders, Lisa brought out the salad bowl, water pitcher, and bread platter. At last, they gathered around the mahogany table, Al at the head, Bernice in the chair closest to the kitchen.

'I must tell them,' Lisa thought, but couldn't begin, not with her mother jumping up like a jack-in-the-box, one time for the salt and pepper she'd forgotten, another to answer the phone. Her father's bulldog face looked contented as he chewed a bite of his chop. Lisa decided to wait until he finished his food before she delivered her speech.

Too nervous to eat, she studied her parents as if they were strangers, her soon-to-be prosecutor-judges. Bernice looked like one of those tall, rangy, fast-talking Hollywood stars from the 1940's. Gold bracelets she'd forgotten to remove jangled on her wrists. Her dark hair was 'frosted' with blond highlights that concealed the encroaching gray. Lisa had always counted herself fortunate to resemble her mother in looks, rather than her broad-shouldered father, who was bald, had a paunch. On occasion, Al used a cane, although his limp was much improved from when he'd returned from the Vallejo clinic. The therapy had helped, but he'd slurred his words, couldn't drive, wasn't able to resume the rigors of work. For a year, Bernice had been the sole breadwinner.

The meal concluded with the usual cups of coffee. Bernice lit a cigarette, and put it in a holder. Narrowing her eyes as the smoke drifted up, she asked Lisa, "Well, did you look for a job today?"

Lisa saw this as her 'cue.' In the college theater productions, she'd always been able to deliver her lines. But now with an audience of only two, stage fright assailed her. She bit her lips, muttered, "I went for a walk in Central Park."

"A walk," Bernice echoed. "Did you look at the newspaper I left for you?"

"I'm sorry…I didn't."

"I see," Bernice said. The fingers on her right hand tapped out a tattoo on the table. She inhaled with her cigarette holder, blew out a plume of smoke, followed by a rush of words. "I would have loved to go to college like you, but I had to work. Your father worked his way through law school. Don't waste the summer by doing nothing."

Al sipped his after-dinner coffee and mused, "I wonder whether Columbia has summer internships for entering graduate students. It's rather late, but someone might have dropped out and left an open slot."

"Al, she doesn't need an internship," Bernice said. "It would be good for her to get her hands dirty."

Lisa felt detached, as if she were invisible, the way she'd been forced to be as a child. Her parents discussed what was best for her, while she scarcely listened. Vaguely she was aware of her mother launching into an account of the family saga, her struggling Russian Jewish immigrant parents, how they'd made a decent living because they worked day and night. They'd sewed pajamas and long underwear. She'd thrown herself into the business too. After her parents died, she banished the flannel pajamas that preceded her tenure, replacing them with shimmering negligees, slips and underwear of her own design. These sexy creations were sold to top of the line stores all over the country.

'Listen to me!' Lisa wanted to scream. 'I don't want to go to Columbia, or any school. It would be nothing but drudgery.' She toyed with her fork, tapped it against the side of her empty water glass. The glass gave out a ringing tone.

"Well, you think you're too good to listen to this," Bernice sputtered. "You've always had everything handed to you on a platter, haven't you?"

The notion that she was spoiled was one that Lisa had heard before. By her mother's lights, Lisa required nothing beyond what she gave her. She'd never asked about Lisa's own desires; not when she was a little girl and desperately wanted satin slippers and was given oxfords instead; not when she picked out where Lisa must go to college.

"Bernie, Lisa's only come home yesterday. Let her settle in and get her bearings." Al's mouth was faintly askew, as it sometimes was after a long day's work. He rose and walked off as Bernice began clearing the dishes and silver.

Her mother's sharp glance reminded Lisa that she must help load plates into the dishwasher. After her chores, Lisa had to proceed to the den to watch television, the next step in her parents' unvarying routine. At least while the TV was blaring, they wouldn't pick on her. She sank into the couch. Images from Saigon flashed on the screen. Helicopters with whirling blades flew above palm trees. Commentators spoke of the escalating American involvement in Vietnam. A protesting Buddhist monk doused himself in gasoline, ignited it, and was surrounded by flames. Tears filled Lisa's eyes. She didn't know whether she was crying for the monk or because she regretted her own cowardice. Her mother handed her a Kleenex.

At eleven, her father clicked the TV off, stretched and said, "Time for bed."

Nightly, Bernice laid out his clothes for the next day. If need be, she took out the ironing board and touched up the shirt and pants she selected. Only after these acts of devotion did she permit herself to go to sleep.

Lisa lingered in the hallway outside her parent's closed door. She'd been reminded this evening that there was no spontaneity in their lives, no stimulus, no adventure, just a dull repetition of days because that was what was safe. Lisa hated being part of it, yearned to get away and didn't know how.

If only she dared to knock, go into their bedroom and speak up about what she wanted. But her mother scared her, and her father made her feel guilty. 'Don't speak. Don't upset him,' was the mantra after he returned from the rehabilitation clinic, and still rang in her ears.

The following morning, Lisa walked over to the stationery store. The woman she'd noticed the previous day, was the owner. She hired Lisa as a salesclerk. It was only a part-time position, but Lisa, according to her mother, was "getting a taste of the working world." When she wasn't working selling greeting cards and boxes of vellum, she chose to spend her time drifting through the Guggenheim or the Metropolitan Museum. Lost in whirls of color, Lisa nearly forgot about the crisis she knew was at the door. One way or another, her parents were going to learn the truth.

On occasion, she met up with friends from college, two young women who lived in

New York. Anne and Charlotte were fellow free spirits. They told her about their plan to hitchhike in Europe. Afterwards, Charlotte was going to trek through the Himalayas with Hannah, another friend. In a burst of enthusiasm, Lisa applied for a passport. She too yearned to have adventures, meet lovers, and see the world. Her passport arrived one morning, its pristine pages, waiting for custom stamps. Lisa hid it in her dresser drawer alongside the bag of marijuana, roach clip, and cigarette papers that Charlotte had given her as a goodbye present before leaving.

Alone in the apartment Lisa would light up, enjoying how 'weed' sharpened her perceptions. The lines of everything in her room were sharper, the colors brighter. She felt as if she were seeing things as an artist would. The best thing was she could relax. A few puffs of marijuana dissipated the tightness in her belly. For an hour or two, she forgot about the explosion that was bound to come.

Towards the end of July, her parents began to ask her about her 'matriculation,' as her father called it. 'Will you take the bus or the train to school?' 'Is there an orientation week?' 'Do you have an advisor yet?' They never guessed the agony their questions caused her. Lisa felt obliged to tell them she'd attended a meeting for in-coming journalism students at Columbia. She envied those who could truth-tell without consequences.

On the morning she was supposed to start her classes, her father came to her bedroom door and called, "Don't over-sleep today, Sweetheart." Lisa feared he'd volunteer to accompany her to Columbia. But, of course, he went off to work, as did Bernice. There were no days off for them.

After they left. Lisa was overwhelmed with self-disgust. She'd let months go by, deluding her parents. Her lies must end.

That evening, her mother prepared dinner, and her father came up to Lisa and said, "Well?"

"'Well,' what?" She knew what he meant, but she pretended she didn't.

"How do you like your classes?"

"Oh, the classes. Umm...umm," She faltered, unable to meet his gaze.

Bernice called them to dinner. Lisa knew her mother would eventually interrogate her too. First, Al's needs for nourishment must be met. Bernice kept track that he received a pat of butter for his rolls, dill sauce for the fish, white wine in his goblet, but only a small bit.

He took a sip, put down the glass and addressed Lisa with a smile. "Tell us all about it. Which was your best class?"

She choked on a bite of roll. Her face burned as she spat out, "I don't want to go to graduate school."

Her father stared uncomprehendingly, blinking his near-sighted eyes. Lisa hated to cause him even the slightest pain. More than that, she was terrified of how such a shock would affect him. But she saw no way out. She'd made a start and had to press on. "I'm sorry if I misled you. I don't want to be a journalist."

"It's a little late in the day to decide"—here Bernice mimicked Lisa—"'I don't want to be a journalist.' You wanted to be a journalist last spring when you applied."

"Actually, I didn't."

Apparently, Bernice thought Lisa was still talking about not wanting to be a journalist. "So why did you apply?" she said. "What's all this about, Lisa? Did you have some little setback today? Whatever it is, get over it. You need to grow up and see this through. You have an obligation. You took up a place that someone else could have had."

Gazing at the remnants of uneaten salmon and wilted salad on her plate, Lisa mumbled, "I didn't take up a place."

"Speak up, Lisa," Bernice shrilled, bringing Lisa to attention.

"I didn't take up a place!"

"How could that be?"

"I never mailed in the application."

Lisa looked up, noticed her father smoothing and crumpling his cloth napkin. It mesmerized her. He tried to speak, but in this moment, there was no interrupting Bernice.

"You what? I don't understand. I sent you money for the application."

"I'll pay you back, Mom."

"You didn't send in the application? You mean to say you lied to us?"

"Yes...yes...yes!" Lisa said. Her mother exasperated her. Why was she so slow to understand? Yes, she, Lisa, was a monster.

"You're telling me that you..." Bernice's face was red and creased with anger. "You're a liar! What have we done to you that you treat us like this? I never thought that you...you..."

While she emitted flustered 'you's,' Al took his opportunity. "Let's hear what she has to say before judging." Lisa didn't know whether he was speaking extra slowly because he was trying to calm Bernice, or because he was stressed. Most likely, it was both.

Once again Lisa told him, "I don't want to be a journalist!"

"I see," Al said softly.

Lisa felt as if she'd cut out his heart. Her own lurched about in her chest like a pebble in a barrel, beating a frantic song of, 'Don't disturb your father'

Bernice asked sarcastically, "What do you want to do? Waste your time?"

"Journalism isn't the only profession," Al said soothingly. "Lisa could study a different field. A smart, talented, beautiful girl like her can be a doctor, lawyer, or a professor. One or two semesters off won't hurt her. She could get some real-life working experience. That's exactly what you've been advocating."

"Okay. I'm waiting. Let's hear what she has to say." Bernice arched an eyebrow.

Lisa's stomach lurched, but she managed to keep her voice steady, a tribute to her dramatic training. "I want to travel."

"Where, pray tell?" her mother asked.

"Europe."

Bernice's mouth fell open. "This is our country, not that cesspool. Did you ever hear of Hitler?"

"The Holocaust was two decades ago...my dream is to go to Paris...to meet artists...to speak French..." What made sense in discussions with Charlotte and Anne sounded weak when Lisa tried to persuade her parents.

"How do you propose to travel?" Bernice asked. "I'm willing to pay tuition for graduate school. Otherwise, you'll have to find a job to support yourself."

"I'll manage on my own." Lisa had no plan, only a need. She wasn't afraid of plopping down in Europe, knowing no one.

"You've had everything," Bernice went on. "Nannies, private schools...music lessons...summer camps. You have the opportunity to further your education. Why are you throwing it away? I don't understand."

"School isn't important! I want to learn about life, to enjoy myself while I'm young...Forgive me, but I don't want to live the way you and Dad do."

"What's wrong with how we live? You're too spoiled to appreciate everything we've given you."

"All you think about is Dad's stroke...and that he might die. That's your single focus. You shut out the rest of the world, including me." Lisa wasn't cruel enough to say that part of her desire to travel came from her desire to leave them. To her mind, they deserved punishment for a lifetime of closing their eyes to her need for affection. Involved with each other, they'd kept her at a distance. She couldn't forget her mother had considered sending her away! Now, she wanted to pay her back by disappearing.

"That's not true," Bernice said. "I never shut you out."

"When I was little, you wanted to send me away."

"Enough, Lisa!" Al cried, striking the table. "This discussion is over."

Scraping the bits of fish skin and bones from the dishes onto a single plate, Bernice said, "Al, go relax in the den. Lisa and I will clear up. I'll put up some coffee and call you when it's ready." Al walked down the hall, leaving them to carry the crockery into the kitchen.

"I don't understand you, Lisa. Is it Women's lib? I never needed it. No one ever took advantage of me as a woman," Bernice said as she rinsed the remains of the meal into the garbage disposal. She ran the water, turned on the noisy disposal. Lisa missed a sentence or two of her mother's monologue. Bernice flipped off the motor. "Or is it about drugs?" Turning to Lisa, she hissed, "Don't think I didn't notice that stink in your room. Don't tell me it's from hairspray or deodorant. You're smoking marijuana, aren't you?"

"You chain smoke. You're hypocritical to criticize me."

"Marijuana is different! Do you want to destroy your brain?" The dirty plates and glasses clattered as Bernice thrust them into the dishwasher.

"Tobacco gives you cancer."

"Aunt Elaine didn't smoke," Bernice muttered. A knife slipped from her hand, fell to the floor. She bent to pick it up.

Lisa started out of the kitchen.

"Where are you going?" Bernice demanded.

"Do you need me?"

"I need you to listen."

They stared at each other. Bernice broke the silence. "Are you on the pill? Answer me..." Sneeringly, she said, "Are you planning to join the sexual revolution?"

"That's my business."

"Not while you're in my home, and enjoying..." Bernice waved her hand, a gesture meant to include the large and small luxuries surrounding them.

"I don't care about living like you," Lisa sputtered. "I don't want to be weighed down by possessions. Life should be light...never ordinary...never vulgar."

Bernice began to cry. The sight of her mother with mascara-smudged cheeks confused Lisa. She didn't want to feel pity. Pity would anchor her here. She hurried off to her room. Soon, the growl of the dishwasher, the screech of the kettle rushed in through her open door. She heard her father's slow footsteps in the hall. He was going to drink his coffee. By now Bernice's face would be washed, her poise recovered. Lisa could make out her father saying resignedly. "She'll be twenty-one in a couple of weeks, Bernie. She has her rights."

What rights? Meaningless blather, Lisa assumed. She shut her door, began to get ready for bed. For once, she'd insist on skipping the TV. The confrontation had exhausted her. While she was undressing, her mother waltzed in without knocking.

Lisa turned away to conceal her breasts, and protested, "I'm changing!"

"We need to talk."

Lisa braced herself for more criticism.

"What's that?" Bernice asked, shrilly.

"What?" Lisa said impatiently.

Her mother touched her shoulder blade. "You have a mole."

"It's nothing. Just let me go to sleep."

"I'm making a dermatology appointment for you first thing tomorrow. You don't play around with moles."

The next day, the doctor removed the growth. Lisa was furious with her mother for forcing her to have a biopsy. The mole was nothing, of course. But Bernice seemed to enjoy medical drama. The doctor said he'd call with the lab results. Every time the phone rang, Bernice rushed to answer with a distraught 'hello,' as if she was about to hear bad news.

When the doctor finally did call, Lisa was home alone. He told her that she had a melanoma. She felt woozy, had to lean against the wall.

"We caught it early. The odds are you won't have any more trouble. To be safe, we'll do a further excision at the site and remove more tissue. Also, I think a lymph node dissection's a good idea."

"Surgery?" Lisa began to cry. She was young, had done none of the things she wanted to do.

"You'll be home the next day. Then you can forget the whole thing."

Numbly, she passed through the ordeals of blood test, chest x-ray, fasting for twelve hours before the surgery. Waking from the anesthetic, she felt sick and confused.

Her mother was at her side. She drove her home and fussed. Her father skipped three days of work to look after her too. Lisa felt that she'd never experienced such attention from them. Her cancer terrified them.

Convalescing, Lisa lay curled up on the couch with *Anna Karenina,* and sipped the lemonade her mother brought her on a tray. Her twenty-first birthday was at the end of the week. It seemed likely her parents would wish to indulge her, particularly, if she insisted. She imagined her father handing her an airplane ticket to Paris, her mother slipping a fat roll of cash into her purse. Hinting for the gifts she wanted, she told them, "No matter what, I want to travel. It's more important than ever to me."

"We'll see. Let's talk about it after we hear from the doctor," Bernice said.

"Dad?" Lisa appealed.

"Your mother's right. We can't make any decisions yet."

Lisa was stunned. It sounded like her parents were waiting for the biopsy report before committing themselves. If she were dying, they'd help her. If she were going to live, they'd resume pressuring her to return to school. She'd have accomplished nothing by telling them her true feelings. Battles that went nowhere were to continue unless the lymph nodes revealed the cancer was spreading. She felt trapped.

Her parents were at work when the doctor phoned. He said, "I have your latest lab report."

Her heart pounded.

"You're cancer-free. You can get on with your life."

Although he seemed in a hurry, Lisa kept him on the telephone. She needed to prolong the contact, hear the news of her reprieve again before she could believe it. Talking with him, she gradually came alive again. "It's my birthday today...You've given me a wonderful present...Thank you..."

After putting down the phone, she wandered restlessly from room to room. Her parents wouldn't come back for hours. She knew she ought to phone to tell them the good news. If she delayed, it was because she couldn't bear for the old futile arguments to resume. 'What are your plans, Lisa? Are you returning to school? Don't waste time.' She thought of how her mother had continued to work even after her father returned to his law practice. Lisa had learned not to become attached to any of the nannies hired to care for her. If she did, the woman was sent away. Probably, Bernice had been jealous, yet she wouldn't give up working. Her job was 'insurance' in case Al had another stroke. Her job was a treadmill from which she couldn't step off.

In the kitchen, Lisa drank a glass of cooking sherry to calm her nerves. Later, she rolled a toke from the last of Charlotte's marijuana, and smoked it in her bedroom. She wandered off to her father's home office. Bookcases of legal books and journals lined three walls. A window looked out on the brick building across the street. Sitting down at Al's desk, Lisa riffled through the papers strewn across it. She wasn't interested in legal matters, only needed something to do with her hands. Opening a folder, she glanced at the first page of a document.

Her name jumped from the text. Ordinarily, she would have found convoluted legal language a struggle, but she read through the pages and easily grasped the exciting news. Her grandparents, made rich by their labors and by her mother's, had set up a trust fund for her. On her twenty-first birthday, this very day, the fund was to start issuing payments of three hundred dollars a month. She knew it wasn't a lot, but suspected that with this money, she could manage to live independently.

Her father had referred to her 'rights.' He must have meant she was entitled to access to this fund. He and Bernice had told her nothing about it. They were her parents! She ought to be able to trust them. Lisa was furious. They'd tried to cheat her out of her inheritance. She was all the more determined to leave home.

During supper, her parents didn't remark on how subdued she was. They expected as much, not knowing the doctor had phoned. A chocolate cake appeared for dessert. Al had picked it up at the bakery for Lisa's birthday. He watched her blow out the candles and congratulated her. As a lawyer, he appreciated her new legal standing. He said, "Now you can vote." Bernice presented her with a gold watch with a delicate gold band. Putting it on her wrist, Lisa thanked her for the valuable gift and said, "I was waiting for this special moment to tell you. The doctor called. Everything's okay."

"Thank God," Al sighed.

"That's what we hoped all along," Bernice said, beaming. "Let's have a toast." She filled wine glasses. "To Lisa. May she live a long healthy life."

Lisa downed a glass, before asking, "Do you have anything special to share with me, Mom and Dad?"

They gazed at her with seeming innocence. She'd have to force them to admit what they'd done! Excusing herself, she ran off to her father's office and brought back the document concerning the trust fund. Her father recognized it and flushed. "So you know about the trust fund."

Her mother cried, "Have you been snooping through your father's papers? I thought we taught you better manners."

"I don't think you can complain about my manners. Not when you've held back what was mine. When were you going to tell me?"

"Your father and I planned on telling you when you were mature enough to handle the money. Your grandparents made a mistake. They should have set up the trust for when you were older and more experienced. If they were alive today, I'm sure that's what they'd want. Money's a responsibility. Let us invest yours. Later when you start your family, you'll have a tidy sum."

"I want it now!"

Turning to Al, Bernice implored, "Help me."

Lisa turned to her father too. "I intend to travel. I should be getting monthly checks. I'd like a fail-proof system for collecting them, no matter where I am."

"I can set that up," Al said in his neutral lawyer's voice.

Later that evening, Lisa was reading in bed when her mother came into her room-- without knocking, as usual. She sat down at the edge of the mattress, took Lisa's hand in hers and said, "I don't think it's a good idea for you leave us. Not now, any way. Be sensible. Wait a year."

"For what, Mom?"

"To…to…to make sure the cancer's not coming back. As I understand it, the first year is when it's most likely to return."

"I'm not waiting a year." Lisa suspected that the purpose of her mother's threats and solicitude was to seduce her into assuming her father's invalid role. The thought of being kept in cotton wool like him was unbearable.

"Stress could bring the cancer back."

Lisa withdrew her hand.

In a breaking voice, Bernice said, "Elaine died young. I don't want to see it happen to you."

"Why are you frightening me?"

"I want to protect you. I always tried to protect you…I didn't let you work at that camp with the sick kids."

"What are you talking about?"

Bernice shrugged, then rose and left. Lisa lay in bed, staring at the ceiling. For the first time, she understood why she'd been forbidden to work at the summer camp for disabled kids. Her mother was terrified of illness. She must have believed such children would infect Lisa, if not with their infirmities then with their bad luck.

The next evening, Lisa was in the kitchen, helping her mother clean up dirty pots and pans from dinner. She said, "I prefer to die young if that's the price of living the life I want."

"You wouldn't talk that way if you actually were facing death." Bernice was bent over the sink, energetically scrubbing a frying pan with Brillo.

"Why do you want me to stay? To help take care of Dad?"

"Would that be such a bad thing?"

"He's doing fine. He doesn't need me."

"I wish I could take off at a moment's notice, but that's not what life's like," Bernice said bitterly. She rinsed the pan, clanged it onto the drainer. Lisa was supposed to dry it.

"You had your chance. Now, I want mine," Lisa said.

Her confidence surprised her. She stood straight, head high and walked off, tossing her dishtowel on a counter. While her mother was busy in the kitchen, Lisa seized her opportunity to speak to her father alone. The sound of a phonograph record came from the living room. Her father was stretched out on the couch, listening to a recording of "The Marriage of Figaro." Out of loyalty to his Jewish heritage, he tried to boycott German products, mostly technology. Wagner he could forgo, but he couldn't renounce Bach, Mozart, and Beethoven.

"You do know why I'm going?" she asked, turning the volume of the music down. She wanted him to understand her reasons, even if Bernice couldn't. Al blinked his assent. It would have been a betrayal to his wife for him to do more.

Two nights later, while Bernice was preparing dinner, Al asked Lisa to come to his office. Just as she'd fantasized, he'd bought her a plane ticket to Paris. The departure date was in two weeks. "Thanks," Lisa said, too moved and grateful to say more.

"I'll worry. You're so young. How are you going to manage?"

"Don't worry about me, Dad. Some of my classmates are in Europe. They're doing fine. I will too."

The next few days, Lisa became organized. She applied for an American Express card. Her father said he could wire her monthly stipends to American Express, so that she'd be able to pick them up at any office abroad. She had medical and dental checkups, bought a new suitcase and walking shoes.

Her mother and father accompanied her to the airport. Lisa hugged them 'goodbye' at the departure gate, then joined the boarding queue. Bernice looked downcast as she waved. Al put his arm around her shoulder and managed to signal Lisa a thumbs-up victory sign behind her back.

Afraid she'd burst into tears in front of them, Lisa was glad to board. As the plane ascended into the clouds, she still couldn't believe that she was setting out. Had her parents left the airport directly? Or had they felt it was necessary to sit down somewhere before they went off? She wondered whether they'd send her letters, begging her to come home. Their need would touch her, but she'd never give up her hard won independence.

She began to feel joyful. Her real life was beginning.

3

Israel, 1982

Karl woke to find his roommate standing at the side of his bed, staring at him intently. Jakob was already dressed, a *keepah* on his head, a white prayer shawl around his shoulders, *tzitzis* strings hanging over his pants.

"Hi," Karl said and threw off his covers.

Jakob shook his head, conveying in dumb show that Karl must not talk. "*Modeha ani.*" he said.

'What's this about?' Karl tried to say. But each time he spoke, Jakob touched his finger to his lips and repeated, "*Modeha ani.*"

"*Modeha ani,*" Karl said, realizing he must parrot Hebrew prayers as he had with Shloime the night before. More prayers were recited while he washed his hands by pouring water from a pitcher over one and then the other, and when he put on his *tzitzis*.

Just as he was wondering whether he'd be stuck in this dumb show the rest of the day, Jakob said, "Hi. I'm Jakob. You can talk now."

"I'm Karl."

They shook hands.

"When's breakfast?" Karl asked. His voice was muffled as he slipped a t-shirt over his head. He was famished. The last meal he'd eaten was on the airplane, three hours before he'd landed.

"Before eating, we have to attend *Mincha,* the first prayer service."

"There's more than one service?" Karl said, incredulously. "Doesn't all the praying we've already done count?"

"Twice a day, a minimum of ten men must come together for a *minyan*."

"A *minyan*?"

"A prayer quorum."

Karl finished dressing, put his *keepah* on his head and, following Jakob's lead again, tucked the velvet bag that contained his phylacteries and prayer shawl under his arm. Like a blind man, he let Jakob steer him from the dorm and into the courtyard where a crowd of boys surged about them, also on the way to *Mincha*. Most of them wore black pants and white shirts and, with *tzitzis* and *kepahs*, looked completely different from the students at Berkeley High. The Berkeley kids--a mixture of all races, not all Caucasian like the Yeshiva boys--had dressed as they'd pleased, or in the style their particular clique dictated.

The students hurried to the main building to the synagogue. The white-walled hall was filled with rows of worn benches. Teachers and staff were on one side, students on the other. Jakob sat beside Karl, providing a whispered commentary. The oil-burning lamp that hung in front was "the eternal light;" the fierce lion embroidered in gold and silver thread on the blue velvet altar curtain, "the lion of Judah;" a large, brass candelabra on a table near the lectern "a menorah."

In the sea of faces, the rabbis stood out with their scant, wispy facial hair, or thick, wavy beards of brown, gray, black, white, gold, or red. "The rabbis wear beards to show God in their faces," Jakob said.

One rabbi was particularly imposing, a broad-shouldered old man who sat on a chair on the raised platform in front of the congregation. According to Jakob, this was Rabbi Tubol, the head of the Yeshiva. With his fluffy white beard, hooknose and black eyes, Rabbi Tubol looked the way Karl imagined God would, that was, if there was a God.

There was a stir in the hall when everyone removed the wooden boxes from the velvet bags and put them on. Jakob showed Karl how to crisscross the leather straps on his left arm and how to tie a *tefillin* box to his forehead. Enclosed in long white *tallis* shawls, the congregation swayed forward and back. How strange they looked, muttering incomprehensible words, and with boxes lashed to their foreheads. Reluctantly, Karl repeated word by word what his roommate read aloud from the gilt-edged prayer book that Jakob called a *siddur*. Jakob took his time, unlike many boys who recited the prayers at lightning speed in a blur of sound, with a resounding 'amen' at the end.

Feeling restless, Karl gazed at Rabbi Tubol and tried to discern whether 'God' was wearing a tie. When Rabbi Levy had visited him in Juvenile Hall, Karl had asked, "Do I have to wear a uniform with a tie at the Yeshiva?" The rabbi had laughed and said that the early Israeli pioneers had given them up, wanting to distinguish themselves from European imperialists. After a while, their informal way of dressing became the general custom. But did a Yeshiva head follow this custom? Karl couldn't tell whether 'God' was wearing a tie because if he was, his beard hid it.

As the service ensued, renewed hunger pains beset Karl. He could think of little else but what would be served for breakfast. At home, he ate cornflakes and toast in the morning. At the jail, there'd been cereal and toast too, but sometimes scrambled eggs or pancakes. Pancakes with plenty of butter and syrup would be delicious. His mouth watered. His stomach rumbled. He couldn't stop yawning, even stretched his arms overhead.

Rabbi Tubol stepped up to the lectern and slowly surveyed the hall. His gaze fell on Karl who shrank at his glare. He didn't know what he'd done wrong. Was it forbidden to yawn and stretch? He couldn't concentrate on prayers he didn't understand. Or did the rabbi somehow know he was the boy who'd been a criminal? The broad-shouldered rabbi reminded Karl of his grandfather. Grandpa Al had refused to speak to Karl from the time he was arrested. Would the head of the Yeshiva shun him too?

At last, Rabbi Tubol spoke. "Welcome students. You have a rich experience ahead of you. Our Yeshiva has a rigorous curriculum and exceptional teachers. I want to urge you to work hard the next two years and receive the full benefit of what we have to offer. Above all, help each other. The failure of one is the failure of all. Let none of you say, 'Am I my brother's keeper?' the words Cain dared say to *HaShem...*"

"*HaShem?*" Karl spoke the strange word aloud. Jakob, who'd been listening raptly to the rabbi, whispered a hasty explanation to Karl. "It means The Name. We don't say the sacred name for God except in prayers. In ordinary conversation, we say The Name..."

Rabbi Tubol said, "This might be your first time in Israel. If it is, one crucial issue you need to hear about is water conservation. Several of you come to us from countries where water is plentiful. Perhaps it rains too much. Our English students complain they must carry umbrellas every day in their home country. Israel is not England. I hope you English boys left your umbrellas at home. You won't need any until the winter."

The boys laughed. The rabbi waited for silence.

"The menorah, the ancient candelabra emblem of the Jewish people, reminds us that water is precious. A renowned scholar at the Hebrew University says the *menorah* signifies the inverted leaves of a palm tree. A parched desert traveler knows palm leaves mean water. Everywhere, but particularly in the desert, water is life. Let me repeat: Water is life! There will be no water rationing as long as you boys act responsibly. Take quick showers. Remember, every drop counts... All right. As you leave, stop at the table outside the door. Each of you will receive a class schedule."

Everyone filed out of the synagogue, went off to breakfast. The Yeshiva's cafeteria resembled the one at Juvenile Hall. The same useless fan stirred hot air. There were the same paper plates, cups, and plastic cutlery. Every boy took a tray and waited his turn for food. Here, though, there was a help-yourself-buffet instead of servers, and boys could heap their plates as high as they liked with salads and a thick, sour-tasting yogurt, not the breakfast Karl expected.

Another difference from Juvenile Hall was that there were no guards who paced the perimeter of the cafeteria. Nonetheless, Karl felt watched. When he raised his fork and was ready to dig, Jakob placed a restraining hand on his arm. "You have to make a blessing over the food first." Noiselessly, Karl moved his lips as if praying. This play-acting embarrassed him, but he had to do it. He must fit in, was terrified to make even the slightest misstep for fear of being expelled, sent back to California, and forced to go to the Youth Authority.

Aside from Jakob, the boys at his table were: two Americans, Zach and Avi; Eli, a redheaded English boy; Leib, a fat kid from Australia. They discussed the Jewish Day Schools they'd attended, used Hebrew expressions, and laughed at jokes Karl didn't understand. The students came from the ends of the world, and yet each of them knew a rabbi or had a relative at the other boys' schools. Looking around, Karl tried to spot someone who appeared as left out as himself, a possible friend. He wanted to meet the *ba'al tshuvahs,* other boys who were new to Judaism. He couldn't tell who they were.

At the meal's conclusion, he discarded his paper dish and cup in the garbage and carried his tray to the rack near the kitchen. Outside the cafeteria, he saw boys checking their schedules, consulting with each other. At least, he wasn't the only one who didn't know where to go. Leib, the Australian kid, glanced at Karl's schedule and said he had the same first class, Hebrew. Together, they searched and found the classroom.

Karl took a seat to the rear, hoping he wouldn't be called on. During class, Hebrew was used freely, and almost non-stop. Karl couldn't understand a word. His mind was drawn elsewhere. He wondered whether Sam Zeiger was still furious. Mr. Zeiger could have followed him to Israel, thirsting for the revenge that the court had denied him. Karl looked towards the classroom door, half-expecting Mr. Zeiger to charge in and shout, 'Shame.'

From Hebrew Karl went to Old Testament class where he sat in the rear again. Rabbi Cohen said that since Rabbi Tubol had spoken of water conservation, he wanted to expand on the subject.

"Tell me," he asked, "what is to be done if two people are stranded in the desert and only one has brought water?"

A consensus emerged among the boys: a person's obligation was to save himself first.

Rabbi Cohen surveyed the room and said, "Yes, an average person is not expected to do more. But what must a scholar do? He is on a higher moral level. As someone ennobled by Torah study, he must share his portion of water, even if it means his death.

Now that you understand that your very life depends on what you learn, we can begin to discuss the Old Testament."

Throughout the morning, Karl felt as lost as a kindergarten kid in a college course. He was glad for the lunch break--and the hour naptime that followed when he could catch up on some of the sleep he'd missed when he'd crossed time zones and changed day into night, and night into day. Jakob offered to forego his nap to help Karl with his schoolwork. Karl was too exhausted and too proud to accept.

It was difficult for Karl to wake from the nap. He was late to his first Modern European History class. Rabbi Wolfe, a heavy-set man in his late fifties, barked, "Come on time in the future. This is not a class you want to interrupt." Turning to the other students, he intoned in a singsong, "This semester, we'll be learning about the conditions in Europe after World War I...the rise of the Nazi party...the appeasement of Hitler by the Western powers...the outbreak of World War II..."

Troubled by his own crimes, Karl had no desire to hear about atrocities committed during the Holocaust. Like it or not, he had to stay in his seat and listen to what was in store for him.

"We're going to visit *Yad Vashem*, the Holocaust memorial museum. We'll read about the horrors in concentration camps. All of you have heard a little about the Nazi crimes before. Now you'll hear about them in detail. This course will be difficult, even painful. If any of you have a need to talk about what you're experiencing, don't be afraid to express your feelings here, or come to see me privately.

"We'll speak about 'the six million'--yes, I repeat, six million Jews slaughtered by the Nazis. We'll celebrate the Jewish survivors, 'the remnant,' those who remember, bear witness, and have assumed a special responsibility for keeping Judaism alive. Even those born long after the war mourn the uncles, aunts and cousins they never met who were lost in the Holocaust. Have any of you lost relatives?"

Jakob's hand shot up. He said his family came from Hungary originally. He spoke of the Arrow Cross Party, Hungarian Nazis who raided houses in the Jewish Ghetto in Budapest. Every night they dragged Jews to the Danube, shot and pushed them in the river. Jakob's grandfather was one of the victims. His fate was particularly tragic because he died shortly before the liberation. If he'd stayed alive a few weeks longer, he'd have been saved.

His voice trembling with emotion, Jakob said, "I'd like to poison the rivers in Hungary to get even with the Nazi collaborators—and if they're no longer alive with their children and grandchildren."

Leib, the Australian boy, said, "You can't blame the children for the crimes of their fathers. Besides, there are children of Nazis who work to build the land of Israel."

Two other students immediately backed up Jakob; one saying in an emotional voice, "What happened in the Holocaust can never be atoned!" The other boy had tears in his eyes and could barely get out his sputter of agreement. "The Nazis and their collaborators, and their descendents are all evil."

All Karl knew about the Nazis was what he'd seen portrayed in films and television programs. That was enough to make him glad that his father wasn't German. If Jakob and most of the Yeshiva students hated Germans, he understood why. But he didn't comprehend why they hated Hungarians. As far as he knew, defeated countries like Hungary had been forced to take orders from Hitler. The men who shot Jakob's grandfather would have been executed if they hadn't killed Jews.

Most people were out to save themselves first. This Karl understood. He'd done it himself. The police would never have caught Reynaldo if he, Karl, hadn't snitched. Reynaldo was older than sixteen at the time of the robbery. His mother didn't have the money to hire a fancy lawyer, a Mr. Huff who might have gotten around that. Most likely, Reynaldo had been sentenced to the hell of Y.A.

If he offered excuses for the Hungarians, Karl knew he'd be condemned as callous. He was astonished at the depth of the students' grief for relatives they'd never met. For them, the Holocaust atrocities inflicted more than three decades ago were taking place now! He shrank from the raw emotions expressed, wanted only to escape. When the class ended, he was the first one out the door.

On the third day, Karl knew it was probably too early for the letter Lisa had promised to have arrived. Even so, he was so homesick that he went to check. Finding his cubby empty, he was disappointed but not surprised. He almost made it out the office door, but before he did, Shloime, looked up from the papers he was sorting at his desk and asked, "Can I help you?"

Flustered, Karl didn't know how to explain why he was checking for mail so soon. But there must be times the mail was efficient. Perhaps Lisa's letter had arrived. He asked, "Did you have a chance to sort today's mail into the cubbies yet?"

"If there's nothing in your cubby, nothing came for you."

"I'm expecting a letter from my mom. Can you look around? Maybe…maybe it got mislaid."

"I've never mislaid a letter!"

Three more days passed. Letters and packages of goodies arrived for other students. Karl tried to find comfort in the thought that it was just as well Lisa didn't send cookies, as they wouldn't be kosher. He'd have to throw them away. But he knew that wouldn't matter. What counted was that he'd have proof she loved him.

On a day when Karl was the only one who hadn't received mail, Shloime took him aside and said, "The Israeli mail system is poor. It's always been, even when the Turks ran things. Either the mail truck breaks down, or there's a flat tire, or the driver's sick. God willing, your letter will arrive soon."

In the middle of the second week, Shloime knocked on Karl's dormitory room door, waking him from his after-lunch nap. "Come with me," he told Karl. Asking for no explanation of why and where, Karl followed him from the dorm to the main building, like he had followed his guard who escorted him to court. Once they were at the office, Shloime instructed, "Go in to see Rabbi Tubol, and pull the door shut behind you."

The old man who looked like God sat at his desk, hunched over a huge book. Its yellow pages seemed ready to crack whenever he turned them. Karl shifted uneasily, bracing himself for a lecture about his crimes, or even to be told that the Yeshiva head regretted accepting him in his school.

In Israel he'd hoped he'd forget about the wrongs he'd done, his time in jail, and how Reynaldo must be suffering in Y.A. But his past tormented him here as much it had in California, particularly after Jakob had showed him a photograph from his *bar mitzvah* party and said, "Whether you have a ceremony or not, you become a man when you're thirteen, responsible for what you do."

The California court had said 'sixteen' marked the age of responsibility. Karl had taken comfort that he'd been less than sixteen when he committed his crimes, an immature, inexperienced, impulsive boy. Jewish law—stricter than the law in an American court—robbed him of his excuse for the bad things he'd done.

Eventually, Rabbi Tubol glanced up and looked Karl over from head to foot as if he were another book to study. "So you're the one who yawns at the prayer services. Take a seat." There was a chair with a pillow, but the rabbi pointed to a bare chair. Karl's legs felt like jelly as he collapsed into it.

"You've had some problems adjusting?"

Karl sighed. Perhaps Rabbi Tubol would restrict himself to speaking about his problems at the Yeshiva. One of his teachers might have reported him for coming late to class. He'd been tardy to other classes besides Rabbi Wolfe's, couldn't help it. Most of the time, he had an upset stomach. The typical Yeshiva meal was *yoghurt*, grilled eggplant, a *tabbuleh* salad of grain, parsley and tomatoes, *falafel*—little balls of fried garbanzo flour topped by *tahini* sauce, and *pita* bread. During meals, Karl ate rapaciously, only to feel a gnawing hunger an hour or two later. He was unaccustomed to eating so many vegetables. Between classes he had to run to the toilet with gas or diarrhea.

"How are you getting on in your studies?" Rabbi Tubol asked.

Karl's face felt warm. Why did the rabbi ask? The teachers must have told him he couldn't keep up. "I study the books the teachers handed out," he mumbled, hoping that would suffice.

Rabbi Tubol spoke to him, but Karl blocked out what the old man was saying about what had been reported about his academic failings by Rabbi Frankel, Rabbi Wolfe, and

Rabbi Cohen. Lisa had trouble concentrating. So did he. That was one reason he was so behind in his Yeshiva studies. Another was, he barely understood how he was supposed to behave in his classes.

At his previous schools, he'd been expected to raise his hand to receive permission to speak. To his amazement, Yeshiva students shouted out answers spontaneously. Or they stood chanting texts, swaying back and forth. Or they broke up into pairs, and studied together. In every class, he was the last one selected as a partner. It reminded him of the shame he'd felt the times when he'd been chosen last for a punch ball or a baseball team when he was younger. The nearly constant noise and chaos gave him a headache.

There was one encouraging sign, though, Karl thought, staring out the office window at the cloudless sky. He'd begun recollecting the meaning of a few basic Hebrew words he must have learnt when he'd lived on the *kibbutz*. '*Cain*' and '*lo*' meant 'yes' and 'no,' and '*ahnee*,' was 'I am.' But his budding Hebrew vocabulary was too miniscule to give meaning to the rapid-fire discussions he heard. Even when these discussions were in English, he didn't understand the references to the Old Testament, Talmud and other Jewish books. None of his classes were as troubling as the one in Modern European History class, but he was barely more comfortable in any of the others.

"Are you making friends?" Rabbi Tubol asked.

Too distracted to hear much else of what the rabbi said, Karl heard this question and shrugged. He didn't know how to talk to the other students. At Berkeley High guys talked about girls and sports. The Yeshiva boys strove to be pure. To discuss girls was considered impure. There was no prohibition against sports, but only Karl wanted to discuss basketball, baseball, and football. He, on the other hand, didn't care anything about the subjects the students loved: genealogy; miracles; angels appearing to holy men;

spontaneous cures from deadly diseases; the chance meetings of relations separated during the Holocaust on a subway platform or in a crowd. There was constant chatter about parents, grandparents, great-grandparents, and ancestors even further back in time. When Karl asked Jakob why the other boys were so interested in dead people, Jakob had explained, "Our dead relatives protect us and plead with *HaShem* on our behalf."

Responding to Karl's shrug, Rabbi Tubol reflected, "Perhaps my question's premature. It takes time to make friends. In a few weeks, I'm sure you'll be able to give an affirmative response. But Jakob is looking after you, isn't he?"

"Yes," Karl said, noting the satisfied smile on Rabbi Tubol's face. Jakob took the role of 'brother's keeper' because Rabbi Tubol said he must.

"I'm glad Jakob's helping."

"Jakob tries hard." Karl conceded. It hurt him that his roommate was more his babysitter than his friend. Why should Jakob patronize anyone? He was far from perfect. When he studied he whirled his hair, and picked his nose. He had a sweet tooth. In his top desk drawer, he kept a secret stock of caramels he never shared.

"You must be wondering why I called you in for this interview," the Yeshiva head said. He rubbed his hands together, as if getting down to work.

Karl stiffened, expecting the long-dreaded lecture about his crimes. The rabbi surprised him.

"I'm not going to say anything about what happened in your past. As far as I'm concerned, that part of your life is over, and the important part is starting. I want you to know that everyone has a new beginning at the Yeshiva."

"Thank you, Rabbi."

Waving Karl's thanks away with a gesture of his hand, Rabbi Tubol said, "Most of the boys find it helpful to have someone in whom they can confide, particularly when they're adjusting to the school. Like every other boy, you've been assigned a spiritual advisor to assist you. Rabbi Blum's young, only thirty-three. You have a lot in common. He's a *ba'al tshuva* from an assimilated family, and he's American. My hope is that you'll speak freely to him. Let him know anything that's troubling you."

Rabbi Blum was Karl's Talmud teacher. The other rabbis were older men with European accents. More formal than the young American teacher, they stood while they taught, kept their backs straight, their arms at their sides. Rabbi Blum moved restlessly about the classroom, and gesticulated. Sometimes, he sat on the edge of his or even a student's desk. Karl liked him but didn't want a spiritual advisor. A spiritual advisor, he guessed, would poke into his feelings and his past.

Rabbi Tubol already knew his crimes, but Karl must keep them secret from everyone else. In jail, there'd been other flawed individuals, kids to whom he could confide and say what he'd done. No one had attempted or even thought about the high standards that existed here.

In his first class with Rabbi Cohen, Karl had learned that a scholar must willingly hand over his portion of water in the desert, must give up his life in order to save another. Karl, on the other hand, was the opposite of a scholar. He'd nearly killed a man. The pious rabbis and students would despise him if they found out. The peaks of perfection were too high and far away for Karl. The prospect of looking towards them with Rabbi Blum made him feel crushed and hopeless.

"Do I have to talk to my spiritual advisor?"

Rabbi Tubol stroked his beard. After a few moments, he said, "This is voluntary."

Instantly, Karl decided he'd never approach Rabbi Blum in the way Rabbi Tubol desired.

"But I do hope you'll confide in him," Rabbi Tubol said.

"I'll…I'll…I'll…" Karl faltered.

"Come closer. Stand up and come around the desk."

Karl stood and approached, his heart thudding. Rabbi Tubol had said he wouldn't refer to his crimes again, but that didn't mean he wouldn't threaten him about what would happen if he didn't conform to the Yeshiva's standards. A complaint might be sent to Judge Thorn. Why did he want him closer? He could say from across the desk that he was going to lodge a complaint.

To his amazement, the rabbi reached towards him and tugged one of the knotted *tzitzis* strings hanging down beneath his shirt. "We'll turn you into a Yeshiva boy yet," he chuckled. "By the way, you need a different name, a Jewish one. Think about it for a day or two. Not too long, because the sooner people start calling you by your new name, the better. I'm sure you understand."

"Is this voluntary too?" Karl asked uneasily.

"No," the rabbi said, and released him from the interview with the agreement that Karl would select a new name and then return to tell him.

Karl hoped more pressing matters would distract Rabbi Tubol, and that he wouldn't notice that his victim hadn't returned. Two days passed. The rabbi summoned him again.

"What's your new name?" he asked soon after Karl was seated.

"Adam," Karl muttered, an answer he'd prepared. Karl meant man in German, and the Hebrew teacher had said that Adam meant man too.

"You'll have to speak up!"

"Adam," Karl repeated.

Rabbi Tubol shook his head. "It's unlucky to pick a name that appears before Abraham in the Torah. The Jewish religion begins with Avram, so in a strict sense the earlier names aren't Jewish."

Karl didn't dare object. "You pick something, Rabbi. I don't care what it is."

The Yeshiva head stared. Seeing Karl was sincere, he nodded. "How about Baruch? It means a blessing."

"Okay."

The rabbi touched Karl's head with outstretched fingers. "From now on, you're Baruch. We'll make an announcement at supper."

After the afternoon services, Karl walked slowly to the cafeteria. Arriving late, he sat in a chair Jakob had saved for him. No one greeted him as it was forbidden to speak until after Rabbi Tubol led the before-meal prayer. The Yeshiva head stood in front of the cafeteria. He glanced at Karl and smiled. Guessing what was to come, Karl shuddered.

"I'd like to call Baruch up to lead the prayer."

A moment of agonizing silence passed. Rabbi Tubol's glasses enlarged his dark eyes. His searing gaze told Karl that he had no choice but to acknowledge he was Baruch. He went to stand beside Rabbi Tubol and stumbled through the prayer. When he finished, Rabbi Tubol said, "From now on, this student is Baruch."

Even in jail, Karl had been allowed to keep his name. Now, he was robbed of who he was. He crept back to his seat and concentrated on finishing his meal. The few times he was addressed, it was as 'Baruch.'

Karl's second Friday at the Yeshiva, the mail truck was delayed, the kind of occurrence Shloime had predicted. After one visit to the office to check his mail, Karl made a second. It was an hour before sundown. The Sabbath was imminent. Once the *shabbes* candles were lit, no work could be done. He couldn't write, cut or tear paper, turn on a light, or ride in a car or bus. Nor would he be able to unseal an envelope. The prohibitions continued until Saturday night. If Lisa's letter came, he didn't want to wait until then to read it.

To Karl's delight, her letter was waiting in his box. He carried it to his dorm room. Jakob was out. He could read in privacy. Despite the letter's brevity, he was grateful for the few lines wishing him well, and for the poem and drawing Lisa had included. At the bottom of the drawing she'd scrawled, "I promise to write a long letter as soon as I hear from you." The date on the letter told him she'd written him the very day he'd left for Israel. The postmark was four days later, not a long delay for Lisa. She was absentminded. At home, on occasion he'd come upon bill payments, birthday cards or letters she'd forgotten to send. When he showed them to her she cried, "Good intentions gone astray," and sent him to the mailbox, or to the post office to purchase the required stamps.

Students called to each other in the hall outside Karl's dorm room, "Time to get ready for *Shabbes*." Their voices were eager. They looked forward to the Sabbath. Karl did not. Experiencing it for the first time the week before, he'd found there was little to do besides attend services, go to the cafeteria for meals, and sleep. He detested the enforced idleness. It reminded him of 'serving time.'

Putting Lisa's letter aside, he began his preparations. He tore the toilet paper he anticipated using until Saturday night, put on a nightlight in the bathroom, and a small lamp in his dorm room to stay lit. As he showered, he thought of Lisa's good points, that she never said a bad word about anyone, enjoyed herself more than other people, and was artistic, poetic, and beautiful. Emerging from the bathroom to put on fresh clothes, he found Jakob, waiting for his chance to bathe.

At the candle-lighting ceremony at sundown, Karl had Lisa's letter in his pocket. The letter was a sign of her devotion. The rest of the evening images of her flooded his mind: Lisa moving gracefully about their flat; watering her ferns; curling up on the couch; writing in her journal; whipping up a meal from refrigerator scraps, a concoction of day old noodles, lettuce, and peanut butter, her talk and laughter making it seem like a feast. When he climbed into bed at midnight, his mind was still busy. He thought about the letter he'd write back. He didn't want to distort or lie and pretend he was happy. Yet, he was determined not to worry her.

The next day, after a big *Shabbes* lunch, Karl decided to skip the after-lunch nap, the only way he dared rebel. Instead of going to his room, he stayed in the courtyard, pacing as he had in the Juvenile Hall recreation yard. Down the road, the *kibbutz* guard dogs barked. The only shade was beneath a stunted olive tree. Otherwise, the sun glared. Karl wished he had on a brimmed hat instead of a yarmulke. The only place to sit was a hard stone bench. He took out his mother's letter and read and reread the onionskin sheet of paper. A dry wind blew dust onto Karl's hair and face. He fled to his dorm room.

Jakob's measured breathing told Karl that his roommate was asleep. He'd taken off his clothes, folded and hung them over a chair. Karl stripped to his underwear too, but left his clothes in a pile on the floor. Unable to doze off, Karl calculated how many hours were left to the suffocating *Shabbes*. He began to masturbate. In Juvenile Hall, all the kids had done it to pass the time while locked in their cells. They'd called it 'choking the chicken,' 'pounding the salami' or 'choking the one-eyed snake.' Karl tried not to make noise, but the bedsprings creaked, louder and louder until he was done. He turned over; lay spent, staring at the cracks in the ceiling.

The slow, audible breaths of sleep no longer came from the next bed. Karl realized he'd woken his roommate. It wasn't the first time Karl had masturbated at the Yeshiva, but it was the first time he'd had a witness.

"You're not supposed to do that," Jakob said.

"Do what?" Karl asked innocently.

"You know."

"That's my business," Karl exploded. He'd been ripped away from his home. He had no friends. Was this one comfort and pleasure to be taken away from him too? "Who gave you to right to tell me I can't?" His legs tangled in his sticky sheet. Turning on his side, he faced away from his roommate.

"Jewish law says a man must not spill his seed on the ground."

Half-raising himself, Karl turned back and hissed, "Even you must do it? Everyone does."

"Sometimes, I violate *Halacha*. But I try not to."

"Why's it a big deal? It's private. Who does it hurt?"

"It could hurt my wife," Jakob said earnestly. He rose and began to dress.

"You're not married. You're not even engaged," Karl snorted. His temper put him at a disadvantage. He hated—and envied—the way Jakob retreated to some far island of calm as he regurgitated the lessons he'd learned from the rabbis.

"I haven't yet met my *beshert*, my intended wife, but I want to be considerate of her."

"What does she care if you jerked off before you met her?"

Jakob buttoned his white shirt. "If I pick up bad habits, I'll bring them to my marriage. Those habits will take away from our pleasure together."

"Once you get married, you won't have to jerk off."

"I'm trying to master my sexual urges. When I have a wife and children, I'll know how to be loyal to them."

"You're worried about your children too?" Karl laughed. His roommate seemed naive and childish.

Acting as if he didn't notice Karl's contempt, Jakob said, "What if I'm attracted to another woman than my wife? It happens to many men. The ones who taught themselves restraint know how to resist." He was standing by the door now, dressed in the usual black pants-white shirt uniform.

"You have wet dreams, don't you? You can't eliminate your urges. You're a man. Men have needs."

"That's why we're advised to marry young. Until my marriage, I'll try to practice self-control, and you should too."

"My sex life is my own business!" Karl said defiantly, outraged that someone would interfere in so personal a matter,

Saying nothing more, Jakob slipped away. Karl was glad to be rid of him, if only for a little while. In the future, he'd take more care not to creak the springs while he whacked off. Or he'd do it in the bathroom with the door closed. Or he'd walk out into the desert and find a solitary spot where he could relieve his tension and loneliness in whatever way he wished.

Rising from his bed, he retrieved his clothes from the floor and dressed. Hours later, at supper, Jakob sat next to him, acting as if their earlier argument hadn't occurred. He tried hard to be pleasant. Infuriating as he was, Karl couldn't stay angry with him.

After three stars appeared in the night sky the students and rabbis gathered in the cafeteria again. Rabbi Tubol lit a braided candle. Everyone sipped wine and sniffed a sweet-smelling spice. The *shabbes* ended. People rushed from the cafeteria to resume their weekday lives. In the courtyard, Rabbi Wolfe sat on a bench and lit a cigarette. A heavy smoker, he'd been deprived since the previous evening. It was forbidden to light fire on the *shabbes*.

The students went to the dormitory. Soon shouts, scuffling noises, and the gush of showers echoed down the hallway. The bus to Jerusalem would come by soon. Hurriedly, the boys prepared themselves for their Saturday night jaunt. They brushed their teeth, combed their hair, put on fresh clothes. Karl was glad he'd escape the Yeshiva.

A half-hour later, a dilapidated vehicle pulled up at a bus stop at the Yeshiva gate. The students and a couple from the *kibbutz* crowded inside. Karl sat next to Zach, the kid from Los Angeles. The bus bumped and shook over the rough road, stopping to pick up two Israeli soldiers. In forty minutes they arrived at the Jerusalem bus terminal.

The streets were hot, noisy, smelly, mobbed with cars, tourists, hawkers, darting children. The jabber of various languages filled the air. On Via Dolorosa, Karl saw black cassocked Greek Orthodox priests, walking in a line and swinging smoking censors. They, in turn, were followed by a procession of Christian pilgrims, dragging large wooden crosses. Stray cats got underfoot in the side streets. Blue-green flies buzzed above food carts and on animals. Donkeys tossed their heads to escape them, jingling their harness bells. Camels dressed up in bridles with red pompoms and tassels, chewed their cuds. The camels emanated rank odors.

Entering a shop on a narrow, winding street, Karl saw a post card with a funny, grinning camel. No sooner had he bought it for Lisa did he notice a far better present in the shop, a delicate silver necklace. Jakob came up to the counter, smiling.

"What do you think of this necklace?" Karl said.

"It's pretty."

Karl asked the dark-haired young Arab at the counter how much it cost. The price was far more money than he had with him. "I can't buy it," he opined.

"Why don't you buy your mom one of those?" Jakob said, pointing to a row of small bottles.

"What are they?"

"It's Holy Land sand. After you die, the sand's put in your coffin and buried with you. When the Messiah comes, the dead awaken. Those who have Holy Land sand make their way to Jerusalem through secret underground tunnels."

Karl paid two shekels for one of the bottles, knowing Lisa would love the story about the underground tunnels. Outside the shop, he fingered the bottle in his pocket. Perhaps the magic sand would keep his mother safe. Tomorrow he'd mail it along with the letter he was going to write. Lisa would probably put the little bottle on the kitchen window ledge at home. Every time she glanced at it, she'd be reminded of him. It might make her remember her life in Israel when Fritz was part of their family. He hoped so.

Saturday after *shabbes* was the big night in Jerusalem for all the Yeshivas. A Yeshiva boy on either side of him, Karl was drawn along. He was wondering when he'd have the opportunity to chat with the opposite sex when a dozen orthodox schoolgirls approached. They walked arm in arm, were dressed in long-sleeved shirts and long skirts. The boys rushed to greet them. Karl was surprised at how easily Yeshiva students spoke to the girls. Like him, they were inexperienced, had never gone out on dates. Yet they were far more relaxed. All Karl could do was stare at the girls.

He singled out one called Rifka. Her round, snub-nosed face and braids made her look like a young girl, but her body was developed like a woman's. Her breasts strained against her white blouse. Reynaldo's renegade voice sounded in Karl's mind with a message Karl didn't dare heed. 'Why don't you cop a feel? All those Yeshiva guys would like to do it but don't have the balls.'

The boys walked and talked with the girls for no more than a half hour before it was time to catch their bus. At the terminal, Karl noticed an older man with sad eyes buying a bus ticket. There was a concentration camp tattoo on his arm, similar to the blue numbers he'd seen on Rabbi Wolfe's arm, and Rabbi Frankel's arm. The Holocaust class had made him aware that Israel was a refuge, a tiny dot of safety for Jews escaping horrors.

On the ride back to the Yeshiva, Karl closed his eyes and half dozed as the bus rattled along. The man at the bus terminal was forgotten. He was thinking of the girls he'd met. A vision appeared to him: Rifka naked in a swimming pool; her breasts bouncing up and down; her long hair streaming behind. With a shake, he brought himself back to full consciousness. He glanced at the postcard he'd bought for Lisa. The camel's lips were stretched in a silly grin. Perhaps she wouldn't like it. He'd send the card to his grandparents.

In jail, he'd learned that they'd set up a college fund for him. Their generosity still touched him, brought back memories of the summer Lisa took refuge with them, before taking him to California. Grandma Bernice had taken him to the zoo, planetarium and Natural History Museum. Grandpa Al treated him to children's plays and a movie. His grandparents had let him hail cabs, slipped him dollar bills to tip doormen and elevator operators. Once in a fancy New York restaurant, Karl had sat stirring water and ice cubes in a goblet with a knife. Grandpa Al had laid a hand on his shoulder and said, "If ever you need help, come to us."

A postcard wouldn't require him to write any more than two or three lines. He'd say, "I'm here at the Yeshiva. Doing okay. Please write! Love from your grandson, Karl." Knowing how angry they were with him, he scarcely dared say more. He hoped they'd respond. As a small boy, he'd loved them. He wanted to do so again.

The next morning, Karl woke at four while Jakob was fast asleep. Trying not to disturb him, Karl tiptoed to his desk. He sat down in his pajamas, put on the lamp, and started his reply to Lisa.

His letter began, "Things are okay. I'm busy every moment. When I'm not in class, I'm studying. Or I'm at services, meals, or praying in my room. At midnight, I go to bed. In the morning, the alarm clock rings at five. The Sabbath is a day to catch up on rest, and everyone sleeps after lunch when it's too hot to do anything else."

Lisa loved learning about exotic tribes and their customs. Karl wrote about keeping kosher--the special foods; the separate dairy and meat dishes; the three-hour wait after a meat meal before observant Jews were permitted to eat dairy foods.

He described the Yeshiva students. "The guys here come from religious schools. A kid told me that in his Jewish high school, the rabbis taught religion in the morning when everyone was fresh. The other stuff like Math and English was for the end of the day, or those subjects got skipped. So I know things these boys don't, like I'm better at Algebra, while they can speak Hebrew and know the bible almost by heart. One boy put a note up in the office that his jacket was missing. He spelled jacket without a 'c.' I guess he was never drilled in spelling..."

Karl wondered when he'd find the time to go to the nearby *kibbutz* store to buy a stamp for his letter. Nearly every second was regulated, although it wasn't as bad as at the jail where guards even dictated when he went to the bathroom. He longed for the freedom he'd had at home. Lisa had never made him do daily chores, hadn't checked his homework and friends, or insisted on regular meal- and bedtimes.

"There's a *kibbutz* down the road," Karl wrote. He described the stucco cottages with red tiled roofs, and the orange orchard. He liked to think of the *kibbutz* as similar to the commune they'd lived on. It was comforting to feel something familiar was nearby.

"The *kibbutz* store sells razors, Kleenex, toothpaste, stamps, stationery. Anything else I need I can buy in Jerusalem. We go there on Saturday nights after the *Shabbes*. I look forward to making the trip. It's a break from the strict schedule.

"I can't wait to hear from you. Write a long letter like you said you would. Tell me stuff from my childhood when I was a little kid. Tell me about our family history too. I was eating my supper the other night, when a kid turned to me and asked, "Are there any rabbis in your family?" Mom, the question may seem like a weird way to start a conversation to you and me, but it's the kind of thing they ask here.

"The kids at my table all got quiet and waited for me to answer. I tossed out, 'My grandfather's a lawyer.' I hoped that would satisfy them. But they had more questions. They wanted to know whether my lawyer grandfather was your father. Was he Ashkenazi, from Eastern Europe? Or was he Sephardic, from Spain or Arabic countries? I didn't know what to say. You never talked to me about our family. Maybe you can write me some of this stuff so I'll know how to answer when it comes up again."

Karl gripped his pen and paused in his writing, remembering how surprised he'd been by the barrage of inquiries. The students had acted as if it was the most natural thing in the world to question him about private matters. The etiquette had been different at Berkeley High where half the kids came from broken homes. Karl had been cautious, had tried not to cause pain or embarrassment with personal questions. He'd never have asked another kid, "What does your father do?"

But that question was put to him soon after he'd said his grandfather was lawyer. He was pained to recall himself stuttering, "My f-f-father's an artist." Fritz was the secret part of his life, never discussed.

"Is he a *frum* artist?" his undeterred tablemates had thrown at him. When they saw he didn't know what *frum* meant their mouths fell open. His ignorance amazed them, as much as their insensitivity did him.

Ever willing to enlighten his charge, Jakob had said, "*Frum* means religious. Observant people often have paintings of rabbis in their homes to feel their presence and to inspire them to do good deeds. But some Jewish artists follow, 'Thou shalt not make graven images.'" When Karl asked what *that* meant, Jakob explained, "Some observant artists believe they're not supposed to make idols, so they never draw people. I know a *frum* artist who shows people by drawing their shadows. What about your dad?"

There was so much Karl had forgotten from that time on the commune. Yet when Jakob asked what kind of pictures Fritz drew, Karl recalled his father's drawings vividly. He was able to say that his father conformed to strict Jewish standards, that he didn't draw people. Fritz had made a small pencil sketch of a cow soon after they moved to Vermont.

Innumerable cow pictures had followed: close-up views of barbed wire surrounding a field with tiny cow figures in the distance; or cows crowded against a fence, their hides pierced by the barbs. Then the cows disappeared from the paintings and his father only drew barbed wire. In one canvas, barbed wire twisted around the bare, slender branches of a sapling. Another canvas had been painted black as night, and Fritz had taken a palette knife and slashed fierce jagged lines across it.

Through his dorm room window, Karl saw the sky lightening. He considered whether to add one last sentence, 'Mom, write me about my dad.' The last eight or nine years, Karl hadn't given Fritz much thought. Now, since his interrogation by the Yeshiva boys, and hearing them speak so often about their own families, he was more curious about his own. Lisa never spoke about Fritz. In a letter, though, she might be more forthcoming. Impulsively, he made his request, then signed off 'Karl.' In a post-script, he added, "I've been given a Hebrew name that everyone calls me. It's Baruch." He put his letter in an envelope, sealed and addressed it. Returning to bed, he dozed off.

A quarter of an hour later, he was woken by Jakob moving about. As was required, Karl didn't greet him. He recited, "*Modeha ani,*" a prayer of thanks to God for letting him wake alive. More prayers were chanted while he washed his hands and when he put on his *tzitzis*. Jakob followed the same routine. They dressed, put *keepahs* on their heads, and carrying prayer bags with phylacteries and prayer shawls, went off to attend *Mincha*, the first prayer service.

It wasn't until after lunch during the Yeshiva *siesta* that Karl had a chance to race over to the *kibbutz* store. A fifteen-year-old girl named Rhonda sold him the stamps, box and wrapping paper he needed to send his bottle of sand. As she assembled what he needed, she peppered him with questions. "Is your face always so red? Are you blushing?

Are you scared of girls?" Her teasing flustered him. He paid Rhonda and ran outside, not waiting for his change.

Back at the dorm, he walked into his room just as Jakob woke from his nap. Jakob sat up in bed and stretched. Seeing Karl red-faced and sweaty, he said, "You shouldn't go out in the middle of the day when it's so hot. You have to be careful, Baruch, or you'll end up with sunstroke." Karl didn't know which annoyed him more, Jakob's interference, or his calling him by the new name.

It wasn't until late that evening that Karl had time to toss the letter and package to Lisa and postcard to his grandparents into the cardboard carton on the floor in front of Shloime's desk. He counted on Shloime meeting the mail truck the following day. In fact, the following afternoon, he glanced out his dorm room window and saw Shloime handing over the box's contents to the mailman.

4

Albany, California, 1982

Overjoyed to receive Karl's long letter, Lisa phoned her parents to tell them she'd heard from him. Her mother and father spoke to her together on separate phones, said they too had heard from him. He'd only written a couple of lines so they didn't know how he was doing. Perhaps she could enlighten them. They hoped he wasn't messing up. How could he manage in Hebrew? Wasn't it hard for him to keep kosher? For that matter how was he able to put up with the Orthodox mumbo-jumbo? Karl wasn't particularly patient, was always blurting whatever popped into his head. Worse, he might have picked up some bad habits and attitudes at jail. The rabbis wouldn't tolerate Juvenile Hall swagger.

Lisa didn't care for her parents' skepticism. "He's fine! He's thriving at the Yeshiva!" she insisted, trying to convince them, and more so, herself. After she hung up, she was shaking. She didn't feel up to writing Karl immediately as she'd intended. Perhaps he'd only write back about a new catastrophe, one that she had the vague feeling could be averted if she never received news of it.

The next few days, she found excuses to delay complying with his request that she describe his childhood. For one thing, first his things must be carted away so that she could turn his room into an office, a proper place to write. Steve, a former boyfriend with strong muscles and a van, promised to help her clear the room, but couldn't come over until the weekend. On Sunday, they negotiated the steep back steps, carrying down a mattress, dresser, bookcase, and cartons filled with Karl's old clothes, books, and a model airplane. Steve's van had a broken muffler. A plume of black smoke rose from the tailpipe as he drove off to the Salvation Army.

Karl's bedroom was empty, the last hint of him gone, except for a ripped poster on the floor, and tape marks on the dingy walls. Standing in the middle of the room, Lisa looked up and contemplated the cracks in the ceiling. Today's effort had tired her, amplifying an exhaustion that went back to when the police had phoned to say Karl had been arrested. "Karl," she sighed. With no furnishings to muffle the sound, her voice echoed against the walls.

The room hadn't been painted since she'd moved in twelve years ago. The landlord agreed to pay for the paint. She chose white for the ceiling and a light yellow for the walls. Little by little over the next few days, she sanded, dusted, and washed. The actual painting took her a day. She left the window open overnight. After the fumes cleared, she went off to buy a desk at a used furniture store on Ashby Avenue. Wooden desks were expensive. She settled for a card table, which was considerably cheaper. Her portable Olivetti had been with her since college. She saw no reason to replace it with an electric typewriter. It would only be too heavy for the card table.

Even after the room was ready, Lisa procrastinated about writing Karl. He'd asked her to tell him about his childhood and about his father. Sitting in the new office, she tried to remember events she would feel comfortable relating to him. He was young, vulnerable, his confidence undercut by having been in jail. The last thing she wished was to upset him with what she wrote. Nor did she want him to think badly of her. At last, she set down a few memories on paper, omitting and reshaping events especially for Karl. When she read over what she'd written, she was dissatisfied. For her own sake, she needed to be honest.

Lisa decided to write freely. Later she could select what she wanted to say to Karl, and omit the other sections. She switched from writing in the first to the third person to help her to be more objective. The old 'Lisa' became someone different from herself. She worked on her project sporadically, but pages began to accumulate, a written record of her experiences, starting with the move to the commune.

Her efforts made her feel as if she was sending dozens of letters to Karl, although she hadn't put anything in the mail yet.

5

Israel, 1982

In Old Testament class, Rabbi Cohen stood in front of the room and talked about the chief temple priest of ancient times, the purity he must maintain—that he must be physically perfect, tall, not lame, not maimed in any way—to enter 'the holy of the holies,' and fulfill his responsibility, sacrificing a red heifer, burning the hooves and pulverizing the ashes into a powder.

The subject excited the other students, but baffled Karl. It sounded like a fairy tale. He withstood his morning classes, and then went to the cafeteria for lunch where he intended to sit with the same group of boys he'd sat with on his first day at the Yeshiva, six weeks ago. Karl had taken all his meals with them until a week ago when a tall boy had approached him on the buffet line and invited him to get to know the few *ba'al tshuva* at the Yeshiva. Karl had been thrilled to meet four boys who, like himself, had come to Orthodox Judaism late. He hoped at least one of them would become a friend.

Since then, he'd been eating meals with the *ba'al tshuva,* finding and not wishing to admit to himself that he was wearied by their endless talk about their 'spiritual journey.' Gradually, Karl had come to see that these students were even fiercer in observance and more judgmental than the kids who'd been born into Orthodoxy. Reuven, the tall kid, experienced an adult circumcision prior to coming to the Yeshiva. Karl was thankful he'd been born at a hospital where circumcision was an automatic procedure for male babies, that he wasn't expected to undergo the procedure now.

At today's breakfast, Reuven had said, "My circumcision made me feel like a real Jew." Hearing this boast, Karl had decided to return to taking his meals at his original table, not to friends, but to boys who tolerated him, and whom he could tolerate.

"Look who's back," Leib remarked when Karl took a seat beside him at lunch. Jakob smiled. There were nods from the other boys. Then they seemed to forget him. Karl knew they would never be deliberately unkind or rude, yet he felt isolated in their midst. These students who'd imbibed Judaism from birth valued what they called *yikus*—status based not only on ability in Torah study, but on an individual's genealogy and the prestige of the Jewish day school the boy had attended. Karl meant little in their world. Still, he preferred them to the *ba'al tshuvas.* And the *ba'al tshuvas* had been his last hope for finding friends.

After lunch, the other boys went to the dorm to nap, but Karl rushed to the office to see if there was a letter from Lisa that might have been delivered late the day before. She'd written only once. He yearned for a second letter, was disappointed when his cubby was empty today when he needed support after his setback with the *ba'al tshuvas.* He felt alone in the world, unwanted by anyone, unprotected.

That evening when he was supposed to be studying at his desk, he began a letter to Lisa, telling her how miserable he was. He paused, wondering whether to beg her to get Grandpa Al to find a way to rescue him, either by hiring a lawyer or doing the legal work himself. Lisa might be able to persuade him to help.

Karl wrote, "Please, convince grandpa to find a way to get out of this place. I hate it here." He underlined hate. "I'm all alone. No one cares about me. The students have nicknamed me 'the gloom-master.' My classes are a waste of time." He went on and on. When he finished he read what he'd said. Dissatisfied with his disjointed reflections, he crumpled the page. He'd put Lisa through enough, wouldn't distress her more.

The next day, he wrote her a letter in which he forced himself to be cheerful. He knew she'd enjoy hearing about Jerusalem, hoped that would entice her to write back. He told her, "For me, the best part of the week is after the *shabbes* ends when we go to Jerusalem. I've been to the mourning wall, Temple, Mount of Olives cemetery, and *Mea*

Shearim where the ultra-orthodox Jews live. In the Arab *shuk* the shop owners sit in front of their little stores smoking *hookahs* and sipping coffee in tiny cups. They sell rugs, shawls and all kinds of tourist stuff. The Christian tourists buy crosses, the Jewish ones buy Jewish stars, *Kiddush* cups, and Seder plates.

"I bought a postcard with a funny picture and sent it to Grandma and Grandpa to give them a laugh. Please ask whether they received it. If you mention my card, maybe they'll write."

Another week and a half passed in which Lisa didn't write. However, Karl received the following letter from his grandfather.

"Karl, let's look to the future rather then dwelling on the past. You're lucky to be in Israel rather than jail. The judge gave you an opportunity. Think long and hard about becoming a better person. You're a smart boy and could still do something productive with your life. I hope you won't waste this chance. Get to work and think about what you want to do when you leave the Yeshiva. Prove to me you're sincerely sorry for what you did by working hard for your future goals. Prove this to me, and you have my full support."

Grandpa Al had made contact, obviously, persuaded by Lisa. The note was a stern lecture, not the affectionate letter Karl needed. But at least his grandfather was talking to him again. A closed door had opened a crack. If only Lisa had written too! He wanted desperately to hear from her.

In a third letter to her, Karl wrote an appeal he was certain his mother would answer. "I've almost used up the spending money you gave me. There's stuff I need like toothpaste, shaving cream, bus fare for the trips to Jerusalem. Also, I'm growing out of my clothes. My shoes pinch, and one of my shirts ripped at the seams. I need new underwear and socks. Please, send me more money. I'll be careful with it. Thank you in advance."

Neither cheer nor need moved Lisa to write. Was she angry because he'd asked her to tell him more about his childhood and Fritz? Karl wished he hadn't. He couldn't stop thinking about her and speculating on why she didn't write.

By the time more than a month and a half had gone by without his hearing from her, he was alarmed, certain a catastrophe must have occurred. He began thinking about a classmate's father who'd grown pale and emaciated, and then died. The Lisa Karl knew was healthy, and never had a cold. But how could he know what had happened to her since he'd left California?

When he was six, he'd overhead her tell a friend, "I had a brush with cancer the summer after I graduated from college." Afterwards, he'd followed her from room to room, asking, "Are you okay, Mommy?" For weeks, he'd tried to conceal his cuts and bruises so she wouldn't worry, cheered her when she was sad, made her laugh with funny stories. After a while, he shrugged off his anxiety. His belief in his mother's immortality returned.

Now, though, the same panic was with him, the same need for reassurance as when he first learned about her cancer. At night, he tossed and turned. It pained him that he was far away, unable to take care of his mother. He had gray circles under his eyes and couldn't stop yawning. Jakob noticed how drawn he looked. He told Karl one morning that while a person slept his soul left and wandered the earth. Tired as he was, Karl could almost credit his soul for having made the long journey to California to check on his mom.

For the first time the prayer services were meaningful to him, an opportunity to beg God to spare Lisa's life. Just in case God did exist, he wanted to pacify him. He tried to say each prayer perfectly. Overwhelmed by worry, he decided one morning he'd skip his first class in order to write another letter to Lisa. He'd beg her to tell him why she hadn't written and whether she was sick. He went from the synagogue to breakfast and barely ate a bite. At the end of the meal, everyone streamed out of the cafeteria. Karl lingered by a bulletin board and scanned the notices. Often, he'd yearned for friendship while chafing at the fishbowl atmosphere of the Yeshiva, the constant presence of others.

Jakob, as usual, was soon at his side, an unwanted Siamese twin.

"Come on. We're late for class."

"I'll catch up," Karl said, pretending to be absorbed by the postings.

There was an announcement of the dates for the winter break. Another notice described a conference of Jewish learning to be held in Toronto, Canada. A third told when the next *shabbes* would start. *Shabbes* commenced at sunset. With winter approaching, it began earlier with every subsequent Friday.

As soon as the hall was empty, Karl left the main building and went to the dorm. It was the first time he'd dared to skip a Yeshiva class. He knew he shouldn't. He dreaded the consequences, feared Judge Thorn be notified. Only two days ago, Rabbi Tubol had made Karl write a statement to be included in a progress report to the judge. Karl had listed his classes and stated that he was leading 'a strict religious life' and learning 'ethical values.' His statement wouldn't matter if Rabbi Tubol slipped a negative report into the envelope.

Karl's panic about Lisa kept him to his purpose. In his dorm room, he sat at his desk. He tore a sheet of paper from his notebook. But where was a pen? He was too impatient to look through his drawers. Three pens were neatly lined up on Jakob's desk. Reaching over, Karl grabbed one and began his letter.

"Mom, you haven't written. When I don't hear from you I think you've forgotten me. Even when I was home you didn't have much time for me. Now that I'm far away, I need you more than ever. I want to know about your health. Please, please, write me and tell me how you are! I need to know the truth. You probably don't realize, but I know you once had cancer. I worry about it coming back. If it does, I want you to tell me."

Karl signed off. There! It was worth missing class. He'd said what he'd had to say. He wrote his home address on an envelope, stuck on postage and an airmail sticker. At the window, he craned his neck and saw the mail truck rattling down the road. He ran downstairs and was just in time to hand his letter to the mailman.

As he walked back across the plaza, he bumped into Shloime who'd also come out to meet the mailman.

"Why aren't you in class?" Shloime asked, sternly.

"I'm sick."

"So, why aren't you in bed?"

"I'm a little better."

Shloime studied him.

Karl swallowed hard. "I had to write my mother."

"It's important to write your mother. Still, you mustn't miss classes!"

Before Karl could stop himself, he blurted. "I'm so far behind. What difference does it make whether I go or not?"

"It's because you're behind that you must not miss a single class."

Karl looked down at his sneakers and mumbled, "What's the point? I'll never catch up."

"Keep trying. I guarantee you will. Now, go to your next class. I won't say anything to Rabbi Tubol as long as you don't skip any more classes."

"Thanks."

Karl walked away. Shloime might keep quiet, but he didn't think the Yeshiva kids would. Yet the day passed without a summons to Rabbi Tubol's office. Perhaps Shloime persuaded the rabbi that the lecture Karl received about truancy was sufficient. No further reprimand was necessary.

Two weeks later, on a Thursday, Karl found a letter in his box. The address was written in the shapely handwriting he recognized as Lisa's calligraphy. Throughout the morning, he carried the unread letter around, afraid to open it. Karl didn't want any of the students about as witnesses if he were to read that Lisa's cancer had returned.

At lunch, he skipped dessert. He returned to his room and sat down at his desk. At last, he had a moment alone. He ripped open the envelope and read:

"Dear Karl, Let me assure you I'm well. I have been for many years. At this point, my risk for cancer is no greater than the average person's. About my not writing, my only excuse is that time flew away from me. Sorry, sorry. I did write once though! You said that you enjoyed my drawing of the cherry tree branch and my poor little poem.

"Karl, if I don't write, it doesn't mean I'm not thinking about you. I think about you often. You asked me to tell you about our past. I've been marshalling my memories, even writing down incidents from my life as honestly as I know how. That effort, indirect as it might be, is my way of showing you attention. I feel this is so even if you never get to read what I write. Can you grasp what I'm saying? I hope you've received all the mental messages I've sent. There, that's enough explanations and *mea culpa*. Let's move on to other subjects.

"Earlier today, I was inspired to sort my books. I came upon *The Odyssey*. As a little boy, you loved me to tell you stories about Odysseus. Do you remember how you liked to hear how Odysseus tricked the Cyclops and put out his eye? I asked you what color the eye was. You said it turned different colors, red when the Cyclops was angry and purple when he was asleep. You said that when you grew up you were going to be like Odysseus and battle monsters.

"Well, you've left home. It's your chance to seek out life. I wish I'd talked with you about this before you left. But 'never too late.' When I was eighteen—a little older than you—I remember how eager I was to go off to college. After I graduated, I traveled about Europe on my own. People would ask, aren't you scared? Aren't you lonely? Don't you miss your family? The truth was, I experienced all of these feelings. But more than anything I was hungry for experience. I wanted to feel alive and free.

"You asked for stories about your father. I met him in Paris. He was studying at the Sorbonne. We had adventures. What I mean by adventures is that everything was unpredictable and exciting. I never knew what would happen from moment to moment. Let me give you an example. Once, we encountered a troupe of gypsies at the train station. The gypsy men played flamenco music on accordions and guitars while the gypsy women and children tugged on people's clothes and begged. Your dad swept me into his arms, and we began dancing to the gypsy music. We twirled, stamped our feet. Fritz dipped me backwards, nearly to the ground. A cheering crowd gathered. We gave a magnificent performance. Bravo!

"One of the gypsies, Lazlo, invited us to perform with them. The rest of week we went to the train station nearly every day. I wore bright ribbons in my hair and banged on a tambourine. Lazlo played the guitar. Fritz pretended to know the gypsy language, and sang nonsense. We passed a hat around. Too bad the gypsies moved on to Rouen. I had to end my days as a *zingerale*.

"I tell you all this because I want you to forget the circumstances that brought you to the Yeshiva. Think of your time in Israel as a great adventure. Do not doubt you're going to be happy there. Of course, this is a period of adjustment for you—and for me too because now, I'm on my own. It's natural to feel lonely or anxious for a while. Use a transition period as an opportunity for creativity. I always do.

"A few days after you left, I went to the art studio on campus. I'd decided to teach myself how to throw pots on a wheel. There's a young man who's supposed to check student identification cards. I managed to slip by the first couple of times. Now, I go every day, and he considers me a regular. I smile. He waves me through. I love digging my hands into big vats of clay. My first pots collapsed on the wheel, but I've improved. Today, I made an enormous pot. It's in the kiln now. I pray it won't crack. I came home, tired, with clay dust all over me. All I wanted was to shower and go to sleep, but I've stayed awake to write to you.

"You don't think I give you enough of my time. I've felt my parents didn't give me enough of theirs. Perhaps there's always a complaint of this sort between the younger and older generations, an inescapable dissatisfaction.

"All my love."

Included in the envelope were a check and a recent photo in which Lisa looked glowing. Avidly reading the first paragraphs of the letter, Karl had been filled with gratitude. Lisa had written, sent a check, and best of all, assured him she was well. She even spoke of Fritz! Surely, now that she'd begun, she'd relate more about that shadowy figure. Maybe she'd tell him where Fritz lived and Karl could write directly to his father.

But when Karl came to the part about the ceramics studio, he nearly stopped breathing. He whipped out the photo she'd included for a closer inspection. Lisa stared out from the picture with a special look he recognized. It was obvious the pottery guy had taken the photo. He was the one Lisa was gazing at so lovingly. The reason she hadn't written all these weeks was a new boyfriend, an all-consuming experience for her. That's how it had always been. Only now, Karl wasn't around to insist she toss him bits of her affection, like scraps to a dog.

Karl now saw almost everything in her letter as false. Her talk about 'freedom' and 'mental letters' disgusted him. He had no freedom, no choices at the Yeshiva, and mental letters weren't the same as real ones. A loving mother would have asked questions about his life, would have wanted to know more about what he'd written to her. Didn't she care? Why, she hadn't even thanked him for the bottle of sand. She'd forgotten about his gift, the way she forgot about him. That was the sort of person Lisa was. He held her letter over his trash basket. His hand shook. He couldn't throw a letter from his mother away.

After pocketing the check, he thrust the letter into the bottom desk drawer. The lunch wouldn't be over for fifteen minutes. He was free to use the hour allotted for naps as he wished. He had plenty of time to walk over to the *kibbutz* store. This time the storekeeper was an older man named Mordechai. After exchanging the check for *shekels*, he asked Karl whether he'd like to see something interesting, then took out some old coins he'd found while poking around the ruins of a deserted Arab village. Karl briefly examined them before running back to the Yeshiva.

He couldn't get Lisa out of his thoughts, not during his classes, and not as he prepared for and participated in the *Shabbes* the next day. He wanted to love his mother, and to believe in her love for him. Excuses for her letter occurred to him. Why hadn't Lisa asked about his life? Because she guessed he was unhappy at the Yeshiva. She didn't want to probe and cause pain. She was putting on a brave face. Possibly the gift he'd sent was lost in the mail. Or she'd received the sand bottle, liked it, meant to thank him but forgot. So what if she forgot? He forgot things too. But he never forgot her.

The thing he couldn't explain away was why she'd ignored him for so long, unless she'd started a new affair. In spite of his efforts to excuse Lisa, the same jealousy he used to feel as a little boy kept overwhelming him.

On Saturday night Karl took the bus to Jerusalem. The closer the Yeshiva students came to their destination, the livelier they became. Joking and laughing, they called Zach, 'L.A.' and Avi, 'Skokie.' Eli addressed Karl as 'Frisco.' Half-heartedly, Karl tried to join in the fun. "Call me Izzy. I was born in Israel." As the only student with that distinction, he felt a quiver of pride, but only for a moment. The distasteful letter soon occupied his thoughts again.

A kid named Gil, declared, "Baruch, you look like you're going to your own funeral."

Karl wasn't in the mood for teasing. "Leave me alone," he snapped back.

"Gloom-master," Gil retaliated.

At the terminal, Jakob touched Karl's shoulder and said, "Wake up dreamer. We're here."

The boys walked towards the *shuk*. There, they dispersed into the little Arab shops that lined the noisy, crowded market. Karl bought the clothes he needed. He had enough *shekels* to cover the cost of a new shirt, underwear and socks, but not enough for shoes—another reason to be angry with Lisa, another stick on the fire. Carrying his purchases in his backpack, he caught up with the other students.

Not uttering a word, he followed them to the religious quarter of *Mea Shearim*. Men dressed in Hasidic-style wool suits, and broad-brimmed hats filled the streets. Karl was glad he didn't have to dress like these ultra-religious Jews, or act like them either. He'd heard that Hasidim threw rocks at the cars of people who drove through their neighborhood on the *Shabbes*. The rock throwing was a far worse desecration of the Sabbath than driving. If one of these weirdoes threw a rock at him, he'd hurl it back. He wished he could throw one at Lisa's new boyfriend.

Two Hasids walked towards him. "*Shalom*. How you doing?" Karl said tauntingly.

Neither Hasid replied. He hadn't expected them to. The street was narrow. Karl could tell they weren't going to make way for him. It was awkward for him to step aside with his bulging backpack, full of his new clothes. Besides, he didn't want to.

One of the Hasids collided with him, then walked past without a word as if Karl were invisible.

Furious, Karl called after them, "Stuck up assholes."

Jakob rushed to his side and hissed, "Quiet. Don't speak like that."

"One of them shoved into me."

"He must not have noticed you were in the way."

"Why didn't they answer me when I spoke?"

"They speak Yiddish."

"They know *shalom*. Everyone knows *shalom*. It's the same in Yiddish and Hebrew."

"Hasidim don't consider outsiders to their group to be truly Jewish."

"So I was right. They are stuck-up assholes."

Jakob shook his head, as if trying to shake Karl's words out of his ears. "When you use bad language it gives the Yeshiva a bad name. More importantly, you should treat people with respect."

Exasperated, Karl cried, "Stop telling me what to do. I can take care of myself!"

Jakob stared. "You don't like me, do you?"

"You're the one who said it."

Jakob walked away. There was no contact between them during the rest of the time in Jerusalem. When they went to the terminal, Jakob seemed as eager as Karl that they not sit next to each other on the bus. The bus stopped at Yeshiva after midnight. Jakob, the first one off, rushed ahead to the dorm. When Karl entered their room, he expected his roommate to be preparing for bed. But Jakob was at his desk, studying. He didn't look up. It was possible he was engrossed in a Jewish text. More likely, he was too upset to speak—or to go to sleep.

Karl walked over to his own desk a few feet away, sat down and arranged and rearranged his notebooks and pencils. After five minutes of silence, he announced, "I'm going to bed." It was like talking to the air. Jakob didn't stir. Karl put on his pajamas, washed up, and climbed into bed. He tried to settle, but couldn't.

At last, Jakob began his preparations for bed. Karl pretended to be asleep, but after the light was off, he called out, "Goodnight." He was glad to hear Jakob say the same. In that one word Karl heard regret and sadness that matched his own.

The next day, Karl was summoned to Rabbi Tubol's office.

"You might be interested in this, Baruch," the rabbi said grimly, showing him a pamphlet with the title, *The Story of Hasidism*.

Riffling the pages, the old man read aloud a sentence here, a sentence there. "Hasidism, a movement emphasizing sincerity over learning or wealth, was founded by the *Baal Shem Tov* in the eighteenth century...Thousands of poor, uneducated Jews joined the movement...The *Baal Shem Tov* conveyed his teachings through stories rather than intellectual lectures..." Closing the pamphlet, Rabbi Tubol slid it across the desk. "Take this with you when you leave. Do you know why I'm giving it to you?"

Karl nodded. One of the other kids had tattled about his encounter with the two Hasids in Jerusalem. He presumed it was Jakob who'd spoken to Rabbi Tubol, but any of the Yeshiva students might have. They considered it their duty to be stool pigeons. He, Karl, may have snitched on Reynaldo, but only after hours of police interrogation.

"When you leave the Yeshiva grounds, you represent this school. I expect you to be on your best behavior."

Karl wanted but didn't dare to put his hands over his ears to block out Rabbi Tubol's voice. He felt utterly alone, abandoned by Lisa, betrayed by the kid who'd tattled. Probably, there'd been more than one.

"I've considered whether to punish you and decided not to because you're a newcomer and not yet fully aware of the high standards expected of you."

The phone in the outer office rang, the sound faint as it came through the closed door. Karl looked out the window and saw a khaki military jeep driving up the road. Further away was the *kibbutz's* orange tree orchard, and beyond, a jagged line of hills.

Karl wished he were hiking in the hills with Mordechai, the *kibbutz* storekeeper, looking for coins from biblical times.

"If you get into trouble again, you won't get off so easily. I hope by next week's trip to Jerusalem, you will have taught yourself to behave with greater courtesy."

Karl nodded again.

"In the meanwhile, avail yourself of Rabbi Blum as a spiritual advisor. Talk to him about your problems."

The suggestion shocked Karl. "You said I didn't have to use him as a spiritual advisor."

"You have problems."

"I lost my temper because someone shoved me. Next time I'm shoved, I won't say anything."

"Let's set aside that incident. I'm talking about other things." The rabbi tapped his fingertips together. His hands were gnarled, heavily veined. "You're having difficulties with your studies."

"Jakob said he'll help me with Hebrew," Karl said, remembering an offer he'd sloughed off.

"I understand your relationship with your roommate is strained. If you're not getting along with other students, you have another reason to talk to Rabbi Blum."

Karl's face burned. Even his fracas with Jakob had been reported. "You said it was voluntary," he insisted.

"Yes, it is. You can't be forced to confide in Rabbi Blum. But I think you need to."

Karl shook his head, meaning he didn't want to do it.

"I mailed your first report to Judge Thorn. In a few months, I'll have to write another report for him. I hope I can tell him that you've made every effort to adjust to the Yeshiva."

Karl stiffened. Rabbi Tubol's threat was obvious. If Karl wanted another good report, he must pour out his guts to Rabbi Blum. Not waiting for a dismissal, he stood up to leave. Rabbi Tubol made sure he took the pamphlet. Karl nearly tossed it into a trashcan as he hurried away from the office. Then he reflected that someone might see and tattle to Rabbi Tubol. He took the tract to his dorm room and stuffed it in the same desk drawer where he'd stowed Lisa's letter, then slammed the drawer shut.

6

Albany, California, 1982

Karl's request to find out more about his childhood became increasingly important to Lisa. For a long time, confusing events from the past had roiled about within her. Now because of Karl, she was attempting to understand them. Every day she tried to remember, if not write about the life they'd shared. Sitting at the desk she'd placed in Karl's room, she often talked aloud to him. She spoke to him more frankly than she'd ever been able to bring herself to do in person. While writing, she referred to herself as Lisa. She hoped the use of the third person voice would confer more objectivity.

Vermont, 1970

Inspired by tales hippie kids visiting their *kibbutz* had told about a commune in Vermont where LSD and marijuana were free and plentiful—Lisa and Fritz departed from Israel with their three-year-old son, Karl. Stopping in Vienna, they introduced Karl to his father's sister, Eva, and her family. A month later, he met his maternal grandparents in New York for the first time, and celebrated his fourth birthday at their home. In September the little family moved on to Vermont. Lisa and Fritz were full of hope for an exciting new life. Both of them wished to experiment with LSD, to be on the forefront, travel like space explorers, find new perspectives, grasp mysteries.

Showing up unannounced, they presented themselves to Mark, the commune's leader, a short, barrel-chested man, solid like a boxer. He offered to take them on a tour of the ramshackle resort he'd bought five years before and turned into his domain. Karl was left to play with a group of children. He made no objection. The *kibbutz* nursery had accustomed him to separations from his parents.

Taking them on a tour of the dining hall, small cottages, orchards, and woods, Mark questioned Lisa and Fritz about their experiences on the *kibbutz* and about their desire to experiment with psychedelic drugs. He smiled and nodded at their enthusiastic answers. Striding along, he looked as if he were in his mid-forties, considerably older than the commune members Lisa saw on the tour.

Mark informed them that most of those who found their way to the commune were impecunious college dropouts whose slogan was 'drop out and turn on,' or runaway teenagers who fit in nowhere but here. Some of them were gay kids who couldn't face their families and conservative communities after 'coming out.' They relied on Mark for their drugs, subsistence, and place in the world. He said he gave them what they needed without asking for a penny. But he didn't have infinite funds. Those who could afford it must pay their expenses.

His uncanny ability to size up people impressed Lisa. He seemed to know down to the last penny how much to demand for room and board, if anything at all. He hadn't inquired about their finances, hadn't been told about her trust fund. Yet he knew to address Lisa rather than Fritz, knew she was the one with money. "You'll have to pay a hundred and fifty dollars a month," he told her. There were other expenses Lisa anticipated. Fritz would have to buy canvasses and oil paints. Karl would need new clothes. He quickly outgrew or wore out whatever she bought him. Even so, she realized she could afford the amount Mark demanded. By the end of the week, she planned to open a bank account in Ayer, the nearest town, and request her father send her trust fund checks there.

An agreement was reached with Mark. Lisa and Fritz moved into a tiny tourist cabin, identical to others spread around the compound. A separate building up the road had communal toilets, sinks and showers. The cabin's only furnishings were a double bed, a cot for Karl, and a dresser. There was no electricity.

All the adults living on the commune had required tasks. Fritz had no opportunity to paint except at night while Lisa and Karl slept. Using a circle of flickering candles for illumination, he'd stand at his easel and work. When the candles burned down to stubs, he'd go to sleep. In the morning, Karl enjoyed picking the soft wax off the floor and playing with it like modeling clay.

Every day, Lisa jumped out of bed, full of enthusiasm for her assigned jobs, whether weeding the garden, gathering kindling, picking apples, or preparing meals. Voluntarily, she organized a jumble of discarded paperback books and constructed shelves for them in an alcove off the dining room. At her turn to set the tables, she picked summer wild flowers to place on the tables, and then when autumn came, red and yellow maple leaves. She folded the napkins in beautiful origami shapes that everyone admired.

Mark provided free drugs. Fritz claimed 'acid' helped him as an artist. "It takes me places, shows me what to paint. I see what's fundamental." Lisa believed in her husband's genius. Thrilled that she was married to an artist, she was willing to make sacrifices for the sake of his art. She cheerfully put up with the irritability and mood swings that tended to follow his LSD trips. The way she saw it, when he was in a dark mood, he was her Zen master, teaching and challenging her.

On occasion, she took acid with Fritz while Mark observed the effects of different potencies and wrote in a notebook. Lisa's first trip, she felt she was receiving a holy wafer. She licked a tiny drop of LSD off a square of white paper. The effects were gentle. She felt like she'd drunk a couple of glasses of white wine. On her next trip, Mark presented her with a small barrel-shaped pill and told her to split it into quarters. Cautiously, she took only an eighth of the pill. It left her stoned and contented for a long time.

The winter arrived, along with freezing, monotonous days. The only distractions from the routines were the free drugs Mark provided. Everyone at the commune seemed to be tripping more frequently than before. This was certainly true for Fritz.

In mid-December, Mark gave Lisa a glob of mucilage on a stamp-size bit of paper, lysergic acid cut with speed. This time, she became anxious and had terrifying visions that wouldn't stop. Sharp-toothed rats gnawed at her hands. Snakes slithered down her throat.

Afterwards, she told Mark, "That's the end. No more LSD for me."

Trying to alter her resolve, Mark urged, "Read the writings of William Blake...Aldous Huxley... Try Coleridge's poetry."

Lisa shook her head. "It won't make any difference."

Despite the bad 'trip,' she still trusted Mark.

Commune members told her, "Mark can perform miracles." They spoke of how he'd transformed their lives.

He was a mysterious man. Some people said he came from Georgia, others that he was from New Hampshire. He was supposed to have had a bitter divorce, and to have lost contact with his two children who lived in Chicago. For Lisa, that meant he'd had significant experiences that had deepened him as a human being. His admiration for Fritz further endeared him to her. He'd once joked that he and Fritz—Fritz was twenty-seven—were the 'elders' of the commune, "a bit older, a bit wiser, and the only two people who can carry on an intelligent conversation."

Lisa was drug-free during the cold and damp of January, February and March. April arrived, but still the unrelenting winter wouldn't loosen its grasp. One evening in early April there was a snowstorm. Waking early, Lisa shuddered at the icy air in the tiny cabin. There was a faint smell of turpentine in the air. During the swirling storm the night before, Fritz had painted a bright, swirling Mandela on a wall. He was asleep now, snoring at her side. Karl lay in his cot, snoring too but more lightly than his father. A ticking clock on the windowsill read six o'clock. There was still time for Lisa to rise and assist with cooking in the commune's kitchen.

Pulling her blanket higher, she wished she could escape the frigid weather. The novelty of the commune had worn off. She yearned for a new, warmer place, fresh adventure. Languorously, she turned on her side. If she drifted into the kitchen after all the work was done as she had several times lately, the commune women on her shift would be furious. Lisa didn't care. Let the others stir the oatmeal and make stacks of toast. No doubt the bread wouldn't scorch as it did on her watch. Later, she'd apologize to the women who'd done her work, and find ways to win them over with flattery and amusing stories. Unfortunately, most of them were unable to see that the uplift she offered was no less a contribution to the commune's overall good than the tasks she was missing, tasks that had begun to seem dreary and distasteful to her.

An hour later, the dining room bell rang. Fritz slept on, but the sound woke Lisa who'd fallen back to sleep. Karl woke too. Jumping out of his cot, he clamored, "Hurry Mommy. Get me dressed." Hastily, Lisa helped him into his clothes and tied his tangled hair into a ponytail, the accepted hairstyle among the commune's boys. Like his father, Karl was fair, blond and blue-eyed, an angelic-looking child.

Knocks sounded on the door. Childish voices called, 'Karl.' With frigid fingers, Lisa zipped up her son's parka, tucked his pants into his boots, and sent him off with the gang of commune kids. She smiled as the door banged behind him, content because Karl was being raised differently than she'd been. He was an independent, free child.

During the first years of his life, the *kibbutz* nannies had watched over him while she, having been appointed head of the 'cultural committee' because of her college drama degree, had organized plays, writing groups, and book discussions. Here at the commune, Karl spent his time with a gang of kids who raced about the snowy woods, built forts of snowballs, played hide and seek, rolled down the hillsides or slid down in cardboard boxes. When they needed help or simply to warm up, they darted into one of the cabins. Doors were never locked. Everyone was responsible for all the children. For the most part, Lisa only saw Karl at mealtimes in the dining room, and at night when he was ready to sleep.

Now that he was gone, she began to dress. Wanting to wear something that reminded her of sunshine and warmth, she searched through the dresser for an embroidered peasant blouse she'd bought years ago in Greece. As she lifted her flannel nightgown and tugged it overhead, a puff of cool air zipped up her thighs. Her teeth chattered as she slipped into her jeans. Quickly, she threw on the rest of her clothes, the peasant shirt, a sweater, wool socks, boots. Her mother had given her a fur-lined hooded coat.

"I'm going to the dining hall, Fritz," Lisa said, standing over him. When they'd met in Paris, she'd thought him the most handsome and smartest man she'd ever met. Now, although he was still in his twenties, he was balding, developing a paunch, and was often lethargic. Before coming to the commune, he'd wanted to spend each moment with her. He'd been passionate, jealous of every man who glanced at her. To her distress, these days he rarely wanted to make love. She found it upsetting that he took acid more frequently than anyone else at the commune. He spent three or four nights a week holed up in Mark's flat, tripping, time she felt he should be spending with her.

She hated Karl witnessing the strange ways LSD could make his father act. Fortunately, many times during the day, he was occupied with his friends, or at night he slept through Fritz's wild streams of talk, hallucinations, stumbling against walls. But the month before, a frightening experience took place on the dining hall's steep roof. Lisa had walked out after lunch and heard Karl calling from two stories up, "Mommy, look at me." He was on the roof-ridge with Fritz, the two of them walking across like tightrope walkers.

Gazing at the gray-white sky, Fritz seemed to be singing to the drifting clouds, "We're going to Austria. To Salzburg, and to Innsbruck too..."

Karl slipped, would have hurtled down, but Fritz grabbed him. They sat down on the ridge as if nothing out of the way had happened.

Fritz warbled, "We're going to Vienna. We're going to the zoo..."

"Help," Lisa screamed. "Help...help!"

People ran out of the dining hall. Soon the whole community stood with their heads tilted up to view the roof. The attic window was ajar. "Go back through the window," Lisa begged Karl. A few of the women cried to Fritz to take Karl back inside. Fritz grinned but did nothing.

"Get the fire department," one woman said. Others in the crowd joined in a chant for the fire department.

Mark took charge. His deep voice rose above the others. "No fire department. They'd bring in the police. They've been looking for excuses to make searches and close the place down."

Panicked, Lisa pleaded, "But Fritz and Karl are up there. We need help. We need to call..."

"I'm aware of that. We'll handle the situation ourselves," Mark said firmly.

"Forget about protecting the drugs! Get the fire department here," Lisa retorted.

Turning, Mark shouted up to Fritz, "Take Karl and go inside." Obedient to Mark, Fritz climbed inside through the attic window, carrying Karl.

In the same authoritative voice in which he'd addressed Fritz, Mark said to Lisa, "You're worked up over nothing. Take a look. The problem's resolved."

Lisa burst into tears of relief. A few minutes later, everyone clapped as Karl emerged from the building. Lisa flung her arms around him. Wriggling free, he raced off with his friends. Then, Fritz appeared. There was more applause. Lisa put her arm about his waist. "Let's go back to the cabin," she coaxed.

After having defied Mark in front of everyone, Lisa dared not look back. Commune members never defied him. They believed in the commune, its values and their leader. Only she had begun to feel doubtful. LSD could be harmful. Fritz said it was worth the risks. But what if her son and husband had toppled from the roof and died?

Once Fritz returned to the cabin, he crawled into bed. Lisa sat on the edge of the bed, pleading, "We have to get out of here... Let's move to San Francisco. We'd be with the flower children...the beat poets... It would be warm there... Are you listening, Fritz?"

He looked at her dully. "Sure," he said, but his eyelids fluttered closed.

After a few hours, Lisa tried speaking to him again. Hearing about the incident on the roof, he looked confused. When he finally grasped what had happened, he shuddered and began to sob. Fritz said he was horrified to have endangered Karl. He'd do whatever she said.

"We have to leave this place. We'll go to California."

"California," he echoed. "Yes... San Francisco. San Francisco's the new Paris, filled with painters and artists. We'll be happy there."

They spoke happily of the adventure ahead, the same hopeful way they used to discuss their future on the commune. They were pioneers ready to start all over, determined to go west.

A few days later, Mark invited Fritz to his flat. Lisa objected, but Fritz said, "The most we'll do is have a beer and smoke a little grass." Fritz didn't return until the following morning. Stumbling into the cabin and mumbling incoherently, he was too helpless to go anywhere but to bed.

After that he seemed to forget about the roof incident. Like many people on the commune, he overlooked disasters, thought his next trip was going to be the good one that would give ultimate insight and calm, a glowing goal that drew him along.

"I'm going to the dining hall, Fritz," Lisa repeated a second time, peering down at her inert husband. As expected, he didn't stir from his stupor. Leaving the cabin, she walked down a path someone had cleared in the snow. Her eyes watered from the cold.

Icicles hanging from cabin roof gutters caught the light, blindingly. Snow weighed down fir tree branches. Everything was blank, crystalline, including the sky and the line of distant mountains. Lisa plunged her mittened hands deeply into her coat pockets and sighed, moved by the beauty around her. She was late for breakfast and for her kitchen chores. Oh, why was she plagued by kitchen chores!

Up ahead was the dining hall building. Mark lived in a flat on the second floor. Lisa stomped inside. Rows of crudely constructed picnic tables and benches filled the large hall. Before collecting her breakfast tray from the kitchen, she went to the potbellied stove in the corner to warm her hands. Karl sat at a nearby table with other children. He was laughing. Lisa was determined to leave the commune, but the thought of separating Karl from his friends saddened her. He loved the kids who sat with him: Zeus, Hermes, Dew, Lunar, and Fire. These children were named after Greek gods and natural phenomena. 'Karl' sounded dull in comparison. When she came to the commune, Lisa had wanted to change his name to Polestar, but Fritz had insisted, "He's Karl, after my grandfather."

Mark sat at the head table. By coming late, Lisa had missed his mealtime ritual. He would enter the dining room and point to those he wished to have sit with him. Since the roof incident, she was never one of the privileged few selected. Today, Jane sat beside the commune's chief. Fritz had said Mark and she were having an affair. The news hadn't surprised Lisa, nor had the gossip about Mark's affairs with other commune women. He was intelligent, self-assured, and not emotionally needy like many of the men on the commune. Mark had many devoted female disciples, ready to walk barefoot over nails to reach his bed.

Lisa had felt attracted to him too, but she wasn't willing to risk losing Fritz's love for the sake of a fling. Before meeting Fritz, she'd reveled in a series of haphazard, impulsive affairs. She stopped having such affairs after she fell in love with Fritz, not because she valued sexual fidelity, but because he became enraged if she so much as flirted with another man. So far, she'd had only two lapses in the years they'd been married. Thankfully, Fritz hadn't found out about either.

Mark's ideas about sexual faithfulness differed from Fritz's ideals. Once, Lisa had seen Mark take a little gold pin out of his pocket. The pin was shaped like the male biological symbol, an arrow protruding from a circle. In this case, the circle had a gap. Attaching the pin to his shirt collar, he'd explained its significance to Lisa and several others who clustered about him that day. The pin meant that he'd had a vasectomy. He'd said, "I advocate every male on the commune does what's necessary to acquire one of these pins. Overpopulation is depleting the earth's resources. We have to stop producing children." Lisa had suspected the individuals hearing Mark's rhetoric, who happened to be parents, were as glad of their kids as she was of Karl. Yet everyone listened attentively as if to a wise father.

Commune members tended to be idealistic. They cared about racial equality, nature, the development of third world countries, and the women's movement. They cared too about sexual freedom, something a vasectomy would facilitate. The majority of the commune saw free sex as a duty, a way to strike a blow against an exploitive system of capitalistic ownership. Lisa was accustomed to statements made around the breakfast or dinner table like: "It's important to sever sex from personal attachment... You can never be a fully-realized person unless you free yourself from sexual hang-ups... All creativity comes from sexuality."

Having warmed herself sufficiently at the dining hall stove, Lisa went to the kitchen to collect her breakfast. Sue, a slender, dark-haired young woman stood by the coffee urn. She gave Lisa a sharp look. "Where were you, Princess? I had to do your chores." The mocking title 'Princess' stung Lisa. Even so, she swallowed her pride, apologized profusely. "You're so much better in the kitchen than me. You're lucky I didn't come. I'd have done things wrong, made a mess. I just get in the way." Hoping to appease and charm, she began a self-effacing story about how when asked to bring baked beans to a college potluck, she'd brought a bag of dried beans because she hadn't known better. She expected Sue to laugh.

Sue held up her hand to stop Lisa's chatter. "What's your point? That you slacked off like you do so often? You'll have to stay after breakfast to clear the tables and wash the dishes. There's nothing you can say that will get you out of it."

"I will." Lisa felt wounded by Sue's sharp manner, but concealed her hurt with a smile that stayed pasted to her lips as she entered the dining hall. Sue followed, carrying her breakfast tray. They sat at different tables. Lisa barely touched her fried eggs, brown rice, and coffee. Who else at the commune called her Princess, she wondered. Behind her back, they probably all did. What harm had she done them? When someone didn't show up for a job and she was there, she did the extra tasks with no complaints. Why couldn't they?

Mark's loud laugh rose above the chatter in the dining room. He guzzled down a mug of coffee. Sometimes he ate almost nothing. Other times, he sensuously relished his meal, licking his lips and fingers. Lisa had been surprised the first time she saw him drink the dressing right out of the big salad bowl. Noticing her stare, he'd called, "Don't you like my table manners?" Then he'd invited her to drink from the salad bowl too. "It's the small things you have to free yourself from first," he'd said. She'd complied. Like almost everyone else, she'd longed to please him.

The only time she'd seen someone defy him was last September in the dining hall when a slight, thin Asian-American woman slapped him in the face. Instantly, Mark had struck her across her cheek. Then he'd sat back down to resume his meal as if nothing had happened. Lisa had been stunned. Afterwards, a few people had whispered about the incident. "What did she expect? She hit him first." Lisa had felt Mark should have done no more than restrain the woman to stop her from hitting him again. She hadn't expressed her opinion. After all, she hadn't known the circumstances that had led to the exchange of slaps. Also she didn't want a critical comment of hers to get back to Mark.

Lisa wanted Mark's praise, not his anger. When he praised someone, the person brightened, perked up, and stood straight. Mark's power was such that he could play with commune members, like a cat playing with prey. Sometimes his narrowed eyes didn't seem to register a person's presence. Other times, he had an intimidating gaze. In the autumn, she'd witnessed him come upon a group who were supposed to be picking apples in the orchard but were lazing about instead. He'd said, "Who's the biggest parasite? Is it you Simon?" Simon shriveled and stared at the ground. "Or is it Helen? Or Rose?" Lisa, who'd been part of the negligent group, had been certain she'd be identified as the parasite. But Mark hadn't shamed her. Afterwards, she'd noticed that Mark made it up to those he humiliated with either a few kind words, special privileges, or release from a work detail. She supposed the earlier hurt made them all the more grateful.

After the meal Karl and the rest of the children rushed outside, as did several of the commune members, including Jane, Mark's current girlfriend. Mark called to those still in the dining hall, "Do I have a volunteer to get the mail?" The mailbox was a mile and a half down the road, a long way to hike on a frigid day. Gray, the guy who usually went for the mail, had the flu.

"I'll go," Lisa offered, wanting to demonstrate that she wasn't a spoiled princess. She could walk through blizzards, if she chose.

"But first she has to wash the dishes," Sue cried fiercely.

"Why don't you wash them, Sue?" Mark said off-handedly.

Mark's taking her side surprised Lisa. Since last month, he'd barely deigned to register her existence.

"But..." Sue began to protest.

Lisa stared at Mark, waiting to find out whether she'd be spared the dishwashing drudgery.

"I need the mail now," Mark declared and waved Lisa off.

The road to the mailbox hadn't been cleared. As Lisa trudged along, snow slipped into her boots. The frigid air was painful to breathe. Yet she felt triumphant. She wouldn't consider turning back and disappointing Mark. He'd stood up for her. Something had shifted. He'd extended his protection to her.

By now, she knew she couldn't get Fritz to leave the commune unless Mark cooperated. She wanted to enlist him as an ally in her battle. Nothing would be accomplished if she accused him of monopolizing her husband, of poisoning him with overloads of drugs, like a drug dealer. No, she must use charm, flattery, humor, gentleness, tact. The rest of the walk she made up wheedling things to say to Mark. *We all love it here…but Fritz needs 'a sabbatical'…a period to restore his body…we'll return to commune…*

Lisa came to the highway, glanced at the telephone poles in either direction, and at the tire tracks in the slushy, gray snow. The commune's over-sized mailbox overflowed with letters, magazines, and two heavy packages. She ought to have brought a carry-bag. On her way back, a few letters slipped from her hands into the snow. Lisa retrieved them, but was nearly in tears because they were damp and dirty. Mark would be irritated! The budding relationship she'd envisioned between them was marred before it began.

The snap of twigs alerted her to a deer racing through the woods. The graceful streak of gray and brown calmed her. It didn't matter if the letters were soiled. The post office often damaged mail. She'd say the letters had been soiled when she got them.

The dining hall was empty when Lisa stepped inside. "Hello," she called, her voice echoing in the vast room. She wondered where to leave the mail. A small table stood at the foot of the flight of stairs leading to Mark's apartment. She plopped her burden on it. The thought of returning to the cabin and seeing Fritz in a stupor made her feel helpless and sick.

Mark appeared at the top of stairs. He told her to bring the mail up to him. "I need to talk to you," he said, smiling.

She climbed the stairs to the landing. Mark waved her into rooms filled with the previous owners' plush rugs and heavy, dark furniture. A large, framed mirror over the living room fireplace reflected the high color and shining dark eyes her walk in the cold had bestowed on her. Snowflakes shone in her hair. She saw herself as if in a painting, a different and lovely girl.

"Take off your coat," Mark said. Lisa did. She handed it to him. He threw it on the antique couch. She began to shiver. "You're cold," he observed. A stove was set into the fireplace He took up a poker, opened its door and stirred the embers. The charred wood sputtered and snapped. Flickering flames shot up. Mark threw a log into the flames, then lit two tokes of marijuana.

Gratefully, Lisa took hers. Inhaling deeply, she felt the grass relaxing her. It always did. The flames in the stove turned a bright gold. The purple curtains looked like velvet. She went over and stroked them. She felt, suddenly, optimistic, happy. Mark was going to help. Fritz would stop taking LSD. Words rose to her lips. Someone else seemed to be speaking.

"I'm worried about Fritz, the changes in him. Tell him to stop tripping... He'll do whatever you say."

Mark smiled. "Is it up to you or I to judge what Fritz should or should not do? Do you really want..."

They were standing close. Had she floated over to him? He was speaking now of American Indians, how the use of peyote gave them insights into nature. Although she stopped following what he said, she was sure every word he uttered was eloquent, confident, powerful. He played with the tassels on the drawstrings of her peasant blouse. She felt a stirring within her. He stroked her hair, kissed her lips. What am I doing, she wondered. Mark's touch on her breasts was electric.

She couldn't stop herself, kissed back, pressed against him. 'Just this once,' rang in her mind. 'Fritz won't find out.' She didn't feel like she was betraying Fritz. She wanted to help him, was laying the groundwork to so.

Transported into a dream world outside of time and judgment, she followed Mark into the white-walled bedroom. He slowly stripped off her shirt, pants, bra. Naked on the big bed, her body throbbed. She was climbing, using every atom of her strength to climb, moaning, panting. Pleasure cascaded within her. She wanted it to go on forever. Then, she was empty, exhausted. Turning onto her side, she fell asleep.

Waking alone, Lisa was confused about what had happened. She dressed and left. The glaring sunlight melted patches of snow. In one spot, a crocus emerged from the dark, moist earth, an encouraging sign of Spring. Hoping to see the deer again, Lisa looked towards the woods. She was like the deer, free and wild, relying on her instincts.

7

Israel, 1982

It had been two days since Rabbi Tubol had told Karl he must consult Rabbi Blum as a spiritual advisor, an instruction Karl had thus far ignored. Sitting in Talmud class, gazing at the young, dark-haired instructor, he recalled Rabbi Tubol's implied threat. If Karl didn't put his troubles before Rabbi Blum, the next report sent to Judge Thorn would be a bad one.

To make matters worse, the topic Rabbi Blum chose to discuss today was criminal law. Karl suspected his teacher had chosen it after colluding with Rabbi Tubol. Every word seemed directed to him, the criminal in the midst of the pure Yeshiva students.

Pacing the perimeter of the room, Rabbi Blum said, "Perhaps the hardest thing in the world is to judge another person. It's difficult to find a balance between justice and compassion. It's almost impossible for a judge to be completely impartial. How did our scholars meet these challenges to achieve justice?"

Students called out—

"Our sages preserved justice by making sure that only learned and fair men were appointed judges."

"There was always more than one judge to offset the bias of the others."

"Judges were instructed to take the defendant's side as much as possible."

"Confession was forbidden because it might encourage prosecutors to engage in torture."

Rabbi Blum smiled at Karl. "How about you, Baruch? Do you want to comment? Let us benefit from your point of view."

Karl shook his head and said nothing. Other times, his silence had been permitted. Today, though, Rabbi Blum kept pressuring him to participate. How about this, Baruch? How about that? What do you think? Karl felt he was being forced into a relationship with him whether Karl wanted it or not. Without thinking, he mumbled, "Leave me alone, you shithead."

Eli, the kid in front of him, whipped around, looking shocked, unable to believe that a student had the temerity to insult a rabbi. "What are you staring at?" Karl hissed. Eli turned away.

Fearful that his insult to Rabbi Blum would be repeated to Rabbi Tubol, Karl began inwardly shaking. Here was another misstep to mention in 'the report.' At least Rabbi

Blum appeared not to have heard. He continued the class, called on other kids. When it was time to leave, Karl was almost out the door when he felt Rabbi Blum's hand on his shoulder. The rabbi said, "I'd like to speak with you. Come by my office tonight."

Throughout afternoon prayers, supper and study-time, Karl felt anxious about the private interview. Rabbi Blum hadn't specified a time for their meeting. Karl decided he'd show up late. The rabbi would have gone to his quarters. Later, if he questioned him, Karl would say that he'd been to his office but no one was there.

At midnight, he walked up to the main building's second floor, passed by empty classrooms. The hall was dark, except for the light from Rabbi's Blum's office. Its open doorway revealed a room half the size of Rabbi Tubol's office. A violin case was tucked in the corner. Nearby were a piece of rosin and a stained rosin rag. Music scores littered the floor as if they were old friends who required no formality, unlike the Jewish books respectfully lined up in the bookcase.

Rabbi Blum stood in the center of the room with his eyes closed, humming and waving his hands. Karl's reluctant knock woke him from his reverie.

The rabbi's face lit up. "You've come. I'm glad! I stayed, just in case."

"What were you doing?" Karl blurted. He closed his eyes and waved his hands to demonstrate what he'd seen.

Rabbi Blum looked flustered. "I got carried away. I was conducting. In my 'other life,' I was an amateur musician."

There'd been mornings Karl had woken believing he'd dreamt of music drifting over the desert, each note a silvery drop of water falling onto the parched earth. Now he knew Rabbi Blum had been playing the violin late at night.

"What was your real job before you became a rabbi?" Karl asked.

"An engineer. I worked for a company in Detroit. It's a life-time away."

Karl was still standing. Rabbi Blum pointed to a chair beside his desk and said, "Please, have a seat." Karl sat and stared at the brown linoleum floor.

"You...you...you seemed uncomfortable in class, Baruch. Did I do anything wrong?"

The rabbi thought *he'd* done something wrong. Karl was astonished.

"I've been waiting for you to come to me...and felt that in a way, what you did this morning...that you made contact...even if it was by calling me 'Shithead.'"

"I'm sorry. I shouldn't have..."

"You don't have to apologize. Do you like it here in Israel?"

"Yeah, sure. It's all right."

"*Emes*? The truth?"

"The truth?" Karl paused, then blurted, "I want to go home." It was not something he would have said to Rabbi Tubol. Rabbi Blum was a kinder, more sympathetic person.

"I'm sorry to hear you're unhappy. Don't you like your friends? Your studies? What is it?" the young rabbi coaxed.

A river of emotions gushed through Karl, washing away the dikes and sandbags of precaution. He'd already admitted he wanted to go home. Now, he felt compelled to explain his reasons. "Everything's wrong," he cried. "The work's too hard for me. I'll never catch up. I feel stupid. No one likes me."

"You're discouraged. It was the same for me when I was in New York, studying at a Yeshiva."

"You say that to make me feel better," Karl protested.

"But it's true. You should have seen what an ignoramus I was. Believe me, if you heard the mistakes I made, you'd find them hilarious." Rabbi Blum shook his head and smiled as if he was remembering a particular error. Then gazing steadily at Karl, he said, "But I caught up, and so will you."

"It's impossible for me to catch up."

"Do you know about Rabbi Akiva?"

"I don't know anything."

Leaning towards Karl, Rabbi Blum said eagerly, "Rabbi Akiva was an illiterate shepherd. Rachel, the daughter of Jerusalem's richest man, fell in love and married him. Her father refused to support them, and they lived in poverty. Poor as they were, Rachel encouraged Akiva to educate himself. He didn't learn to read until the age of forty. Baruch, you're only sixteen."

"How old were you when you started studying Talmud?"

"I? You want to know about me? I was twenty-five when I went to the seminary."

"Why'd you become religious?"

The rabbi frowned. "Because I...I experienced a tragedy...a personal tragedy." He turned and gazed out the office window.

Karl found it reassuring that his advisor had secrets also. Maybe he could be trusted.

Facing Karl again, the rabbi said quietly, "Let's talk about Rabbi Akiva, not about me. You might expect Akiva's starting late in life would put him at a disadvantage. It didn't. To this day, he's venerated as a great sage. Be patient, Baruch. Keep working and you'll do well."

"Akiva must have been a genius."

"Maybe, but I like to see him as an ordinary human being, like you or me. Because he was older and more experienced, he had deeper insights and a different perspective than other students. In this way, his late start was an advantage."

"I'm not a Rabbi Akiva."

"The greater your effort, the more the merit. In Judaism, it's sincerity and enthusiasm that count."

"Really? It doesn't sound that way when I talk to the other boys. They say..."

"Don't be afraid. Tell me."

"They boast that their fathers, their grandfathers and their great grandfathers were rabbis, and that's why they can study well. I don't come from a long line of rabbis."

"Neither do I. Neither did Rabbi Akiva. His father was a convert, or perhaps it was his grandfather. It's not certain, and it's not important. What is important is what you achieve on your own. Do you feel some of the boys are less mature than you?"

"Yes!"

"They've led protected lives."

Karl nodded. He'd come to believe that, on the whole, the other students had been pampered, and kept apart from people who were different from them. Jakob, who grew up in South Africa, had said the only blacks he'd known personally in Johannesburg were the maids who came to clean the homes in his neighborhood. *Eema,* his mother, had made sure Jakob's clothes were always clean and pressed. Unlike Karl, Jakob had never had nits in his hair, or rashes on his skin. If he cut himself, *Eema* had antiseptic ointment and a bandage ready, or *Abba*, his father, drove him to the doctor's. Jakob had never had to bake his own birthday cake, let alone prepare his own meals. Not once had he been left alone all night, cowering at every sound and shadow.

"The other boys offer you their learning, but you can offer the benefit of your experience. It's not good to lack either. When you were paired with Jakob as a roommate, it was to benefit him too. You have something to offer the other boys as well. I wish you'd participate more in class. Tell me, why do you always sit in the back of the class? Why don't you join in more?"

Karl shrugged. "I don't mind sitting in back. I'm used to it. My first grade teacher told me to sit in the back, because I interrupted too much."

"Don't sit in the back any more. Sit up in front and ask questions. Give your opinions. Be spontaneous."

"The back's where I belong," Baruch said gloomily.

"Even if you were the slowest student, I'd want to see you participate."

"Why? What's the point?"

"The only way the Yeshiva can help a student sharpen his mental abilities is if the student comes up with a position and states it. Then the teacher can ask him and the others in the class for alternative positions. This technique will force you to see weak and ambiguous points, if any, in your thinking."

"I don't have much to contribute because I don't know much about Judaism."

"You can use your unique background to draw fresh conclusions. Let me give myself as an example. I love music, so when I look at Torah, I see music. A story in the Bible is like a symphonic movement to me. Life is limitless. Jewish learning is limitless. There's always room for an individual to create something new, even if it's a joke. Perhaps all you want to say is: 'The Beatles are like Samson—all those guys think their power's in their hairdo.' For that matter, a lot of women do too."

Karl hadn't laughed hard at a joke for a long time. It was a relief, a marvel to laugh, to feel the quavering sensation deep in his belly bubbling up, and to let go, and then relax.

The rabbi became serious again. "When you speak up, your teachers will also make you look for common denominators between your argument and everyone else's, no matter how far-flung the connection. That will expand your intellectual powers too."

Karl nodded, although he felt doubtful.

"I want you to participate. You'll challenge yourself, your fellow students and your teachers. It's exciting. Don't deprive yourself. Don't deprive others of your perspective. There will be other benefits. You'll fit in better here if you participate more. We can talk about this more, but it's late. You must be tired. I'd like you to come back again for another talk." Smiling, he added, "but earlier in the evening."

"When do you want me?"

"Tomorrow."

With the slightest nod, Karl agreed.

"Good, Baruch."

"My name's Karl!"

"Michael was my American name. I changed it to Mikel when I entered the Yeshiva. We both have new names. It takes a while to get used to them. Do you prefer for me to call you Karl?"

Karl mumbled, "Baruch's all right."

They parted with a handshake that sealed a commitment the rabbi made. Starting tomorrow, he'd meet with Karl every day except on the *shabbes*, and tutor him until he caught up with the other students. The private lessons would have to be suspended during the four weeks of long winter break that would take place the following month, but the tutoring would resume immediately afterwards.

Usually, when Karl returned to his room for the night, he marked off the day on his calendar, glad that there was one less day until he was freed from serving time at the Yeshiva. Tonight, he didn't feel a need to cross off the day.

The room was dark, but he could see that Jakob had kicked off his blanket. Karl smoothed it back over him, remembering a favor he'd received from his roommate that morning. Jakob knew Karl's shoes pinched. Apparently, he'd asked around and found a benefactor. A used pair of sandals had appeared on the floor of Karl's closet. Karl had tried them on, walked around the room and pronounced, "They fit." To wear hand-me-downs embarrassed him. But seeing the smile that lit Jakob's face, he'd decided to wear the shoes, and had worn them all day. He took them off now as he undressed for bed.

The earlier conversation with Rabbi Blum sounded in his head after Karl slipped into bed. He went over every word that was said, thrilled at the prospect of Rabbi Blum's friendship. The trouble was, he found it hard to believe that the rabbi truly cared about him, or that he'd honor the promise he'd made to tutor him. There'd been too many times in his life that he'd been disappointed by men who took the role of his friend and mentor, starting with his father.

A few of Lisa's lovers took the trouble to read stories, wrestle, and toss a ball to Karl. But the moment inevitably came when he was slipped a couple of dollars and told, "Go to the toy store," or "Go to the movies." Karl was furious when Howie, one of his mother's boyfriends, refused to play with him. He'd charged into Howie, butting him like a goat. Howie head-locked Karl and began to punch him. During the beating, Lisa skittered off to a corner like a frightened child while red-faced Howie screamed at Karl, "I hope you've learned your lesson." With all his heart, Karl hoped he had a better teacher now, one who wouldn't hurt or abandon him.

The next day, Karl forced himself to take a front row seat in Rabbi Sobel's class.

Although it was a course in ancient history, the class discussion drifted to the current status of women in Judaism. Rabbi Sobel's position was that Judaism honored and protected women.

"I don't agree," Karl said. Several boys had responded at the same time, and he assumed he'd be ignored.

To his surprise Rabbi Sobel said, "Very good! Baruch has the opposite position to mine. Let's hear why."

"It's wrong for women to have to isolate and inconvenience themselves because of male weaknesses," Karl said.

"Give us examples."

Karl spoke timidly at first, then with growing confidence. "Women have to sit separately in synagogue so the men won't be distracted from their prayers. They have to wear long sleeves even when it's hot in order that men don't have impure thoughts. I think men should develop self-control."

"What about the rest of you? What do you think?" Rabbi Sobel asked.

As the discussion resumed, Karl sank into his seat, trembling, but excited. He'd stated what he'd thought.

Not that everyone had agreed with him. "Inherent male impulses can't be controlled," one boy said. Two other students argued that women should take care not to be provocative. But Karl's perspective had been accepted. His ideas were seen as valid as anyone else's!

That evening when he went to meet with Rabbi Blum, he recounted all that had happened in class.

Propelled from his seat with obvious pleasure and excitement, the rabbi half-rose and cried, "Well done! I'm proud of you. You had the courage to state your opinion. I hope what you did today will be a turning point. Now, let's begin our Hebrew tutoring."

They sat side by side while Karl attempted to translate a text. Karl had to turn to him every other word for help. His earlier confidence disappeared. "This isn't going to work. I'm hopeless. Don't waste your time," he said.

"I'm not wasting my time... Be patient. In a way, your Hebrew is better than mine. As far as I can tell, your accent is pure, almost as if you were born here."

"I *was* born here. I lived on a *kibbutz* until I was nearly four," Karl said, surprised and heartened by the praise he'd received. Perhaps, there was hope for him.

"So you've come back... To make *aliyah* to Israel means to ascend."

"And *yored*, to leave Israel, is to descend?" Karl didn't know how he recollected the word, only that Rabbi Blum's kindness fished it from his memory.

After their meeting Karl walked across the courtyard towards the dorm. Glancing up at the starry sky, he felt light, floating. He'd heard in the rabbi's warm words something unsaid but implied—'I care for you.' Perhaps Rabbi Blum's affection wouldn't endure. But in this moment, he was hopeful.

8

Vermont, 1971

The snowstorm in early April marked the end of the winter. As the weather warmed, adults and children at the commune stripped off their clothes and walked about nude. The free sex many residents advocated blossomed. Mark, the puppet master who'd hooked Fritz on LSD, now exercised his power over Lisa. One afternoon, the last week in May, she crept furtively up the steps to his flat for a tryst. With Mark, she became a different Lisa, the Lisa he hypnotized. He liked having sex a certain rough way, pinning her down, holding her wrists tightly. She'd have preferred him to be gentler. When she protested, he became angry. Lisa stopped objecting. For her, there was a mysterious inaccessible something in Mark. She kept struggling to reach it. The next few days, she returned daily as if he were some kind of drug.

There were benefits to her week-old affair with the lord and master of the commune. Almost at once, a few of the men began to act in courtly ways and flirted with her. They found her more attractive because Mark desired her. The women began to treat her with deference. Sue, for one, stopped objecting when Lisa didn't turn up for her kitchen shifts. Jane didn't dare to complain that she'd been supplanted. Overall, Lisa fit in better at the commune. Still, it was discomforting that her affair was generally known.

Lisa kept studying Fritz's face, trying to decipher whether he suspected. She was certain he'd find out. When he did, he'd explode with fury. She felt confused, out of control, uncertain whether the risks she was taking weren't too high. Three more days passed. It was June. Lisa knew Fritz would never give up LSD without Mark's support and consent. She continued to offer her body to Mark, kept making him swear he'd stop giving Fritz drugs. And Mark did keep his promise!

One morning, fifteen days after she'd commenced her affair, Fritz told her that he was going to renounce LSD. There were ups and downs to his recovery. After a week of being drug-free, he lapsed. A fortnight passed, and he forswore LSD again. This time, he seemed determined to master himself. Lisa felt richly rewarded as she watched him transform to his clear-headed, energetic, passionate old self. After watching how hard he'd struggled to master his cravings, she determined to give up something too. She stopped visiting Mark's bed, a step towards leaving the commune.

California was on the horizon. Fritz hoped to sell some of his paintings. There'd be fewer to transport, and he'd make extra money for the trip. One hot July afternoon, he borrowed Mark's station wagon, loaded it with his canvasses, and drove to Ayer, a tourist town with art galleries. One of the gallery owners agreed to exhibit Fritz's work. Four days later, a check came in the mail. Two paintings had been sold!

That night, Fritz celebrated with an acid trip. Lisa didn't know whether it was because he credited LSD with inspiring the pictures, and didn't think he could paint without its aid, or simply because his success made him relax his guard. She felt crushed and helpless.

Three evenings later, the summer heat was sweltering in the little cabin. Karl wore nothing but underpants, had already kicked off the light sheet with which Lisa had covered him

"I want Daddy to put me to sleep," he whined.

"He's with Mark."

"I want to stay up until Daddy comes back."

"Stop it, Karl. You have to go to bed right now," Lisa cried.

"Don't be mad," he beseeched her.

Feeling guilty for her harsh tone, Lisa comforted him with kisses, and sang him a lullaby, "Hush, little baby…"

Finally, he put his head on the pillow. His eyelids fluttered shut. She expected that later in the night, there'd be one of the brief but frequent thunder and lightning storms that lit up the mountains during the summer. Anticipating that the storm would bring a chill, she drew the sheet over Karl again. Then she tiptoed to the double bed, sank into its soft mattress and fell asleep.

Later, stirring in her sleep, Lisa wasn't sure whether she was dreaming, or a storm was actually taking place. The storm turned out to be the bright moonlight shining in the window, and Fritz clomping through the door. Sleepily, she glanced at Karl's cot, was reassured that he was still asleep.

Fritz moved over to where she lay, bent down and brought his face close to hers. His features were twisted, his skin mottled red. With a contraction of her heart, she heard him hiss, "You slept with Mark!"

"I did it for you…" she murmured in a voice that didn't sound like her own, but a small, pleading creature's.

"For me!" he laughed.

"To make you see that this isn't the right place for us, that we have to leave."

"You slut. You bitch. You fucking whore..." He slapped her across her face, once, twice, three times, snapping her neck.

Lying there while he cursed and excoriated her, she waited for his rage to exhaust itself. Mercifully, Karl did not wake. Mercifully, Fritz did not hit her again.

Bringing his mouth right up to her ear, he spat out, "*Drecklick Jude.*" Filthy Jew.

The words roused her. She felt as if she'd received an electric shock. Using all her strength, she pushed him away. He stumbled backwards like a drunkard, attempted to right himself, and pitched forward onto the bed. She was able to slip out of the way as he fell. Taking her opportunity, she ran off to crouch by Karl's bed. Fritz lay on their bed without moving, as if he'd passed out. His breathing deepened. His snores rolled out, seeming to rasp, *Drecklick Jude.*

Lisa touched Karl's hand in order to calm herself. His hand was the inert hand of a sleeper. She stroked his arm. His skin was cool from the chilly night air. Quietly, Lisa crossed the room. Instead of going for a blanket as she'd first intended, she stopped at her bed. She pulled her suitcase from beneath, edged it out inch by inch until it was free. Grabbing handfuls of clothes for Karl and herself from the dresser, she hurriedly packed, dressed, and removed her shoulder bag from a drawer. Inside the bag was three hundred dollars in cash, as well as her passport, a credit card, and checkbooks for the local bank.

Gently, she shook Karl, whispering, "You have to get dressed."

"No," he whimpered, kept his eyes shut, grasped his pillow. He drifted back to sleep.

Lifting his limp arms and legs, Lisa dressed him then left him to doze on his bed as she carried the suitcase and her shoulder bag outside. She wondered whether to leave a note. Fritz adored Karl. He'd be furious at her for taking him away. No, she wouldn't write a note. It would slow her down, and might even weaken her resolve to go. She reentered the cabin in order to get Karl.

Fritz moaned. She froze. There was always a chance he might wake and come after them. Picking up Karl, she rushed outside. If there'd been a key, she'd have locked the cabin door after her in order to slow Fritz down. With her free hand, she grabbed the suitcase and bag she'd left by the door. Weighed down with a child and luggage, she staggered down the road as quickly as she could.

The full moon lit the path towards the main house. Pussy willows lined the sides of the road. Gravel crunched beneath her feet. After a few yards, she had to stop to catch her breath. Awake now, Karl slipped to the ground, ready to walk on his own, curious about where they were going and why.

"It's a surprise, Karl. You're not supposed to tell when it's a surprise."

"Is it my birthday?"

"That's in a few weeks. It's a different surprise."

"Does Daddy know?"

"It's a surprise for him too."

Inside the dining hall building, she set her bags down and told Karl to wait for her at the foot of the steps. "I'll be back soon," she whispered as she started up to Mark's flat. She wanted Mark to give her a lift to the bus station. The lights were out, the door to his bedroom closed. She'd hoped he was still up, but it looked like she'd have to wake him. She wondered whether he'd try to dissuade her from leaving. Opening the bedroom door, and peering into the darkness, Lisa was astonished. There was someone with Mark, although she couldn't tell who it was.

Lisa was barely able to control her urge to shake Mark awake and say how much she despised him. A month ago, she'd stopped coming to his bed! His revenge was to inform Fritz of their affair. Duplicitous as Mark was, she must not make a scene, not with Karl waiting for her below. Grasping the doorknob, she pulled the bedroom door shut without making a sound. She used Mark's phone to call for a cab.

Twenty minutes later a taxi pulled up to the main building. The driver took Lisa and Karl to the bus terminal in Ayer. During the bus ride to New York City, Karl curled up against Lisa and fell asleep. She was tense and fearful but tried to sit still and not wake him. *Drecklick Jude*. How could Fritz utter something so awful? It must have been dredged from a sewer of boyhood memories. The ugly words enraged and hurt her more than the slaps, or his saying, 'You slut. You whore.'

Sleeping passengers sprawled in the bus seats. Motels and restaurants flashed along the dark borders of the highway. Lisa barely noticed them. The bewildering scene kept exploding in her mind, Fritz screaming she was a filthy Jew. She'd thought he liked her being Jewish. Why, when she became pregnant, he'd said their child must be born in Israel. At Fritz's insistence, they'd gone to live on a *kibbutz*. For over three years Fritz had labored as a *kibbutznik*, building up the Jewish land with his labor and sweat.

For him to speak as a Jew-hater meant Fritz was no longer himself! He was mentally ill. Lisa shuddered. If he'd been suffering from a physical ailment, like cancer, she'd have stayed with him. The darkness outside the bus was dissipating. The new day brought no hope and many regrets. Oh, she'd done something terrible. She'd abandoned a sick husband, without as much as a goodbye. She'd torn Karl from his father, and from a life where he felt safe and had friends. How was she going to care for a child alone? She'd been impulsive and stupid.

The bus pulled into the Port of Authority. When she lifted Karl from his seat he awoke, but only for a few moments. Once again, Lisa had to carry him and drag the suitcase. Her shoulder bag cut into her shoulder. Stopping frequently, she made her way to the taxi queue. A cab took her to her parents' building on Park Avenue. It was Sunday, the traffic light. Karl woke during the drive and looked about. "Where are we?" he asked with astonishment. "Look at the tall buildings!"

And a few minutes later: "Are other kids from the commune coming to New York?"

The doorman recognized Lisa and relieved her of her suitcase. He'd begun to work at her parents' building last summer, the very week that she, Fritz, and Karl had arrived from Europe for a visit with her parents. Lisa stepped into the air-conditioned lobby. Everything looked the same as before she'd left for the commune, blue walls, potted plants and brown leather easy chairs. The sound of splashing water came from the small corner fountain.

At the elevator, the doorman handed back her suitcase. She rode up with Karl. Her parents would demand explanations of why she'd come. With every floor she ascended, her anxiety increased. She neither wanted, nor knew how to tell them what had happened since she'd seen them a year ago.

Standing at her parents' door with Karl and her suitcase, she gathered her courage and knocked timidly. Her mother opened the door. Bernice was dressed in a dark blue bathrobe. Her face looked pale without her usual makeup.

"Oh, Lisa," she gasped, called Lisa's father to come. In a flustered voice, she invited her daughter and grandson inside the vestibule.

Al appeared with a puzzled expression on his face. He pushed his gold wire glasses up on his nose and peered at Karl. There was a brief exchange of greetings as everyone stood in the flat's entry hall, not knowing how to proceed.

"Give Grandma and Grandpa hugs," Lisa told Karl, although she assumed he'd forgotten his grandparents. Yet Karl let his grandfather shake his hand, and didn't protest when his grandmother picked him up.

Holding him like a radioactive package, Bernice rushed Karl to the bathroom. Lisa followed. Standing in the bathroom's doorway, she watched her mother run the bath, and pour scented bubble bath in the tub. Karl cooperated as Grandma stripped off the pants and long-sleeved shirt with which Lisa had dressed him in the middle of the night. The cuffs of Bernice's silk bathrobe got soaked as she lowered Karl into the tub. She rolled them up.

"Lisa, my purse's in my bedroom. Take my credit card out of my wallet. Go buy Karl new clothes." Pointing to the shabby pile on the floor, Bernice added, "And throw these in the incinerator."

Lisa winced. She ventured, "I've got clothes for him in the suitcase."

"Toss them out too."

Lisa nodded. This place wasn't her home any more. She'd have to abide by her mother's rules. She yawned, felt exhausted from her trip. "It's Sunday. The stores will be closed."

"Maybe they're closed in a little town in Vermont. In New York City, Sundays are the days stores make the most money. Or have you forgotten? Lots of stores are open."

"I just got here. I'm tired..." Lisa protested. "Can't I go later?"

"Karl needs new clothes. He can't go around naked. You can see I'm busy. And I'm not sending your father out. He wouldn't know what to buy."

"Okay! I'll go!"

As Lisa was about to leave, Al called to her from the kitchen, "Come in here a moment." She entered the kitchen, a large room with high cabinets, and old-fashioned fixtures. There was a deep porcelain sink and a six-burner stove, identical to the one in the commune's kitchen.

"Have a cup of tea with me," Al said, smiling genially.

Grateful for the invitation, and hoping for sympathy, Lisa sank into a sturdy wooden chair. She watched her father fill the kettle and set it to boil. He put out two mugs, each with a tea bag.

"Your husband's not here," Al mused, as he crossed the room and rummaged in a cabinet for a box of biscuits.

"His name is Fritz," Lisa said irritably to his back.

Al sat down across from her. "I know his name. Where is he? Back in Europe?"

She understood that her father wanted to know whether she'd separated from Fritz. He'd be happy if she had. Her parents had been polite to Fritz when he'd come last year. But she knew they'd cringed every time they heard his German accent. Her parents admired German technology but wouldn't buy a German car. Nor did they want an Austrian son-in-law. The Holocaust must not be forgotten.

"He's staying on the commune for a while," Lisa said as casually as she could manage. The teakettle's piercing whistle scratched her nerves.

Al poured steaming water into the cups, and swished about the tea bags. "That's all you're going to tell me? What are your plans?"

"I really have to go out. Mom wants me to buy clothes for Karl."

"But your tea..."

Lisa took a few sips, pushed the mug away and left.

Outside, nannies wheeled prams and strollers. A dog walker strode by with half a dozen dogs. Lisa recalled a small shop that sold stylish children's clothing from France. If it still existed, she could walk over in ten minutes. On the way, she pondered her father's question about her future. She couldn't stay with her parents for long without old tensions erupting. Beyond her intention to leave in a week or two, she had no plans. The only thing she could think to do was to take Karl to San Francisco. After they were settled—she'd work out the details later—she'd bring Fritz to their new California home and nurse him back to health. Away from the commune, surely, he'd become his old self again.

The red striped awning of the children's clothing store fluttered in the breeze. The shop was open. Lisa bought Karl shirts, pants and underwear, as well as a less practical purchase, a little, black velvet suit that would please her mother. She left the shop weighed down by two shopping bags full of clothes.

Her father let her back into the flat. Piano music floated from the living room. Lisa was drawn to it. She saw her mother seated at the Steinway, playing and singing, "Three Blind Mice." Sitting beside her, Karl laughed and banged away randomly. Lisa was astonished that Bernice let him pound on her precious piano. As far as she could remember, her mother had never done such a thing for her.

A scent teased Lisa's nose. She sniffed, recognized the odor of the bubble bath from Karl's bath. It was still emanating from his skin. He was dressed in a t-shirt that hung down like a dress. His long hair was gone. Her mother must have snipped it off. Lisa was shocked that Bernice hadn't asked permission. At least she hadn't shaved Karl's head on the supposition that he had lice.

Bernice rose, took Lisa's two bags and peered inside them. She trilled, "Karl, you have lovely, new clothes. Let's get you dressed."

"I'll do it, Mom."

Karl chirped, "I want Grandma to do it."

Hurt to see him trip off with his grandmother, Lisa went to her old bedroom. Although she ached to stretch out on her bed and sleep, she sat down at her desk to write a letter. After topping a sheet of paper with "August, 1971," she wrote, "Dearest Fritz, I'm visiting my parents." She wanted to apologize for her affair, and for abandoning him, but decided these subjects must be discussed face-to-face.

She wrote only a brief note. "At the end of the week, I'll take Karl to San Francisco and find a place for all of us to live. If you get this before next Saturday, you can reach Karl and me at..." After writing her parents' phone number, sending her love, and signing off, she slipped the letter in an envelope. She mailed it the same day.

Nearly a week passed without Fritz telephoning. Lisa was miserable without him. Was he too wasted to call? Was he too angry? She wanted to know. Aside from a letter or telegram, the only way for her to reach Fritz was to phone and leave a message with Mark. No one else at the commune had a telephone. One evening after she'd put Karl to bed, Lisa went to her father's den. Finding it empty, she dialed Mark's number. After two rings, she hung up. She didn't trust Mark. Best to leave him out.

In the living room, her father was relaxing on the brown leather couch with *The Wall Street Journal*. Her mother sat in an easy chair, flipping through *Vogue*. The blinds were drawn. The sound of traffic from the street below was faint, a pleasant thrum like the beat of ocean waves. A sleepy feeling stole over Lisa. The large room enveloped her. Nothing had changed since her childhood. The thick Persian carpet was the same, as were the satin drapes, lit oil paintings. The bookcase contained the old set of encyclopedias and classic books

Shaking herself awake, she said, "Mom, Dad."

They looked up.

"I'm leaving for California the day after tomorrow."

"What?" The magazine slipped from her mother's hands.

"Why California?" Al asked mildly.

Lisa didn't know whether she'd be able to convince Fritz to join her in California, and whether he'd fare better there, but she spoke resolutely. "Fritz and I want to live in San Francisco!"

"Whom do you know there?" her father asked.

"No one, Dad. Does that matter? I traveled all over Europe on my own."

"It would be different if it was just you. But you're dragging a small child to a city where you know no one."

"If you argue with me, I'm going to walk out of this room, take Karl and leave right now."

"Please, Lisa, I'm concerned. Think about it a little longer."

"I'm not going to change my mind."

Bernice said, "You could leave Karl with us until you're settled. I'll bring him to San Francisco myself when you're ready."

How sensible the offer sounded. It was clear that Karl adored his grandmother, and she him. For a moment, Lisa was tempted. She couldn't bring herself to accept, was jealous of her mother's closeness to Karl. After a month or two, he might not want to return to her. "Thank you," she said, "but Karl's coming with me."

The next evening at supper—a week before the actual date of his fifth birthday—Bernice made a party for Karl. She brought out a decorated cake as dessert. Karl blew out the candles and opened his presents. There were five picture books from Grandma and

Grandpa. Afterwards, he refused to go to bed until Lisa read him every one of his new books.

In the morning, her parents took them to the airport, accompanying them to the departure gate. The waiting area was filled with passengers.

While Bernice played with Karl, Al took Lisa aside. "I guess you're really going."

"Looks like it," Lisa said, forcing a smile.

Al took an envelope from his jacket pocket. "Here's some extra cash to get settled. If you need anything else when you get there, let me know."

"Thanks, Dad. I'm okay. Just send me the trust fund checks."

"As soon as you send me an address."

"I will. And don't worry about us. I saved some money on the commune." Earlier this week, she'd transferred her money to the checking account she had with the Vermont bank. She'd paid for the airplane tickets by check.

"Take the cash anyway. It will come in handy. Think of it as a scholarship," Al said, passing her the envelope.

Lisa held back the tears, moved that her father seemed to understand how frightened she was. There'd only be her looking after Karl now. There was no one to help her with him or with the many things she had to accomplish.

9

Israel, 1982

The Yeshiva's mid-year break was coming up in December. Two weeks before the 1983 New Year, it was shutting down for a month. Judge Thorn had not allowed for vacation breaks when he'd sentenced Karl. All the students were to leave except for him. Jakob was flying home to Johannesburg, Gil visiting his Israeli relatives, Avi, his relations in Europe. Gobby who was related to Rabbi Wolfe's wife would accompany the Wolfe family to a kosher resort in Netanya. Other rabbis were taking their wives and children to the Dead Sea.

Rabbi Blum planned to go to Detroit to see his parents. The afternoon before he was to depart, he welcomed Karl to his office for their regular meeting. Karl looked around the cluttered office. After many weeks of nearly daily meetings, he'd come to feel at home. He was accustomed to mulling over the rabbi's intriguing questions, and often repeated his mentor's ideas to other boys. They'd become his ideas too.

With a newfound ability to concentrate, Karl had been studying longer hours. He strained his eyes. Two weeks ago, he'd gone to a Jerusalem ophthalmology clinic, and a doctor had prescribed glasses that helped. Rabbi Blum handed him a Hebrew text to read aloud and translate. Karl put on his glasses.

The text was about the *lamed vov tzadikim*, the thirty-six ordinary seeming individuals throughout the world who upheld the universe with their goodness. Rabbi Blum listened with the same unwavering attention and respect he always showed, even when Karl stumbled over words.

Usually they conversed for a half-hour before concluding their meetings. This afternoon, the rabbi departed from their routine. After an hour of study, he began to shuffle some papers together, and said calmly, "I'm afraid our time's over. I have to pack." He stood up, and put his hand out to shake Karl's.

Karl forced himself to extend his hand. "I'll see you when you come back from Detroit." His mouth was dry. He could barely spit out the word 'Detroit.' All he knew about the city was that it made cars and music, but he hated Detroit because it was taking his teacher away. He hadn't realized how attached he'd become.

As if he could read Karl's agitation and wished to calm him, Rabbi Blum sank back into his chair. "Actually, I scarcely have anything to pack. I don't have to run off. Let's go on with our discussion."

For Karl, each tick of the clock seemed to say, 'You can rely on your teacher.' The room filled with shadows. Rabbi Blum let time slip by. He put on a lamp. The window became opaque, reflecting back only the little world of the office, as if nothing existed outside of it. They ignored the hurrying footsteps in the hall beyond the door. People were rushing to the prayer services and then would go to supper.

Rabbi Blum spoke about the *lamed vov tzadikim*. Karl gazed at the slender, graceful man beside him. The rabbi could be one of 'the thirty-six,' except for one flaw. He was single. Rabbi Frankel had said marriage was exalted in the Jewish religion, that in ancient times, no childless, unmarried man qualified to be a member of the twenty-three judge Jewish court, the *Sanhedrei Ketana*. A bachelor was considered less compassionate than a man who'd experienced family life.

"Can I ask you something?" Karl asked, emboldened because Rabbi Blum's departure was imminent. He must ask now. People disappeared overnight, his father, Lisa's boyfriends. Perhaps he'd never again have the chance to ask. "Why aren't you married?"

Rabbi Blum rotated his neck as if he had a crick. "It's hard for me to explain. I...I'll tell you another time."

"So not all questions are permitted?"

"Almost all," Rabbi Blum said. "Try me. Ask me something else."

Permission was given. Karl intended to take it. He posed a question that he wouldn't dare ask anyone else at the Yeshiva. "What do you think about God?"

"You're not going to let me off easy tonight, are you?" With a sigh, Rabbi Blum leaned back in his chair and glanced up at the perforated ceiling tiles. "Ah, God. *HaShem* is complicated."

"Don't I have to believe?"

"Either way, you're still a Jew. To study the Talmud, you don't need great reverence or faith, only a sincere willingness to learn."

"You don't believe?" Karl blurted.

Shaking his head, his teacher said, "The other rabbis would give you a different answer than me about whether it's an obligation or a requirement. I...I struggle. You're surprised?"

"Yes."

Gazing at Karl, Rabbi Blum spoke eagerly. "It's like the story of Yakov wrestling all night with an angel. I wrestle too. To doubt, to struggle—to me, those are Jewish qualities. The word 'God' is an abstraction. I'm trying to not accept a generic fairy tale concept. I don't want superficial answers. There's a lot of freedom in Judaism. You don't have to contort your mind and feelings to fit a doctrine. Actually, you're supposed to keep questioning. You have not only the right but the duty to do so."

Karl was too astounded to speak. He'd assumed faith was automatic to everyone at the Yeshiva. Now he knew that the ultimate could be questioned in Judaism, that he could find or not find God on his own terms. There'd been many influences drawing him to Judaism, but none as powerful as what he'd heard from Rabbi Blum tonight.

The loud rumbling of Karl's stomach interrupted the discussion.

Rabbi Blum laughed. "There's a voice that can't be ignored. You're hungry! Come on. I know where we can get a snack."

In the big kitchen off the cafeteria they encountered the dishwasher, a young man whose facial features showed he had Downs' Syndrome. Supper was long over. He'd just finished his shift. Before hanging up his apron, he brought them juice, and plates of fruit and rolls. They sat on stools, eating, their voices echoing off the kitchen's tile walls. Karl felt lucky to have Rabbi Blum to himself for so long. He felt more relaxed than in the office.

Rabbi Blum flicked a crumb off his trim beard, smiled, and said, "If you keep doing so well, I'll be out of the tutoring business. You'll soon reach the level of the other students. I'm proud of you."

The compliment made Karl glow. Rabbi Blum seemed the kindest person he'd ever met.

He entreated Karl, "While I'm gone I want you to study on your own. Don't lose your momentum."

"I promise!"

They finished eating in silence. Rabbi Blum brought their plates to the sink, scraped them, and turned on the faucet. He dried the washed plates with a dishcloth, then folded it neatly, and hung it on a towel bar. Karl drank in his every motion.

10

Albany, California, 1971

Walking down Franklin Street with Karl one afternoon, Lisa saw a boy's bike with training wheels left lying on a lawn. She smoothed Karl's long, unruly hair with her hands, then took him across the grass to the house and rang the bell. He needed friends like he'd had at the commune. Since coming to California two and a half weeks ago, he'd clung to her constantly. On the way home from the grocery yesterday, he asked her to carry him. When she refused—her arms were filled with bundles—he flung himself down on the sidewalk and sobbed. Once they were home, there'd been more tears because she'd forgotten to buy milk. After he calmed down and began playing with a toy car, she flew to the grocery and back. She wasn't away more then ten minutes. Still, the moment she stepped into the flat, Karl charged into her, sobbing, "You left me, Mommy."

Lisa rang the buzzer. A woman and dark-haired boy about Karl's age came to the door. The two boys stared at each other while Lisa trilled brightly, "We're new neighbors." They were invited inside. After fifteen minutes of conversation, Lisa said, "I have some errands to run. Can Karl stay and play?" At the commune, children had been welcome everywhere. She assumed that would be the case here too.

It seemed like it was. The mother agreed to watch Karl. Lisa's only concern was that Karl would balk at being separated from her. To her delight, he disappeared into the boy's room. For the moment, he was the old, independent Karl. Lisa felt free to go off for two or three hours.

She caught a bus headed to Telegraph Avenue, a street off the Berkeley campus. Through the bus window she glimpsed the university's tall buildings and green lawns. In time, she hoped to audit classes, attend cultural events, and meet young people. When Fritz came, he'd be happy that she'd established a circle of friends with whom he could have philosophical discussions. Her intention, today, was to visit a coffee shop where she'd heard students hung out.

Entering the dim interior of Enrico's, she bought an Espresso and sat at a marble-topped table in the rear. A hippy couple sat two tables over. They stared at Lisa, whispered together.

"Lisa?" the man asked. He was a burly, longhaired guy dressed in camouflage clothing and combat boots

"Do you know me?"

"From the commune in Vermont. Alice and Terry. We left the commune a few days after you guys arrived."

"Ahh," Lisa said, pretending to remember. There'd been a constant flux of people coming and going at the commune, too many for her to keep all of them straight. "May I join you?" she asked, and when they nodded enthusiastic assent, she carried her Espresso over to their table and pulled out a chair.

Alice, a pale, blonde young woman, sat with her hands between her knees "It's nice to meet someone we knew before," she shyly offered

"Yes!" Lisa concurred.

Her companions reminisced about Mark, and other mutual acquaintances. It meant a lot to her that they knew Fritz. They began to seem like old friends. She learned that neither of them worked, that they received S.S.I. checks from the government. Their big problem was their landlord.

Terry said, "The fucker's at us all the time. We're looking for a new place. Do you have any leads?"

"I'm not the one to ask," Lisa laughed, recalling her futile search for a flat in San Francisco. Her heart had been set on living among the 'flower children,' beatniks and poets in the Haight. But the affordable apartments had been either too small, located on a high crime block, or had no bathroom other than one shared by all the tenants. Finally, she'd bowed to practicality. Rents were cheaper in the East Bay.

"Housing's fuckin' tight here too." Terry's comment was accompanied by a paroxysm of head scratching that seemed to express his frustration about high living costs.

"I know," Lisa sighed. She'd looked for a flat near the university, but finally settled for one in Albany, a working class town just north of Berkeley. Her landlord slashed the rent because an apartment complex was about to be built across the street. Months of dust, noise, and mess were ahead.

"So what's the blood-sucker getting?" Terry asked.

"Sixty-five a month."

"Fuckin' fantastic! Alice and me pay more for a room."

Glancing at her watch, Lisa was distressed to note that two hours had passed since she'd left Karl. Soon he'd be clamoring for her, if he weren't already. She craved more time apart from him. If only she could arrange something that would give her the freedom to go out whenever she pleased. Perhaps, she could.

Her father had already sent a trust fund check to the local bank she was using. He would continue to make deposits every month. She could afford the cost of two more people at her table. "I can give you a place to sleep and free food in exchange for your looking after Karl three or four hours a day," she proposed.

"We'll need our own bedroom," Terry asserted.

"I'll...I'll give you my bedroom...I'll sleep in Karl's, and he'll bed down on the living room floor...The arrangement will be temporary, until Fritz comes."

"Exactly when's that?"

"Don't know," Lisa shrugged, masking the anxiety the question caused. She'd sent Fritz a letter the day after she'd moved into the Albany flat and had given her phone number and address. She'd been confident Fritz would call to find out about Karl. He hadn't phoned. Perhaps that was because Mark had the only telephone on the commune.

"I have to go," she said. "I have to pick up Karl. Come with me. I'll show you my place."

Alice and Terry accompanied her on the bus.

"Before we left, me and your old man smoked some pot and talked politics," Terry said.

At the commune, there'd been many boring political discussions. Lisa preferred not to be subjected to another, but there seemed no way to stop Terry from expounding his views in a loud voice that made the other bus passengers stare.

"I'm a Syndacalist," he informed Lisa, proudly. "You know what that's about."

"Oh, of course," Lisa said. She assumed it was something akin to being a communist or anarchist, something that would shock her mother, a fervent believer in free enterprise.

They came to Lisa's bus stop, walked to Franklin Street, a block of small stucco cottages. The two-story corner house was the exception. She rented the upper flat.

Leaving her new friends standing in front, she hurried three houses down to the neighbor's to pick up Karl. The moment he saw her he leapt into her arms.

"We have some visitors," she told him. "People we knew on the commune."

Karl was excited, ran ahead, eager to see who'd come.

"Hey, buddy. Remember me?" Terry called. He shook Karl's hand, as did Alice.

The entrance to the upper flat was around the back of the house, up a flight of steps. Karl danced after them as they climbed the stairs, and as Lisa took Alice and Terry on a tour of the flat. She pointed out the freshly painted walls and carpeted floors, amenities that had been in place before she moved in. Showing the living room, she felt self-conscious at her haphazard furnishings like the three-legged couch that had telephone books supporting the end with the missing leg.

"A gift of the gods," she said, hoping Alice and Terry wouldn't be put off. She related how the couch had appeared in the street with a 'Free' sign. Just as she'd been contemplating how to move it, two students had walked by. Fortunately, she'd been able to charm them into the donkey's work of carrying it up the steep back stairs. One of those students, it turned out, was going off to graduate school in the Mid-west. He'd sold her linens, dishes, and additional furniture.

The two bedrooms were small, Karl's minute. Lisa feared he'd balk at giving up his tiny bit of space. For a moment, she considered making the sacrifice of her bedroom. But no, she needed her privacy more than a child did. After they'd seen the bedrooms, Lisa served Alice and Terry herbal tea in the kitchen. They sat at the round table, another item the student had sold her. She was proud of the table. It might have a gouge across its top but it was oak, and worth more than the thirty-five dollars she'd paid.

"When can we move in?" Terry asked, scratching his head furiously again.

The habit disgusted Lisa. She considered making an excuse and sending him and Alice away. But then she thought that if they were here, she could go anywhere she wished...to the university...to San Francisco. Freedom was everything to her. "Right away!" she blurted.

The next day, Alice and Terry were installed.

11

Israel, 1983

The Yeshiva closed. The only people left were an elderly caretaker, the dishwasher, cook, and Karl. He was surprised at how lost he felt without the usual routines. With a predictable schedule, he'd always had something to do and knew what was expected. This orderliness was different and better than the chaotic life he'd led with Lisa.

As the days passed, he missed the other boys. Karl knew the glass wall that separated him from the students would never shatter. Yet in the last month and a half, he'd begun to walk around it, joined the joking, horsing around, and stepped into the warmth of friendship. The British kid, Eli, had invited him to play chess. Karl loved chess since he was six. One of Lisa's boyfriends had taught him to play. For a year or two, he'd challenged every person who'd walked through the door of the Franklin Street flat. He'd been elated to win, and distraught when it looked like he'd lose. Sometimes, he'd cheated or resorted to overturning the board to avoid a checkmate.

With Eli away, he replayed the games they'd had in his head. He and Eli were well matched. During their games, Eli put on a comical cockney or an upper class British accent and called his castles Balmoral and Buckingham. His chessboard fascinated Karl. It was only plastic, but Eli said it was a replica of a hundreds-of-years-old set found in Scotland at a place called the Isle of Lewis. To Karl, the pieces looked like cartoon characters, short and squat, with silly expressions that made him smile. He missed handling them, missed the strategy discussions he'd had with Eli at meals, and between classes.

"Hey, why'd you use that opening last game?"

"I felt like it. By the way, you protected your queen a lot."

"You came out too fast with your knight."

"Fast? You made all your moves too fast."

Time passed slowly at the deserted Yeshiva. Cold and rain confined Karl, making the place seem like a jail. The habit of masturbation asserted itself because he was alone. In prison, kids had boasted about how frequently they jerked off. Karl had too. Not that he expected or wanted to be pure now, but he preferred not to act the way he had in prison. He tried to occupy himself by keeping up the hours of study he maintained when school was in session. When Rabbi Blum returned, Karl wished to surprise him with the progress he'd made in all his subjects, but particularly in Hebrew.

Mostly he was in his room, except when he took his meals in the kitchen with the cook, dishwasher, and caretaker. As the three workers conversed in Hebrew, more and more Hebrew phrases kept popping into Karl's head, ones he must have heard as a toddler. It was strange, one moment, he didn't understand what was said, and the next, words from his childhood surfaced. This had happened in the months before, but never so frequently as now, as if he'd crossed over some barbed-wire boundary.

The rain began to let up. In mid-January, there were a few clear days. One afternoon, Karl put on his sneakers. Without stretching or warming up, he blazed off into the desert. Breathing hard, perspiring, he ran past bare acacia trees, jumped from stone to stone. His heartbeat quickened at the thought that in only two days, the students and rabbis would be back. He couldn't wait, even yearned to hear the name 'Baruch' pronounced again.

Rabbi Blum had changed his name to Mikel, viewing the change as an opportunity for a new life. Karl wanted to be like him. 'I'm Baruch,' he thought with wonder as he raced back towards the Yeshiva. The name that had been chasing him for six months had finally caught up.

12

Albany, California, 1971

To Lisa's delight, Karl adored Terry. Terry was a substitute father to the boy. The two of them would stand mesmerized at the living room window, watching workmen with bulldozers and wrecking balls raze the vacated houses on the site across the street. One moment a house was standing, the next it was split in half amidst clouds of dust.

"Bull's eye...rat-tat-tat," they shouted, as walls crumpled like paper. Terry blew the tip of his finger, his 'gun,' and called out, "Stand-by. New target. Set sights." They crept around the floor on their stomachs like soldiers crawling through the jungle in Vietnam. Sometimes, Terry played 'dead,' and Karl jumped on his back, bounced on his rear and smacked him like a punching bag. Then Terry bucked to life and growled, "Come on, you geek...Come on, you damned water buffalo! I'm ready for you."

Before her new housemates had moved in, Lisa had felt imprisoned, hadn't even been able to take a few moments to sit in the garden behind her house. There was a small stretch of lawn and a leafy tree, ideal to sit under and write poems. Now, she sat there often. She could go wherever she pleased—museums, concerts, films, lectures. She loved meeting new people, stopping for a cup of coffee and conversation. There were men who flirted with her. She flirted back, but never went beyond that. Fritz was joining her soon. Lisa didn't want to risk sexual encounters that Fritz might discover.

Terry and Alice were companions to Karl and provided freedom for Lisa. In her gratitude, she ignored Terry's blackened nails, pungent body odor, and head scratching. Then Karl began scratching his head too. She took him to a clinic. A nurse pronounced he had lice, shaved his hair, and put stinging lotion on his scalp. Thankfully, Lisa didn't need the treatment. Alice and Terry did. The problem was solved. The household arrangement continued.

Three weeks later, Lisa returned one night from a poetry reading and was alarmed to find Karl sobbing. A frightened-looking Alice relayed that Karl had sucked on a LSD-laced sugar cube Terry had left on a saucer in the refrigerator. Lisa comforted Karl. When he stopped crying, she sat him at the kitchen table with his coloring book and crayons. He complained the Mickey Mouse and Donald Duck pictures were jumping from the pages.

"They'll stop jumping," she assured him. They did. If they hadn't, she'd have taken him to the Emergency Room. Karl put his head down on the table and fell asleep. Gently, Lisa lifted him in her arms. She carried him to the living room and placed him inside the sleeping bag he'd been using on the floor ever since Alice and Terry had come.

When he woke late the following morning, he seemed his usual self. She gave him a bowl of cheerios doused with milk.

"Where are Alice and Terry?" he asked, his mouth full of cereal.

"They had to go," she told him. She'd made sure they were out of the house before he woke.

Karl burst into tears.

13

Israel, 1983

His first day back at the Yeshiva Rabbi Blum wore informal clothes, chinos, a checked shirt and white sneakers. His eyes lit up when he encountered Baruch in a hallway. At a meeting the next afternoon, he asked Baruch about the studying he'd accomplished. At the end of their discussion, he pronounced himself pleased with his student's work. Two weeks into the spring semester, the rabbi confirmed Baruch's academic progress by reducing their private tutoring sessions. The almost-daily meetings at the rabbi's office were reduced to once a week. This vote of confidence, as well as a newfound ability to concentrate on his studies, gave Baruch the courage to begin participating more fully in his classes. He started expressing strong opinions, and found he could win support for them. Suddenly, four boys wanted him for a study partner.

The slacker who'd sat at the back of the class progressed to more forward seats. Baruch was sitting in the front row of Talmud class one afternoon in February. Rabbi

Blum stood before him, surveying the class. The sunlight streaming in the window bothered his eyes. He moved a few inches to a more shaded spot.

The rabbi asked, "If a poor man and a rich man commit the same crime, should the judge exact the same fines from both?"

Voices rang out. Most of the students stated that they felt poor criminals should be treated more leniently.

Baruch objected with an adamancy he'd not have dared express the previous semester, "Nobody should get special privileges."

"What if the poor man can't afford the fine?" Zach countered.

Baruch was determined to demonstrate that he had truly caught up with the other students. He wanted to justify his teacher's confidence in him. Rabbi Blum must see how quickly he marshaled arguments, how logically and persuasively he made his presentation.

He said, "Let's say the man is a thief. Stealing is always wrong! That's what 'Thou shalt not steal,' means. The man should have asked for charity or found another legitimate way to obtain the money he needed before he stole. Besides, the law should treat everyone equally. If not, there's no real punishment. The court would be phony, and everybody would know it. If a thief was poor, he wouldn't care if he was caught because he'd know the judge would let him go."

In his enthusiasm, Baruch began to quote a Talmud text from memory. Ever since he'd learned to read, he'd had a photographic memory. In first grade, he used to show off by glancing at an upside book, then closing his eyes and reciting the page to an audience of rapt little classmates. The Hebrew words—even those he didn't understand—tripped off his tongue. To conclude his argument, he made a traditional Talmudic comment, "*Vedilma ipkha?* And perhaps the opposite is true?" He glanced at Rabbi Blum to see whether he was impressed. A word of praise would make Baruch joyful. He'd worked hard to deserve it.

Without praising or criticizing him, the rabbi moved ahead and called on another boy. Baruch was hurt. Had his analysis been shallow? He couldn't bear the rabbi's disapproval. Leaving class, he felt not just confused but inferior for not grasping what his teacher wanted. He brooded about how he might have responded differently to Rabbi Blum's question.

That night, as he lay in bed, he was still thinking about his failure to impress Rabbi Blum. A scene flashed in his mind. He was in Judge Thorn's courtroom, awaiting his sentence with Mr. Huff, his lawyer, beside him. The judge had ruled favorably. The ignorant boy Baruch had been hadn't worried whether the verdict was fair, whether he'd had any undue advantage over the poor boys also tried that day.

Nor had Karl judged Lisa when she'd driven him away, and pulled her blue Ford into a parking spot a block from the courthouse. She'd stopped so she could light a toke of marijuana. "I need this after today's ordeal," she'd said, oblivious to the police cars streaming by. One toke didn't suffice. She'd lit another and driven onto the freeway, once again endangering his life and freedom.

Lisa had scarcely taught him the difference between right and wrong. He'd suffered for it. Baruch was tempted to fault her for his own moral obtuseness, his inability to find the answers that would please Rabbi Blum. He struggled not to blame her, not to judge her by the high Yeshiva standards he'd begun to absorb.

Perhaps it was impossible for anyone to live by Jewish ethics, let alone Lisa. You were supposed to control your tongue, neither criticize nor praise a person behind his back, not boast, not hurt anyone's feelings. There were many rules, but no simple formula to know how to apply them. Every human action was complex and had repercussions. In addition, there were special situations in which a particular rule had to be broken in order to practice kindness. No matter how much he studied, he wasn't sure he'd ever understand what was required.

Over the next month, Baruch's relationship with Rabbi Blum seemed to be unraveling. The rabbi's eyes no longer lit up when they met. He was still friendly to Baruch, but a certain spark disappeared from their encounters. During their private conferences, he was subdued, and at times, even though he never said anything outright, he seemed upset. Once he told Baruch, "Every word and every gesture counts." With such a high standard, Baruch didn't understand what his teacher wanted—let alone how to achieve it. Still, he persevered and worked harder for his approval.

One afternoon at the beginning of May, Baruch took an opportunity in Talmud class to stand up and recite by heart the laws of damages, the penalty to a man if his ox destroyed a shed by rubbing against it for creature comfort, and the penalty if the ox knocked the shed down in anger. The night before, he'd looked up the words he didn't know. After his recitation in Hebrew, he gave an English translation, thinking that surely, this would please Rabbi Blum. The rabbi made no comment.

After class, Eli asked Baruch, "How many pages of Talmud do you think you could memorize?"

Baruch shrugged.

"Two or three?"

"More than that."

"How many?"

Other boys had gathered around, and were waiting for Baruch's answer.

"Five," he said. His heart thudded. Five pages were too much. Now that he'd made a boast, they might insist he prove himself. In his previous schools, he'd never refused when other boys challenged him to a race or a fight. It hadn't mattered what the odds were. Even if a kid were larger, he'd wrestle with him. He wasn't going to back down. If they did challenge him, he must try and memorize the pages.

"Make it six, then you can rest on the seventh, and let me choose the text, and we have a bet."

"What are you putting up?" Baruch asked.

"What do you want?" Eli asked.

"Your chess set."

With a surprised laugh, Eli replied, "Sure. It's a deal."

"What text should I memorize?"

"Start with *shomrim*, the laws on safekeeping objects," Eli said. He'd selected a section they hadn't studied in class, one with which Baruch wasn't familiar.

The boys made bets on the upcoming sporting event.

Baruch had one week. One day, he memorized a page or two of text. The next he devoted to reviewing what he'd learned the day before. It was difficult. There were times when he was discouraged. He regretted boasting. At the conclusion of the week, the boys came early to Talmud class before their teacher. Baruch stood up and began reciting while they followed from their texts. If there were even one word wrong, they'd notice.

Shortly after Baruch began, Zach called, "Go, Baruch." He was one of the few who'd bet on him.

From the corner of his eye, Baruch saw Jakob flash his fingers in a 'v' for victory sign. He too had faith in Baruch.

Baruch was glad of the encouragement.

Rabbi Blum entered the classroom and stood, observing Baruch reel off the text. Baruch sweated. He had moments when he almost stumbled, almost stuttered, but always he saved himself. At last he came to his last page, and he knew he could do it. Happiness surged through him. The words streamed from his lips, every one correct to the last. He'd done it!

The class was in an uproar. The boys cheered and called out congratulations. "Baruch...Baruch," they chanted. Baruch was hoisted up in a chair by a couple of boys and paraded around the classroom. Kids reached out to touch his hands. He'd done more than win a chess set. He was happy, happier than he'd been in his whole life. He had friends, felt admired, liked, supported.

Only Rabbi Blum was silent. He walked out, choosing not to teach the day's class. No longer triumphant, Baruch now hated being jostled up and down in the chair. His head ached from the noise. If Rabbi Blum was no longer his friend, then he wanted to escape the class, to run away from the Yeshiva. That night he had to force himself to go to Rabbi Blum's office for their scheduled weekly meeting, something he used to look forward to doing.

The rabbi sat hunched at his desk, absorbed in a book. Looking up, he said, "Oh, Baruch."

Baruch swallowed. "Did I do something wrong in class?" He'd prepared the question in advance. Rabbi Blum had asked a similar one at their first private meeting. At that time, Baruch had deserved a rebuke. But he didn't deserve one now.

Yet the rabbi nodded and said, "Yes."

That simple 'yes' felt like a slap. None of his classmates thought he'd done anything wrong. Quite the contrary, they praised him for his accomplishment.

"You wanted me to participate more. I was trying to please you," he blurted resentfully.

"I know."

"So why are you mad at me?"

"Baruch, sit down," the rabbi said gently.

Baruch complied. Until tonight, he'd loved this room because it was Rabbi Blum's. Now, everything looked ugly. The clutter of papers and books on the desk irritated him. His own desk looked the same. He'd tried hard to be studious, to acquire knowledge, to do everything his teacher wanted.

In a measured voice, Rabbi Blum said, "Try to understand, Baruch. You have to be humble in your learning. The greatest pleasures are not in display. It's important to look inward. Use the Talmud as a knife to shape yourself, not as a spotlight for your talents. While we're having this discussion, I'd like to add that it's important to respect other people's opinions. I want you to be tolerant. When you conclude your arguments and say, '*Vedilma ipkha*? Perhaps the opposite is true?'… it shouldn't mean 'See how clever I am. No one can match me.'" Sighing, Rabbi Blum said, "I'm at fault. I wasn't teaching you correctly. In my enthusiasm, I was taking you along too quickly. It would have been better if I'd held you back."

"I don't get it." Baruch slapped his forehead. All the hard work he'd done was for Rabbi Blum's sake. And now, he was saying, 'Stay behind. Be stupid.'

"What don't you get?"

"I started out behind. You're supposed to help me get ahead, not hold me back! I wanted to show you how hard I've been working. That's what you said you wanted. Now you've turned it against me."

The rabbi's brow creased. He pressed his palms together, brought them to his chin. "It's hard for me to explain, and for you to understand. The development of your character has to keep pace with your learning. For some individuals, study corrupts more than it enlightens. That's why not all of the Talmud is open to everyone."

"Which part isn't open?"

"There are certain esoteric passages reserved for mature individuals. These passages are supposed to produce mystical states known as *pardess*, which means entering the orchard."

Blah, blah, blah, Baruch thought. It was all just a lot of talk. Lisa said she'd reached 'mystical states' with LSD. "It's much faster to take drugs than to sweat over the Talmud."

"There's no comparison, and I think you know it," Rabbi Blum said with a flash of anger.

Baruch's shoulders hunched. He felt rejected, lost. He pushed his glasses' back on the bridge of his nose. Everything was blurring, spinning about him, the ripped window shade, dingy white walls, cracks in the ceiling, a sheet of paper on the desk covered with the rabbi's small, neat handwriting. Was it a bad evaluation of him for Rabbi Tubol to read? He could barely keep himself from grabbing it to see. "What do you want from me?"

"To be patient, to listen."

"I'm listening," Baruch said dully.

The rabbi nodded. He rose and paced the small space of the office. "The surface meaning of *Ma'aseh Bereshit* can mislead an inexperienced person. That's why a rabbi instructs only one disciple. Initially, he'll teach only the outlines of the subject. That's to test the student to see if he's prepared for more. There's a Talmudic story that says four rabbis entered *pardess*. One rabbi died. The second went mad. The third became a heretic. Only Rabbi Akiva came out whole."

"What does this have to do with me? You're not teaching me *Ma'aseh Bereshit.*"

Rabbi Blum pressed the long fingers on his left hand as far back as they'd go. His knuckles cracked. The phrase 'bending over backwards' leapt into Baruch's mind. No, he mustn't be tricked. The rabbi didn't love him. He was no different from Lisa's boyfriends who'd pretended affection for a while. No different from Lisa, who scarcely wrote. She seemed to have abandoned him. That's why he'd counted on Rabbi Blum, but no more.

"For me, the whole Talmud is *Ma'aseh Bereshit!* Study has to be approached with care. I should have taken my time, and tested you as we went along." Pausing in his pacing, he touched Baruch's shoulder.

Baruch pulled away as if he'd been burned.

"I'm on your side, Baruch. Please listen."

"I'm listening!"

"You're not going to run off on me?"

Baruch wished he could. But Rabbi Blum's question forestalled his leaving. "I won't run off," he said. Tears welled up in his eyes. Ashamed for the rabbi to see them, he pretended not to notice when Rabbi Blum proffered his handkerchief. The rabbi left it on the desk nearby, and sat down in the chair beside Baruch.

"An individual might be brilliant but his intelligence matters only if he's grounded in good values. Without good values, he'll use the Talmud superficially, coarsely, and even cruelly..."

The rabbi continued to speak but only the word 'brilliant' seeped through Baruch's confusion and misery. So many times he'd heard people describe his mother as brilliant. Yes, Lisa did shine, made witty remarks, possessed artistic talents. But what good was all that to him? He couldn't count on her.

What if she was a Yeshiva student and was asked what she would do if she and a friend walked out into the desert with insufficient water? She'd relish the challenge of coming up with innumerable clever explanations of why she, not someone else, should have the water. Her ability to argue might make her appear to be an excellent Talmudic student. Yet nothing she learned would change the person she was.

Barely aware he was picking up the rabbi's handkerchief, Baruch wiped his eyes and blew his nose with it. "So where does a person get these values?" he asked, hoarsely.

The rabbi stared at Baruch and smiled.

Joy coursed through Baruch. Rabbi Blum didn't hate him. On the contrary, he was trying valiantly to help him understand something essential.

"Instead of parading what you learned before your friends, you should come to Talmud on your own, naked, all lies and pretensions stripped way. The values you need to learn are in the Talmud. You reshape your soul as you learn...I see the Talmud as music. Any monkey can learn to play the notes. But to play with all your heart, to give yourself over to what you learn—that's the only way that's worthy!"

Baruch saw that the rabbi was throwing him a lifeline. Was he capable of doing what his teacher demanded? If he were to be completely honest, he'd have to confess the crimes that had brought him to the Yeshiva. He felt he couldn't tell Rabbi Blum, that he couldn't risk his disgust. He'd just seen how horrible the rabbi's only seeming-rejection had felt. How much worse if he truly turned away.

"You look discouraged, Baruch," Rabbi Blum said. "Don't be. Everything will come in time. I have great confidence in you. You'll use the Talmud to help you look inward, and you'll discover your strengths and weaknesses. It will give you detachment, and you'll have control over yourself. You might stumble from time to time, but you'll soon be moving ahead. You have depth of feeling, enthusiasm, ability..."

Receiving the praise he'd yearned for from his teacher, he was pierced with guilt. He should confess his crimes right this moment. He could begin by posing a Talmudic problem. Can a near-murderer ever approach the Talmud the right way, or is his soul too soiled? The words were harsh. If he said them and conveyed his full meaning, the affection he saw in Rabbi Blum's eyes might disappear. He wasn't ready to dredge up what he'd done, not now, and perhaps not ever.

"I have to go."

After parting from Rabbi Blum, Baruch ran down the hall and outside. A full moon shone in the night sky. He stood in the plaza, reliving the contest, his recitation of the laws of *shomrim*. Those laws illuminated his flaws. To safe-keep the property of another person meant you didn't take as much as a minuscule fraction of what didn't belong to you. Yet he'd broken into a house to help Reynaldo steal. Then, he'd nearly stolen someone's life. He deeply regretted his boastful performance in class. What Rabbi Blum said was true. Every word and gesture counted.

Gazing up, he attempted to pray. It didn't work now and hadn't during services. Many times Baruch had wished the prayers he recited had meaning for him, that he could find comfort in that simple way. Something Rabbi Frankel said in class came back to him, that faith in the Messiah and in God sustained many people in the Nazi death camps. Only now did Baruch grasp he must have been referring to the faith that had upheld him. He envied Rabbi Frankel. Even while living in hell, his faith had raised him up and brought him peace.

Much as he wished he could, Baruch didn't believe in God. Most of his teachers and classmates assumed he did. He'd said nothing to disabuse them. At least he didn't lie to himself. Instead of speaking to God, Baruch asked the pale moon to witness how he longed to learn to be good.

14

Albany, California 1972

After Alice and Terry left, Lisa was determined not to invite other people into her home as live-in babysitters. Instead, she looked about for new neighborhood kids she could recruit to play with Karl. In two weeks, she found three, and introduced herself to their mothers. The problem was none of the moms were willing to keep him more than a few hours. Nor were they always available when she needed help.

Karl missed Terry. When there was no child with whom he could play, he clung to Lisa. One morning when she took him to supermarket, he insisted on riding in the shopping cart at the supermarket as if he were a much younger child. Then as they were leaving the store, he spotted a young woman in front, trying to give away cats. Inside her cardboard box were four kittens, little fur balls with slits for eyes, mewling, and stretching their necks. Karl wanted one badly. Lisa had to drag him away.

At home, he tried to enlist Lisa to wrestle with him, a poor substitute for big, burly Terry. She said, 'no,' had never felt comfortable with Terry's horseplay, preferred more refined activities for her son, like reading. Once he could read, there'd be an added benefit. He'd be able to occupy himself.

When she offered to read to him, Karl started sobbing. Her pity changed to frustration as he refused everything she suggested, playing with his toy cars, building blocks, coloring pictures, baking cookies.

"I want Terry," he said obstinately.

"There must be something you want besides Terry."

"No…Get him back!"

"Terry's not coming back! So tell me something else," she said, wishing the husband whom she desperately missed was at her side. There'd have been no necessity to take in Terry and Alice if Fritz had come to stay with her. Karl would have had his real father. But since leaving the commune, she'd had no word from Fritz. He hadn't answered any of the three letters she'd sent from California. In her last letter, she'd said, "I need you. I can't do this alone." When Fritz didn't reply, she'd telephoned Mark for news of Fritz. The trouble was Mark never answered, at least, not the five times she called.

"Terry!" Karl insisted.

Expecting Karl to reject the possibility as he did everything else, Lisa blurted, "Do you want to get a kitty?"

"Yes!" he cried, surprising her with his smile.

Lisa didn't know what to do. She didn't want the cat. Nor did she want to go back to fighting with Karl. "All right," she sighed, "we'll go to the store. But you have to promise not to talk about Terry any more."

"I promise."

On the way to the supermarket, Karl worried that all the kittens would have been taken. But the woman they saw earlier was still in front of the store with her cardboard box. While attempting to make a choice, Karl squeezed Lisa's hand. He selected a black female cat, the smallest of the litter. The woman lifted the kittten out of the box and set her in Karl's arms.

"What shall we call her?" Lisa asked.

"Is Blacky good?"

"That's nice, but wouldn't you like to call her something more special?"

"You pick, Mommy."

"Let's see." Walking home, she considered Cinderella, 'cinder' being a more subtle way of saying 'blacky.' Other names flashed in her mind, including that of a character in a French play. That name, Aztac, was the one she liked. "Let's call her Aztac," she said. Karl agreed.

When they came to their house, they ran into Phil, the elderly gentleman who lived in the adjoining house. He'd just pulled his blue Ford into the alley and was stepping out of the car. A tall, lanky Texan, he had on a beige suit, white shirt with a string tie, shiny wingtip brown shoes, and a Stetson hat.

"I got a kitty," Karl boasted, cradling the cat in his arms.

"Do you? Well, look at that. Do you have a litter box so she knows where to go? I don't want to be stepping in cat poop when I come out to my car."

"I didn't have a chance to buy a litter box yet," Lisa said, irritably. The truth was that until this moment, she hadn't thought of such a thing.

She climbed the stairs to her door. Entering the flat, she spread newspapers on the kitchen floor, put out a saucer of milk. The little black cat evacuated. Lisa managed to scoop up the turds with tissues and flush everything down the toilet bowl. She repeatedly soaped and rinsed her hands.

As the water flowed over them, she wished she could cleanse away her recent failure, her bringing Terry and Alice into her home. Perhaps Aztac would be another disaster. Cats took care and time and even carried diseases. Litter and cat food had to be purchased, and God knew what else. Probably there would be veterinarian bills. She felt overwhelmed, desperate to have Fritz at her side. These last three months, she'd worked hard to set up a new home, longed for him to be part of it. She didn't regret having yanked herself and Karl out of the commune. Her escape was a miracle. She needed another, to get Fritz out.

While Karl played with Aztac in the kitchen, Lisa went down the hall to the living room where she turned on the radio to a Bach cantata. Lying down on the couch, she let the music wash over her. The volume was on loud, but not loud enough to drown out the question pounding in her head: 'Was Fritz ever coming?' If only she knew what he was feeling? Whether he still loved her? She yearned to hear his voice, touch and smell him, for them to be close as they'd once been.

She didn't hear Karl when he came up to her side. Her eyes were closed. Absorbed by the music, she was startled when he whined, "Mommy..."

"One moment..." Was he tired of the cat already? It enraged her to think that he was going to start clinging and whining again.

"Mommy...I want you," he screamed above the radio sound, forcing her back to a reality she wished to escape.

She sat up quickly. Her hand lifted of its own volition, struck and left a red mark on his cheek. He raced off to his room, hid in the closet. She was mortified when she couldn't coax him out. The rest of the day, she berated herself for what she'd done.

After she put Karl to sleep, she dialed Mark again. She didn't expect anyone to answer. To her surprise, he picked up.

With little preamble, she said, "Where's Fritz? Why haven't I heard from him?"

"Oh, he's gone," was Mark's, laconic answer.

"When did he leave?"

"Ummm...I think two or three days ago, or maybe last week."

"Where did he go?" Lisa pressed, hoping the answer would be 'California.'

"I don't know," Mark said, irritably. "For that matter, you vanished like a thief too."

Exasperated, Lisa cried, "A thief. How dare you! What'd you do, kick Fritz out because I wasn't paying the monthly fees any more?"

"Don't be ridiculous."

"Or did he decide he didn't want to be around someone who'd seduced his wife?"

"I was his friend. I told him what happened. You're the one who kept it secret."

Lisa hung up. She couldn't trust anything Mark said. Fritz probably detested him too. Hunched on the couch, she tried to piece together what had happened. Fritz's departure from the commune was exactly what she desired. Perhaps he was hitchhiking to California. The summer they left Israel, they'd entrusted Karl to Eva, Fritz's sister in Vienna, then spent a month hitchhiking across Europe. Right this moment Fritz might be in the passenger seat of a big rig truck, rattling along at ninety miles an hour over the Kansas plains. She hoped he was on his way to her, wanted to believe he was. If only he'd notified her he was coming, she'd feel less worried.

15

Israel, 1983

The Yeshiva closed down for the six-week summer break. Two days later, Baruch caught the bus to Jerusalem and reported for the volunteer job Rabbi Blum had set up for him at a center for disadvantaged Moroccan boys. Mr. Nussbaum, the director, led him around a former store, partitioned into spaces of various sizes, and furnished with tables, bookcases, couches, and a ping-pong table. "Some of the boys come from broken homes," Mr. Nussbaum explained. "Others have a history of truancy, or have committed a petty crime like shoplifting. They all have difficulty with schoolwork."

Baruch spent the day playing ping-pong, checkers, and cards, and tutoring boys in Hebrew, the language in which he communicated with them. He strove to emulate the tact Rabbi Blum had shown him at every turn. In the evening, he took the bus back to the Yeshiva. The week ahead was free. It wasn't until the following Thursday that he'd work at the center again.

Before leaving for Detroit, Rabbi Blum had set up a schedule of study for Baruch to follow. With everyone away, he worked harder than ever. To break up the monotony of studying, he took long walks. The walks distracted him, lessened his urge to masturbate four or five times a day as he had in jail. "I don't want to be a slave to my body," one or another of his Yeshiva friends had told him. These boys believed that self-control couldn't be achieved unless one made it a daily habit. At first one must master small challenges, then move on to larger ones. The idea had inveighled its way into Baruch's consciousness.

During the day, the summer heat was fierce. He walked only at dawn or twilight when it was cool, strolling past acacias, low-lying juniper bushes, and yucca plants with stiff knife-like leaves. The desert was silent. A small sound like a seedpod rattling in the wind was startling. With little to distract him, his thoughts flowed freely. Moses, himself, had wandered over these sands while he 'received' the Torah. Baruch was thrilled at his own small insights into his Talmud studies. He looked forward to relating them to Rabbi Blum. His teacher had left his office unlocked so that he could be contacted by phone. He'd said he hoped their conversations would help Baruch stay involved in his work.

During a telephone conversation the first week of the break, the rabbi said, "Please feel free to use my phone to call your mother."

"Thank you, but I don't have to," Baruch demurred, hoping the subject would be dropped.

"Why?"

"It's expensive. Wouldn't Rabbi Tubol object if I used the phone?"

"Rabbi Tubol won't be involved. I'll take care of it."

"I don't want to cause you expense."

"You'd rather not call her?" the rabbi asked bluntly.

"I'd rather not," Baruch admitted. He'd let Lisa know that he worried and suffered when she didn't write. Even so, except for a rare note, she'd forgotten him. The thought of reaching out to her yet again hurt his pride. Baruch resisted the temptation to remind

Rabbi Blum that once, during a class discussion, even he'd conceded that some parents were difficult, that the capacity to reproduce was not always connected to the ability to be a good parent, or even a good person. Perhaps Rabbi Blum was recalling this too, and that was why he didn't respond immediately.

Finally, the rabbi said, "It's natural for a child to struggle with his mother or his father at your age. But a parent, even a bad parent, is fundamental to an individual's life. 'Honor Thy Father and Mother,' is among the first five commandments. The last five commandments are between man and man. The first five between God and man are considered more imperative to obey. I'd like you to phone your mother."

Baruch said goodbye. The conversation troubled him. Must he phone? Lisa's neglect had wounded him. If only she were less self-absorbed, more devoted to him. If only she were religious, dressed and acted modestly. As far as he knew, she was still married to his father. That meant she ought not to have lovers. If only…she was like the mothers of other boys at the Yeshiva. Then it would be easy to call her.

He glanced at the Jewish books on the rabbi's shelves. Which tome explored the commandment 'Honor thy father and mother?' Even if he were to find and read that section, he trusted his mentor's interpretation of the text far more than his own. In the spring, he'd been admonished for having a false approach to Talmud. Since then, he'd been trying to follow Rabbi Blum's guidance.

The rest of the day, he struggled over what to do. By the next morning, he was still torn. He realized he wouldn't have peace until he did what the rabbi wished. He intended to go to lunch before he phoned. Over the break, the cook served light meals in the cafeteria kitchen. Usually a pot of soup simmered on the stove, and he helped himself. On the way to the kitchen, he changed course. Fearing he'd change his mind if he stopped to eat, he took the stairs up to the next floor. He hurried to Rabbi Blum's office where he sat down in his teacher's chair and telephoned home.

The phone rang and rang. Eventually, Lisa answered. "Who is it?" she asked groggily. Baruch had forgotten to take the ten-hour time difference into account. Fortunately, it never bothered his mother to be awakened. Like a cat, she could curl up and fall back to asleep instantly.

"It's me."

"Karl!" she cried with delight. "Where are you? Are you calling from a pay phone?"

"I'm not," Baruch assured her. "My rabbi said I could use his phone."

"Wonderful. How are you?"

"You didn't write," he accused in a preemptory tone.

"Surely, I must have." She sounded bewildered. "I think about you all the time."

"How am I to know that?"

"I'm not good at writing letters, Karl."

"You write poetry and keep a journal." He recalled her saying she'd begun a manuscript of her memories of their past.

"That's different. A letter needs an envelope, a stamp, a trip to a mailbox, or the post office," she laughed.

He wasn't drawn into her humor. The pain she'd caused him wasn't a joke. Closing his eyes, he saw her with a bewildered look on her face. She didn't comprehend what she'd done wrong.

Even so, she said, "I hope you'll forgive me."

He stiffened. Apologies came easily to her lips, followed by a rush of words that were meant to sway whoever was angry with her into a good humor.

"Thank you for phoning. I've missed you, Karl. Are you doing anything interesting this summer? How are your classes?"

"The Yeshiva closed down for a break. I'm alone," he said angrily. Here was one more thing about him that she'd forgotten.

"Alone," she echoed, and then in a sober voice, "I am too."

"What do you mean?"

"Steve and I aren't together any more."

Steve, he assumed, was her latest boyfriend. He remembered her anguish after previous breakups, her dragging about the flat, sad and lethargic. No wonder she hadn't written. How old was she now, about forty? Would it be hard for her to find someone new? Pity surged up in him. "I'm sorry, Mom. Are you okay?"

"I'm terrific," she insisted, brightly. "Let's talk about something else."

She wasn't a complainer, had never been. Baruch admired her for that. Complying with her request to change the subject, he said, "I've been going into Jerusalem once a week to do volunteer work with Moroccan kids."

"Oh, Moroccans," she breathed. "I wish I knew more about them. You'll have to tell me every detail." Lisa sounded ready to be ecstatic about Moroccans—for his sake.

Baruch described his activities with the boys, the ping pong games, the Hebrew tutoring. Warming to the subject, he said proudly, "The director said he wants me to continue working there during the winter break."

"That's marvelous," Lisa said.

She spoke lovingly to him. His resentment dissolved. Perhaps, a letter was something she couldn't manage. But a telephone conversation was delightful to her, even if she'd been wakened in the middle of the night. She was a naturally hospitable person. Baruch recalled people stopping by the flat with no advance notice. She'd drop everything, serve tea and snacks, and chat for hours.

In the midst of her goodbyes, she half-apologized. "I should have written you more than I have. You see, I was a bit distracted..."

"I know, Mom," he interrupted. "It's better talking on the phone anyway. I'll phone soon." He knew she wasn't going to change. It was he who must improve. On the spot, he decided that from now on, he'd take the initiative rather than wait for her to make contact.

In their second conversation a few days later, she sounded more cheerful than before. She talked about the archeology course she was auditing. "The professor said he's planning a trip to Quinto Roo in Mexico for a dig. Doesn't that sound exciting?" The subject came up again during the third phone call.

The following day, Baruch phoned Rabbi Blum to discuss his studies, as they'd agreed to do. When they were done, the rabbi asked whether Baruch had been talking to his mother.

"I have."

"How's it working out?"

"Good...it's working out good," Baruch said, "but...but I don't see how I can keep doing it while you're paying the bills. I don't like taking advantage of you. I'll figure something else out."

"Please, don't worry about the bit of money I'm paying," Rabbi Blum interjected. "The cost of losing contact with your mother is much greater. Promise me you'll keep phoning her."

Baruch was silent.

"It's what I want you to do. You'll give me a lot of pleasure if you keep in touch with her."

"Okay. I will."

"And you won't worry?"

"I won't."

The conversation had reassured Baruch, relieved him of the agitation he'd been feeling about the phone bill. Two days later, he called his mother a fourth time.

"You again?" Lisa said. She seemed pleased but surprised by his constancy.

"I'm trying to be a good son," he teased. Despite his flippant tone, he meant it. He wanted to be a good Jew and obey the fifth commandment.

At first, the only part of the commandment he considered fulfilling was to honor Lisa. But gradually he began to wonder whether he oughtn't to honor his father too. He was unsure. Did he owe devotion to a father who'd deserted him? More troubling was his belief that Fritz had committed a crime. They were alike. How alike, Baruch was afraid to find out. His father might be in prison for a new crime, or he may have become a drugged-out derelict. Or was he simply living peacefully somewhere in Austria? Lisa could tell him the truth, but Baruch didn't dare ask her. In recent years, whenever he'd mentioned his father, she'd turned away or left the room. To even think about Fritz had seemed to violate the ban of silence she imposed.

During the solitary days of the break, Baruch found himself speculating about Fritz's whereabouts. Perhaps he was living with his sister, Eva. Baruch had met Aunt Eva, Uncle Dietrich, and their twin boys when his parents left the Israeli *kibbutz* and dropped him off at their home in Vienna. Although he'd stayed with his Austrian relations several weeks, he scarcely remembered them. However, he did recall Eva's married name. This was because in fourth grade he'd brought home a boy named Clark Biederman, and Lisa had said, "Karl has cousins in Vienna with the same last name as you." The name had stayed in Baruch's memory because it had been so rare that Lisa let slip anything related to Fritz.

Long forgotten memories about his father began to flutter into Baruch's consciousness. Fritz had whittled little animals for him from bars of soap. He'd bounced him on his knee and yodeled, or invented funny songs half-English, half-German. Out walking in the desert at dusk, Baruch recalled a line, then two, then a whole song his father had made up. He couldn't get the silly words and melody out of his head.

'We're going to Ostrich

To every place we like

We're going to Salzburg

And to Innsbruck too

We're waltzing to Vienna

To the Schonbrunn Zoo

We're climbing high in the Tyrol

We're sailing down the blue

We drink our beer

In great big steins

Yodel, yodel-o-o-o-o"

At the conclusion of his walk, Baruch went to Rabbi Blum's office and found a book of maps. At one of their meetings, the rabbi had taken it off his shelf to help Baruch understand certain questions he'd asked about World War II. Now, Baruch studied a map that included Austria and Israel, concluding they weren't far from each other. After his two years at the Yeshiva, he could stop in Vienna and find Fritz. He wasn't sure what they'd do. Go to the Schonbrunn Zoo? Stroll past elephants and tigers? Sing the very song rattling in his brain? Perhaps, it was only a whim, not worth pursuing.

Even so, the day of his birthday, he phoned Lisa, intending to ask for Fritz's address and phone number. They exchanged greetings, she, wishing him a happy birthday. He was pleased she remembered.

"I have something to ask you," he ventured,

"What is it, Karl?"

"I want to know where…" The words died on his tongue. He couldn't bring himself to mention his father's name. Secrets were thick concrete walls. If they came crashing down, something essential to him or his mother, or both, would be destroyed.

"Never mind. I forgot."

16

Albany, California 1972

Lisa had no idea where Fritz was. Mark had said over the phone that he'd left the commune. Did that mean Fritz was on the way to her? She couldn't sleep that night. Her longing for Fritz kept her tossing and turning. Memories of their time together in Paris flooded her mind. Around three, she dozed off, and then woke at eight, too tired to move.

Lying on her side, she felt something warm brush against the back of her head. Her heart leapt. Perhaps Fritz was here! She turned over. Aztac was curled on the pillow besides hers, her tail twitching.

With a light-footed bound, the cat leapt from the mattress and followed Lisa to the kitchen to receive her morning bowl of milk. Karl was already at the table, coloring. He wore the pale blue pajamas with a teddy bear print that Bernice had sent.

The cat began meowing. Lisa set her bowl of milk on the floor, then poured Fruit Loops and milk into a bowl for Karl. She ate nothing herself. Her wakeful night had destroyed her appetite.

Sitting across from Karl, she watched him eat. He gripped his spoon with his thumb opposing four fingers together as if it were a hatchet. Bits of cereal scattered on the table and milk dripped down his chin.

Lisa lacked the will and energy to entertain Karl today. She said, "You should go play with Robby." Robby's house was around the corner.

Karl shook his head at her request. "I can't go there."

"But why?" Lisa said with consternation.

"They don't want me."

"What do you mean?" Lisa asked, trying to keep her voice even. Aztac was on her lap now. Automatically, Lisa stroked the cat's fur. The kitten was more her cat than Karl's.

"I don't want to say."

"It's all right to tell me, Karl."

"I knock on the door, and the mom says, 'Go away.'"

"She'd never say that. You're no bother to her. You and Robby keep each other busy, don't you?"

"She said I'm too wild."

"What about your other friends? Their mothers are nicer."

"All the moms say I'm wild. They all don't want me."

Lisa was furious. What bullies the neighbors were, ganging together against a five-year-old. She lifted Aztac off her lap so she could go hug Karl. Her arms about him, she promised, "I'll make it up to you."

As a treat, she took him to the Albany library that morning. They selected a stack of ten books from the children's section. The clerk at the checkout desk said the only requirement for obtaining a card was that the patron should be able to sign his name. Lisa looked on proudly while Karl signed his name in large, clumsy letters.

At home, she settled on the living room couch with Karl and Aztac, and read one picture book after another, "Baby Bird," "Goodnight Moon," "Curious George." Although she felt too tired to read with enthusiasm, she acted out the various characters in different voices. Her hope was Karl would forget how the neighborhood mothers had behaved. She wanted to show she loved him!

After reading the last library book, Lisa said, "All done." The effort had drained her.

"Read them again," Karl insisted.

"It's time for Mommy to rest." Lisa handed Karl his favorite truck. "Play while I take a little nap."

She stretched out on the couch, nearly drifted off, when she became aware of Karl standing near her shoulder. "Where's Daddy?' he asked. The question pierced her. Had he read her mind? Did he know that she hadn't had a moment's peace since last night when she'd talked to Mark?

Instead of answering Karl, she took him into the kitchen and sat him at the table. Aztac jumped up on the counter and watched while she rummaged in the cabinets for the box of hard candies she'd bought for emergency bribes.

Karl's cheeks bulged from the three lozenges he stuffed into his mouth. Counting on a few moments of quiet, Lisa crossed to the window and looked outside. Below, she noticed her next-door neighbor hosing down his car in the alley between their houses. All she could see was the top and brim of Phil's Stetson and the black plastic smock he wore to protect his suit. The sight of the water spray calmed her, allowed her to consider a hopeful possibility that would answer a pressing need. She wished it had occurred to her before.

An older person would welcome a child's visits, and might not expect payment. Phil was married. Perhaps his wife would become a substitute grandmother to Karl. During his stay in New York, Karl had adored his grandmother—so much so that Lisa had been jealous. Perhaps that was why it had taken her so long to think of Phil's wife as the solution to her childcare problem.

Fired by her new idea, Lisa poured the rest of the candies from the box on the kitchen table. Aztac was frightened by the rat-tat-tat as they dropped on the oak surface. The cat scampered down the hall while Karl eagerly grabbed the candies. Busy stuffing them into his mouth, he barely noticed when Lisa said, "I have to take down the garbage. I'll be right back."

The garbage pails were under the steps. Lisa deposited a half-full bag, then strolled into the alley, and called out a friendly, "Hi."

Phil aimed the hose to the ground. "Hi there." His eyebrows raised in surprise.

"How are you?" she asked. She felt awkward. Until now, she'd rarely done more than nod when they passed.

"Dandy."

"And your wife?"

"Joy's at work."

"Is it a full-time job?"

"Yup, full-time. She's a secretary for the city."

"Oh," Lisa said, disappointed to hear Joy was away all day.

Half-heartedly, she persisted, "What about you? Are you retired?"

"Me? I haven't worked for over a decade. I've got emphysema."

"I'm sorry." She noted his sallow complexion and hollow cheeks. He wasn't a good candidate as a babysitter.

"It keeps me at home, washing the car, whether or not it needs it." A wheeze interrupted him. He struggled for breath, and then began talking again, garrulous like any old person who has had little opportunity for conversation.

Unable to break into his flow of words, Lisa pointed up to her flat. "I have to get back to my son."

"Cute little tyke. Me and Joy never had kids."

The following day, Lisa and Karl were out for a walk. He asked again, "When's Daddy coming?"

"Maybe today," slipped from Lisa's lips. Karl became excited. All he could do was jabber about Fritz. When they came up to their house, he refused to climb the steps to their flat. "I want to wait here for Daddy." He squatted in the middle of the gravel driveway between their house and Phil's.

"He may not be coming today. Maybe tomorrow, or the next day."

"Daddy won't know which is our house. I gotta wait here to show him where to go."

"Okay, Karl. Come up when you're tired of sitting out here."

Lisa slowly climbed the stairs to the flat. Aztac was in the litter box. A noxious odor told Lisa she'd have to clean it. But she couldn't bring herself to do it now. Going to the living room, she looked out the window and checked on Karl. He sifted pebbles through his hands while he patiently waited.

Rarely had she felt so lonely. The air in the room seemed thick, unbreathable. Fritz might have returned to Europe. For all she knew, he'd dropped into some black hole. She should never have told Karl he was coming.

In her bedroom, she curled up on the mattress, drew the blanket over her, and fell into a deep sleep.

The sound of pounding on the outside door woke Lisa. She didn't know how long Karl had been standing on the porch, crying, "Let me in."

Her arms and legs were leaden. She wanted to but couldn't move.

Before she could stir, she heard Phil calling up to Karl from the alley, "You the one making that commotion? You come downstairs and I'll give you something real good to eat." She remembered that she hadn't given Karl lunch. Beef jerky was the sort of food Phil would offer. Perhaps Karl would like it.

Hearing Karl's light footsteps as he descended, she relaxed. Phil was going to be the babysitter. Overcome by lassitude, she lay in bed another twenty minutes. Then, she forced herself to rise. She felt she'd better get Karl.

Aztac lay purring on a warm patch of linoleum in the kitchen. She'd give the cat some cat food when she returned. Going down the back steps, she spotted Karl in Phil's garden. He had a bucket of birdseed. Taking handfuls out, Karl scattered them over the small stretch of lawn and beneath Phil's two fruit trees. Robins gathered and pecked. His screen door banging, Phil came through his back door, holding a pair of opera glasses. He helped Karl focus them on the birds.

"You two look like you're enjoying the birds," Lisa trilled from the alley.

Phil popped out the garden gate with Karl. "I wanna talk to you," he drawled before she could say a word. "Take this boy of yours upstairs. Give him something to do that will keep him busy for ten minutes."

Not a good sign, Lisa thought. She was about to apologize, to say, 'I hope Karl wasn't bothering you.' But Phil's glare silenced her. She took Karl to the flat, gave him a dish of ice cream. Remembering Aztac must be hungry, she dropped a few dabs of the ice cream on the floor. Hurrying away, Lisa left the carton on the counter, instead of returning it to the freezer. Down the stairs, she ran.

Phil was pacing back and forth in the alley. The moment he saw her, he stopped short and said, "Your boy was hungry. Here. This is for groceries." He tried to press a roll of bills into her hand.

Laughing nervously, Lisa pushed the money away. "Thank you. It's kind of you. But we're fine."

"Take the money," Phil persisted. "You can get him a haircut and some new clothes. Spruce him up." He had more of a Texas accent than the last time they'd spoken.

Stiffening, Lisa said, "I don't need charity. I have my own money."

"From your job?"

She would have said, 'none of your business.' However, he deserved some consideration after babysitting. She told him the truth. "I receive a monthly check from my family."

Phil thrust the bills into his pocket and exploded, "You mean you don't work! Then why the hell ain't you taking care of your kid? I'm no babysitting service, you know!"

Lisa didn't want to hear what he had to say, couldn't bear to be criticized. He didn't know what she was going through, that her husband had disappeared from the face of the earth, that half the time she was worried sick about him, and the other half, filled with hope that he was about to walk in the door.

The rest of the day, she wondered whether there was any point in remaining in California. She couldn't care for a small child on her own. No one here was going to assist her, not the neighborhood mothers, certainly not Phil. If only she could count on Fritz coming to join them to start the new life they'd planned together.

To her surprise, the next day, Karl rushed down to the alley to help Phil hose his car, and Phil let him. Afterwards, Karl was permitted to follow him into his flat and remained there the rest of the morning. When Karl returned home, he was full of stories about Phil. He didn't ask, "Where's Daddy?"

In the following weeks, Karl spent more and more time with Phil, helped wash the

Ford daily, accompanied him on errands to the store. Lisa was grateful to Phil for caring for Karl even though her attempts to be gracious to him were received coolly. His reserve, she decided, was part of his gruff cowboy manner, natural to him, and not meant to offend. He was far superior to Terry whom she blamed for Karl's ostracism by the neighborhood mothers. Terry had involved Karl in war games and bad language. Fortunately, Karl was in better hands now.

17

Israel, 1983

The Yeshiva reopened in late August. At their first meeting, Rabbi Blum told Baruch, who was reading aloud a Talmud tract, "Whoa! Not so fast." Baruch began reading again, slowly at first, but soon, without even realizing it, he resumed the breakneck pace to which he'd become accustomed.

"You don't gulp down a fine wine," Rabbi Blum chided.

Baruch looked up. "You never objected before if I read fast."

"Before was before. Your first year here you made several changes: dressed differently in *keepah* and *tzitis*; mastered basic Hebrew; learned to recite prayers by heart. Now, you're starting your second year. From today on, I want you to strive to make deeper, more internal changes."

"How do I do that? By reading slowly?" Baruch joked.

The rabbi smiled. "Exactly! You have to slow down...linger over what you learn.

Ask of every word you read, 'How does this apply to my life?' Sometimes it helps to close your eyes, relax, and let your mind wander. The answers will rise up spontaneously. You must use Talmud as a key to unlock your heart. I want you to have skills that make you self-reliant. When you leave here in a year, depending on what you do, you might have to be your own teacher."

Baruch felt perplexed, yet willing to try what Rabbi Blum demanded. In the next few weeks, he paused from time to time as he studied, closed his eyes, and attempted to relate what he read to his own life. There were obvious connections between his criminal experiences and the legal discussions he read, but he felt Rabbi Blum had meant something altogether different. It saddened him that he couldn't grasp what was wanted.

Then one evening he came to a Talmudic line that said, 'He who eats in the street is likened to a dog.' Closing his eyes, he recalled how Lisa used to give him an apple or cookie, and send him out to wander around in the street like a stray dog. The Talmud line was an open sesame to the floodgates of memory. He remembered how he'd find sticks for sword-fights and challenge other boys, "Let's see who is stronger;" how he'd push kids down, roll in the dirt and wrestle with them; how the mothers on the block treated him like he had rabies. But most of all he remembered Phil.

He was the only neighbor willing to put up with a stray dog kid. Karl knocked on his door every morning, and Phil, even if he were still in his pajamas, invited him in and offered him a Pepsi. Taking out his tin of tobacco and cigarette papers from the back of a high kitchen cupboard shelf, he'd take Karl to the back room, a laundry room with a big sink. Phil referred to the room as 'my cowboy bunkhouse.' There was scarcely space for the cot he'd squeezed into it. At night, he slept on the cot so his coughing didn't disturb Joy.

"This here is happiness," Phil would sigh, sprawled on the cot with a lit cigarette. His dark eyes narrowed as he exhaled smoke and told stories about growing up on a ranch where his mother was the cook. Spellbound, Karl sat cross-legged on the floor, sipping Pepsi while he listened to Phil describe the Texas rolling prairie, dust and tumbleweed, or heard him relate how Lady, his border collie, got caught in a barbed wire fence and lost a leg.

Karl felt like he was in a real cowboy bunkhouse. He loved the manly tobacco scent that filled the narrow room, and the rifle propped up in the corner. Phil knew all about rifles. He told Karl, "By the time I was twelve I was clearing out vermin, rats and such on the ranch. I'd go out on the prairie and shoot rabbits. My ma cooked them up in stews for the help." Phil puffed away until he lost his breath from coughing. Then, he stubbed out the butt in a special flat metal container, and opened the back door to get rid of the smell. "Our little secret," he said about his smoking.

After this ritual, it was time for the next. Karl was permitted to watch as Phil shaved with a shaving cream cup, brush and old-fashioned straightedge at the backroom sink. Then Phil dressed up in his suit and boots, and put on his Stetson. Before he'd go out, he had to adjust the hat a fraction of an inch to the right or to the left, until it was exactly where he wanted it. Phil had to look good, even if he was only going out to wash the Ford.

On days he was feeling energetic, he took Karl on excursions. They rode the old-time steam train in the Berkeley hills, wagered bets at the Albany racetrack, went to the Grizzly Peak stables to admire the horses, watched planes take off at the Oakland airport. Another favorite destination was Siegle's gun shop where Phil enjoyed sauntering past racks of rifles. When he found one he liked, he picked it up. Karl would watch him look through the sights and demonstrate its action.

"This here buggy is getting a workout nowadays," Phil once said on the drive home from the gun shop.

Now, a dozen years later, Baruch was astonished that an ill man like Phil had taken so much trouble. The effort to entertain the 'stray dog' kid must have exhausted him. Five-year-old Karl hadn't even been a particularly appealing child. Looking back, Baruch cringed at the savage he'd been.

Phil's wife wore an elevated shoe on her left foot. One weekend when Joy was home from her secretary job, Karl had poked around in her closet, looking for one of her orthopedic shoes. Right in front of her, he'd put it on, clomped up and down, and imitated her limp. Instead of throwing him out, Phil had talked to him patiently and explained that what he'd done was cruel, and not funny.

'He who eats in the street is likened to a dog' brought together Karl and the person he was now. Phil had taught him basic sanitation like hand washing before meals and after using the toilet. At the Yeshiva, he learned the significance of these lessons, that washing his hands was not merely a physical but a spiritual act. His *keepah* reminded him of the cowboy hat Phil wore because he believed going out bareheaded was disrespectful to others.

Another Talmud adage Baruch knew applied to Phil—'Greater are the deeds of a righteous person than the deeds of Heaven.' Baruch couldn't think of him as a perfect teacher who was all wisdom and kindness like Rabbi Blum. Yet Phil had loved him enough to throw himself into the difficult battle of teaching him how to be decent.

Once on their way home from the racetrack, Phil stopped at a Dairy Queen, reminiscing to Karl about a Dairy Queen in Texas, a little white shack that stood alone, at the bend of a Texas highway. "Nothing ever tasted good as ice-cold Dairy Queen in the Texas heat!" He bought two chocolate cones. As they licked them, they strolled past a Chinese restaurant, dry cleaners and medical supply store.

An airplane flew overhead, a silver streak in the sky. Shading his eyes, Phil squinted and said, "Hey, will you look at that baby. You gonna be a pilot, Karl?" As a young man, this had been Phil's ambition. But the TB he'd suffered in his early twenties had kept him out of the air force.

"Yeah."

"What do you say?"

"Yes, sir. I will, sir."

"Good, Karl. That's a snappy answer. You're learning. If I had a boy, I'd tell him the same. I'd want my son to be like you."

Karl threw himself at Phil, hugging him and crying, "I love you!"

"Now, now, what's this about?" Phil said.

The braiding together of the Talmud and Baruch's memories was like learning to ride a bicycle. At first he'd kept crashing to the ground. But suddenly the ability came to him to enjoy forever after. The Talmud opened trails he could follow. All through the autumn, he kept thinking about Phil, recalling good qualities that it had been too painful to think about for the last decade.

Shortly after his sixth birthday, his substitute father had died in his sleep, abandoning him the way his real father had done. Or so it had seemed to little Karl. Hearing the news of Phil's death, he'd cried uncontrollably.

A week after Phil died, Lisa took Karl to pay Joy a condolence visit. They sat with her at the small Formica-topped table in the kitchen, drinking sodas. Joy's face was pale, swollen. She said, "Phil was a sick man. It wasn't like I wasn't expecting it. What with his lungs so poor, I'm grateful he lived as long as he did."

"Can I have Phil's hat?" Karl piped up.

"His hat?" Joy looked confused.

"The big hat."

"You mean his cowboy hat."

Karl nodded.

"What a shame. I would have given it to you. Really, I would have. But I've already cleared out Phil's things."

"Everything?"

"Yes."

"You shouldn't have!" Karl spat out angrily.

Lisa rose. "Come on, Karl, let's get going."

While she said her goodbyes, Karl ran out into the alley. Blinded by tears, he crashed into Phil's Ford. The collision knocked him off his feet. He plopped down next to the car. Along came Lisa.

"Come on, Karl," she said.

He refused to move. His face felt hot. His fists were tightly clenched.

Lisa asked Karl again. When he didn't come, she left him sitting in the driveway.

That evening, Joy came to see Lisa. The moment she stepped into the flat, Karl scampered away to his room. He could hear Joy telling Lisa that someone had taken a sharp rock and run it down the side of the Ford, making a long, jagged scratch. The sight of it so upset her that she wanted to sell the car.

After she left, Lisa called excitedly, "Karl...Karl."

He wouldn't come out of his bedroom. He was afraid she knew he was the one who'd scratched the car. Lisa opened his door.

Instead of rebuking him, she jingled a key and chirped, "Guess what? I bought Phil's car. Joy practically gave it to me."

Looking back, Baruch assumed that the reason Lisa didn't scold him was because she saw he was suffering. That evening, she even gave him a special treat. At an empty parking lot, she let him sit on her lap and steer her new car while she worked the gas and brake.

The Talmud did more than restore such memories. It allowed Baruch to see that Phil hadn't deserted him. He had only to reach out and Phil came to him in his imagination.

In December the Yeshiva closed down for a month. Students and teachers went off for the break. The night before his departure Rabbi Blum talked to Baruch about the topics he'd be studying during the break, and the volunteer work he'd do at the center in Jerusalem. At dawn the next morning, Baruch glanced out his dorm room window and saw a gray figure in the courtyard. It was Rabbi Blum waiting for a taxi to take him to Ben Gurion airport. Wanting to say a final farewell, he ran out of the dorm in his pajamas and bathrobe.

Rabbi Blum's face lit up with a smile, but seeing Baruch had no coat and was shivering, he said, "You don't have to wait with me."

"I want to."

"It's supposed to rain."

Baruch remained by his teacher's side. The rabbis had taught him that to see off a friend or guest followed the example of Abraham, who'd accompanied two visiting angels part of their way after they departed from his home. This was how one demonstrated courtesy and protected a visitor from harm.

It was light out when a cab turned into the Yeshiva courtyard and pulled up in front of them. The driver was a thin, dark-skinned man. He climbed out and jerked open the trunk, revealing a television set that he said he had to deliver to his brother-in-law. Rabbi Blum hesitated, but when the driver insisted there was room, he handed over his suitcase. Luckily, there was space. Climbing into the cab's back seat, the rabbi carefully set his violin beside him. He rolled down his window and said, "Call me in a day or two." Baruch nodded.

It was the rainy season. Rain began to splatter the plaza, and dampen his clothes. But he remained outside, watching the taxi drive down the road. After it disappeared around a bend, he returned to the now-quiet dorm. Stripping off his wet clothes, he stepped into a hot shower.

After his shower, he shaved carefully, in preparation for going off to his volunteer work. The medicine cabinet mirror was clouded over. He had the uncanny feeling of seeing a stranger's features reflected through the steam. With the side of his hand he wiped the surface clear, and saw it was himself. But he was struck by how much he'd changed since coming to the Yeshiva. Somehow, without his noticing, he'd acquired a man's face. The nose seemed longer, more defined. His blond hair was darker, his shoulders broader.

Baruch left the Yeshiva for the bus stop. There were still threatening gray clouds gathered in the sky, but the rain had stopped. The bus drew up. Recognizing his passenger, the Arab driver called out, "Hey, California boy." After paying the fare, Baruch took the seat behind him. The bus rattled along, putting Baruch into a soporific state. He thought of Phil, and how he wished to devote himself to the boys at the center, as Phil had devoted himself to little Karl.

In Jerusalem, the bus pulled into the large terminal. From there, Baruch walked to the center for disadvantaged boys. Mr. Nussbaum shook his hand and said, "I'm desperate for more help. Is it possible you could work more than one day a week this time?" Baruch eagerly agreed. If he could, he'd come into the center every single day of the break. But it was closed weekends. He realized too that it was better if he didn't volunteer on Fridays. The days were short in winter. With the infrequent bus service between Jerusalem and the Yeshiva, he might not get back before sunset, the start of the *shabbes*.

Most of the boys were familiar. They seemed glad to see him. A new kid, a twelve-year-old named Maurie, got into a fight. Baruch had to pull him off another boy and see to it that Maurie didn't start fighting all over again. He was reminded of how little Karl used to challenge other kids, "Let's see who's stronger," and then throw himself at them. Other than several incidents with Maurie, the day went smoothly. He worked five hours at the center, then hurried to the terminal to catch his bus to the Yeshiva.

After having a meal of chicken soup in the kitchen, he went to Rabbi Blum's office. He would have liked to call his teacher to tell him his first day back at the center was a success, and that he was going to be volunteering four days a week instead of one.

However, Rabbi Blum was still on his plane. Even if he were home by now, he'd be too exhausted to have a telephone conversation.

Baruch phoned Lisa. When she picked up, he said, "I'm back with the Moroccan kids."

Like the first time he told her about his volunteer work, she fussed about the exotic connection it had conferred on him. Nothing was more romantic to her than travel and meeting people from faraway places. She told him, she too was going to learn about another culture.

"I'm so glad you called because I'm going away for two or three weeks, and I wanted you to know."

"Going away," Baruch echoed, trying to absorb the news. He hesitated, not sure he wanted to know, but felt compelled to ask. "Are you going with someone?"

She laughed nervously. "Roger."

"Roger?"

"I told you about Roger."

"No, you didn't."

"My archeology professor…the dig… Quinto Roo."

Chattering on, Lisa didn't seem to notice how quiet he became. When she was about to hang up, he remembered to ask, "What's your phone number in Mexico? I'd like to have it in case I have to contact you."

"Don't be silly. You won't be able to reach me while I'm on a dig."

"It's the vacation break here. I'm on my own. I thought that…"

Interrupting, she said, "I'll write. I'll send you a post card with a picture of a sombrero, or of parrots."

Everyone at the Yeshiva was gone, and so was Lisa. Without being able to call her, Baruch felt all the more lonely. Four days a week, he worked at the center in Jerusalem. On the bus, at the terminal, or walking to the center, he was hyper-aware of the women he saw in a way he'd never been before. The dark eyes and black hair of the Arab women enchanted him. He yearned to exchange glances, or better yet, to talk to them. Several were thin. Others had voluptuous bodies. Nearly all of the women aroused him in some way. Either he desired their kisses, or with the older ones, their motherly carresses. Baruch's strange, unsettling feelings disturbed him until he came to the center. Then they disappeared.

At the center, he felt like he was in his world, the right place where he could be a role model the way Rabbi Blum was to him, and Phil had once been. The boy Baruch was most concerned about was Maurie, the new kid. Maurie was small for his age. Other kids picked on him. There were pokes, nudges, name-calling, and even vulgar comments about Maurie's mother. "Don't pay attention and they'll stop it," Baruch urged. But with each provocation Maurie exploded, hitting and punching in every direction. Every day, Baruch had to jump into the fray and separate him from other boys.

The breathlessness he felt after one Maurie incident brought back a recollection of Phil wheezing while he tried to admonish little Karl. Baruch hadn't realized how working with a troubled kid would demand every ounce of his strength and patience. How much more difficult it must have been for a sick, old man.

One afternoon, instead of striking back at a name-caller, Maurie ran out of the center. Baruch chased after, calling, "Maurie, wait for me." Rain poured down. Baruch slipped on the wet cobblestoned street and fell to the ground. He was surprised to see Maurie pause and glance back.

Rising to his feet, Baruch said, "I'm all right." Then he begged Maurie to wait.

"Leave me alone," Maurie hissed, but he'd stopped running, was only walking quickly.

"Where are you going?" Baruch said, following a few paces behind. His soaked sneakers squished with every step. "Come back to the center where it's dry."

"You go back if you want. I'm not going back."

Baruch didn't know what to say or do. Then, unbidden, an image of Phil rose in his mind. Phil smiled and said, 'You tell that little kid you're one hell of an Indian scout, and you're gonna keep tracking him.'

Baruch told Maurie, "Okay, I'll go wherever you go."

Maurie slowed down. They walked side by side in silence.

A small black and white cat came out of nowhere, the usual Jerusalem stray, half-starved, ribs sticking out, the rain making its matted coat more bedraggled. The creature brushed against Maurie's legs. The boy knelt down and ran a finger over its back. The cat gave a plaintive meow. Most wild cats in Jerusalem hissed and scratched when touched. This one was tame. It responded to Maurie's stroking its back with a low purring hum of satisfaction. The boy's tight face softened. He picked the cat up, held it awkwardly at first, then more securely.

Phil hadn't cared for cats, but had known how to act in a loving way to a forlorn child. Baruch imagined him saying, 'What are you waiting for? Tell the kid the critter needs him. Go ahead and put your hand on him like you need him too.'

Reaching out, Baruch touched Maurie's thin shoulder, and said, "This little cat came to you for help. Let's take him to the center where you can get him a saucer of milk. Come on." He was surprised that Maurie followed him back to the center.

At the threshold, the boy stopped short and said, "Nobody wants me here."

Baruch was baffled about how to respond. The other boys did reject Maurie! But Phil had ready advice. 'Emphasize the positive. Tell him he's making progress. He is, ain't he?' Baruch said, "Last time he called you a name, you hit Benjamin. This time, you ran out and didn't hurt anyone. That's a step forward. You're doing better. Everything takes time. Be patient."

Maurie accompanied him into the center. Baruch inwardly rejoiced that he hadn't let Maurie run off, alone and uncomforted. Phil hadn't let him. For the first time, he glimpsed what the other Yeshiva students meant when they claimed their ancestors guided them. Of course, Phil wasn't like the generations-back-relatives the students spoke about. Baruch had had to resurrect him by dreaming and remembering as he studied Talmud.

18

Albany, California, 1972

A month had passed since Mark had told her that Fritz was no longer at the commune. Lisa reasoned he should have come by now. As he hadn't, she felt a need to do something that she hoped would free her from her perpetual expectation and waiting.

Returning from a walk with Karl, she encouraged him to visit with Phil. Earlier, Phil had gone to a doctor's appointment. But the blue Ford was in the driveway now. Karl flew up the three steps to the porch. Phil answered his knock. With a curt nod to Lisa, he welcomed Karl inside.

Knowing Karl would be well looked after, Lisa went off to the small shoe repair shop a few blocks away. The tall black man who ran the business greeted her with a smile of recognition. In addition to offering repairs, he also made custom-made sandals. Shortly after she'd arrived in California, he'd fitted her for a pair. During the fitting, she'd laughed at his flirtatious compliments. "I'm married," she'd said, and when he'd held onto her feet, she pulled them away.

This time, Lisa was the seducer. If Fritz weren't coming, why shouldn't she sleep with the sandal-maker? She wanted to do just that. A sexual encounter with this stranger would denote a new beginning. The affair was brief, as were the ones that followed. In the next two months, there were four one-night stands with men whose names she forgot in a day. Her strategy failed. Much as she tried, she couldn't stop hoping Fritz would show up.

In the spring, she met John, a burly, dark-haired guy with a long ponytail, who'd grown up in the mid-west. His father and three brothers did construction work. John did too, but he also attended classes at the university. Five years younger than herself, he reminded her of a young Fritz, lively, irrepressible, full of ideas. She was drawn to, but not in love with him, as he soon was with her. Lisa felt obligated to warn him he mustn't take their relationship too seriously.

"I want you to be prepared. If my husband turns up, I'm going to break it off with you," she warned one evening while lying in John's arms. He pulled away and turned on his side. In the tense silence that followed, Lisa wondered whether she'd regret it if he'd walked out on her. She felt confused, afraid of being alone.

Then she heard him say in a choked voice, "I guess I have no choice but to accept your terms." She felt relieved he wasn't going to leave, but glad she had spoken. Having expressed her devotion to Fritz, she was free to cast off her lover if her circumstances changed. Fritz might still turn up. He'd always been full of surprises.

She asked John to visit at night, afraid that at other times, Karl might walk in on their lovemaking. The thought horrified her. She had a certain delicacy about children in relation to sexuality. They must be kept innocent of it, must not hear it spoken about, and certainly not see the sex act performed. John came by after midnight, long after Karl had gone to bed. Once settled into a deep sleep, nothing disturbed Karl, not even John roaring into the alley on his motorcycle. It never occurred to Lisa that the noise might bother someone else.

One morning, hearing a pounding on her door, she threw on a bathrobe and rushed to open it. Aztac bounded out the door. Phil stood before Lisa. His face was flushed. Wheezing from the climb up the back steps, he said, "You gotta do something about your damn cat." Aztac was weaving in and out between his legs.

"What's the problem?" Lisa asked. She picked up the cat, stroked her fur. Aztac purred.

"My wife works. She needs her sleep, and she ain't gettin' any. That critter of yours is in heat. The tomcats come round and serenade all night." Phil began coughing. Finally, recovering, he said, "I'm afraid I'll come down with a cold that won't get better 'cause I don't get my rest."

"She's only a kitten. It's some other cat," Lisa protested.

"No. It's your cat keeping me up!"

"What am I supposed to do?"

"Just keep her locked up. Or you take her to the pound."

That evening, Lisa was sitting in the kitchen, trying to talk quietly to John. She did not wish to disturb Karl who was down the hall, asleep in his bedroom. A half-full gallon of Gallo wine stood on the table. They'd been drinking steadily for the last hour. Lisa told John about the morning's conversation.

"He's a real kook. Every time I turn into the alley and he hears my motorcycle, he switches the light in his back room on and off," John said.

"From now on, turn off the motorcycle on the street and wheel it into the alley quietly." Lisa hoped that would satisfy Phil. His goodwill was important to her, and meant even more to Karl.

"Sure, I'll do that. And I'll wheel my bike out when I leave. But it won't help him sleep any better. The reason he can't sleep is because it drives him crazy that we're having sex. It wasn't the cat he was talking about. It was you."

"Oh," Lisa said, feeling degraded by John's words. She comforted herself with a swallow of wine.

"He wishes he was screwing you." John kept on.

"He helps me out with Karl," Lisa said in a thin voice. "He probably thinks that for Karl's sake, I shouldn't have an affair. He's an old-fashioned man with old-fashioned values…"

"Why are you defending him?" John interrupted. "Do you think he's right?" He drained his glass of wine, and refilled his and hers.

"I'm just saying that he deserves gratitude and respect, and so…" She searched about for the second point she meant to make, but what she wished to say eluded her. Then it flashed in her mind. "Joy does too!"

"Who's she?" John asked, slurring his words.

"She is…his wife…and…and…"

Lisa felt a tug at her heart, thinking about Joy. Other than the over-sized black elevated shoe she dragged about, she was a dainty woman in her pastel-colored dresses, with her shiny white purse, and with every strand of her gray hair in place, rolled into tight ringlets. The other day, they'd met on the street and chatted. Lisa had helped carry in Joy's groceries, and then stayed for a cup of coffee. Joy wasn't standoffish like Phil, and like the neighborhood mothers who'd banded against Karl.

"Which one is she? The cripple?"

"Oh, why do you have to use that ugly word?" She stared at John—saw he wasn't like Fritz at all. Fritz, when he was himself, not on drugs, was a far more sensitive man. The only reason she'd been drinking tonight was so as not to see the difference. Not to see that John was temporary. Not to see he was a distraction from her yearning for Fritz, and not someone to replace him.

"S..s..sorry, I offended you," John said testily.

"I think you better go," Lisa said coldly.

"Oh, come on, Lisa. Don't be that way."

"Go!"

"It's over between us?"

"Yes."

John put on his shoes, grabbed his leather jacket. "You didn't really give me a chance. Right from the beginning, you didn't."

Slamming the door behind him, he ran down the steps. Lisa heard the vroom of his motorcycle. She glanced out the kitchen window, saw John drive out of the alley. Phil's back room light began flickering on and off. It reminded her of a lighthouse warning ships not to crash against treacherous rocks.

19

Israel, 1984

At the New Year, the deserted Yeshiva dorm transformed to a noisy place. Students returned for their final term of study. Encountering each other, they shook hands eagerly like travelers from the ends of the world reuniting—which they were. Jakob brought back a gift for Baruch, a t-shirt that said 'Jo-town,' for Johannesburg. Baruch immediately put it on and wore it to the afternoon's prayer service.

There, he glimpsed Rabbi Blum amidst the other rabbis. The sight of his teacher's kind face lifted his spirits. Wrapped in his prayer shawl, Rabbi Blum swayed, his eyes closed. The services ended. Everyone left the prayer hall to go to the cafeteria. Baruch darted through the crowd to walk beside Rabbi Blum. They greeted each other warmly, raising their voices to be heard above the din in the hallway.

The rabbis sat separately from the students in the cafeteria. Reluctantly, Baruch parted from his teacher. At the buffet, he filled a plate with cold salads, then sat down with Jakob and other students. They were excitedly discussing what they intended to do after concluding the two years in Israel. During the break, plans had been finalized to attend college, enter a rabbinical seminary, or join a family business. Two boys had become engaged and would marry in the next year.

Baruch found it painful to field inquiries about his own future. He knew he had to leave the Yeshiva in six months, but didn't want to think, no less talk about it. The thought of parting from Rabbi Blum forever made him sick. For months, he'd put off talking to Lisa about his return to California, what he would do, how they would manage together. She wasn't religious. He needed to ask whether she was willing to give him the support he needed to be observant.

They hadn't spoken since she'd gone off to Mexico. Presumably, she'd returned four days ago. Wanting to renew contact, Baruch had phoned twice but failed to reach her. He'd try again tonight, since Rabbi Blum had said he wasn't using his office when Baruch consulted with him at the end of the meal. Baruch went directly to the office and dialed his mother.

"Oh, Karl," she greeted him and began to chatter about Mexico, the jungle, parrots, pyramid ruins and orchids. "I'm sorry I didn't send you your postcard," she apologized. "I bought one. My intentions were good. I meant to send it. But I needed a bookmark. Your card did service as one. Before I knew it, the card was lost."

"Don't worry about the card." Baruch couldn't be annoyed since he never expected her to keep her promise. To keep kosher was far more trouble than sending a post card. She'd have to be scrupulous. With a sinking feeling, he realized that the woman speaking excitedly about her trip wasn't, and never could be scrupulous. She sounded like a child.

"It's a treasure hunt, Karl. You dig carefully and, if you're lucky, you find something. It's thrilling. I hope you can go on a dig. They have them in Israel, you know."

He mentioned the ancient coins the *kibbutz* storekeeper had once shown him.

"Marvelous…marvelous," she said, "dig up some coins for me."

"Sure," he replied, half-heartedly. At one time, he'd have loved to dig up the little metal coins she wanted. But in this moment, he knew he'd changed, wasn't that boy any more.

He thought of Rabbi Frankel, a Holocaust survivor. In one of his classes, he'd said that when the Messiah came, he'd ask people to cross over an iron or a paper bridge. Those who chose the iron would fall into the sea and drown. But those who followed across the paper bridge would be safe. At the time, Baruch had listened without fully registering the meaning until the rabbi explained that iron meant guns and tanks. It could also mean the gold and silver greedy people struggled to acquire. Paper meant books, learning and Torah. Karl had chosen iron. Baruch wanted to choose the paper bridge now, and in the future.

He said goodbye to his mother, and sat staring at the phone, lost in thought. If he were to live with Lisa after he left the Yeshiva—and where else could he go but to her— he feared he was bound to become slack, even lackadaisical in his Jewish commitment. He might even revert to being Karl. His past self reacted to events without thought, the way an animal does. Baruch didn't want to be that kind of person ever again. In the next six months, he had to strengthen his will and resolve to be observant.

He recalled a class lecture in the autumn. Rabbi Cohen had spoken about the Musar movement that had swept through East European Yeshivas during the early part of the century. Musar followers engaged in a rigorous curbing of their impulses, appetites, and even underwent self-humiliation. Rabbi Cohen had concluded his lecture by saying, "Musar practices are extreme. Nothing I'd recommend."

Deterred by the rabbi's warning, Baruch hadn't tried to find out any more. But now, after speaking with Lisa, he wondered whether Musar could toughen him, and prepare him for returning home. He went to the library and obtained a slender volume about Musar. It took two hours to read through at his dorm room desk.

After he was done, he sat perfectly still and stared into space. Inwardly, he was trembling. What he'd read revealed his own superficiality. Musar must be used for only one fundamental purpose. He must transform himself into a good man!

The next day, Baruch began a regime of self-discipline that included punishments for past and present transgressions. At various times, he placed a pebble in his sock, a rubber band tight about his ankle, slept without his pillow. After each trial, he'd ask, *'Am I a good person?'*

The night he stretched out on the floor instead of in his bed, an astonished Jakob asked, "Why are you down on the floor?"

"I'm in training."

"For what?"

"To get control over my body."

"Ah, I see," Jakob said, approvingly.

Like the Musar-niks, Baruch also seized on fasting as a way to expiate sins.

One morning, Leib, the fat kid, followed Baruch out of the cafeteria. "Are you sick?" he asked. He'd noticed Baruch had had only juice and a cracker.

"I'm healthy."

"Aren't you hungry?"

"Sort of."

"I get it. You're not a slave to your stomach like me. I can't help it, I have to stuff myself." Tears welled up in the boy's eyes. "I saw sandwiches in an Arab shop in Jerusalem and couldn't resist. I ate one even though it wasn't kosher."

The admiration he received motivated Baruch to further deprivations. But just as he was feeling better about himself, an old fault reasserted itself. He'd never been patient with less gifted individuals. In class one morning, another boy read haltingly from the Torah. Bored, Baruch interrupted and began to recite the passage from memory. Then he remembered how Rabbi Blum had once rebuked him for being a show-off. He stopped reciting mid-sentence, muttered, "I forgot," and sat down.

During the rest of the class, he could barely concentrate. He wondered whether it was a futile effort to try to transform himself into a better person. The Musars had had a passionate commitment. To quench their pride, some had walked about in rags, or with snot dripping from their noses. He lacked the courage to expose or humiliate himself.

After class, he went up to the boy who'd read slowly and forced himself to apologize. But that was scarcely enough. Walking away, he tried to think of another sacrifice. He recollected how much he looked forward to the weekly trips to Jerusalem with the other students. Must he give them up? 'Yes,' came a stern voice from within.

On Saturday night, Baruch sat at his desk while he watched Jakob change into a fresh white shirt, comb his hair.

"Hurry up," Jakob said, noticing Baruch wasn't preparing for the trip to Jerusalem.

"I'm not going. I have to study," Baruch said.

Jakob tried to dissuade him, but then went into the hall to the join the other boys. Before they left, Avi poked his head in the door and said, "It won't be the same without you, Baruch. You're working too hard. Change your mind."

"Another time."

"Okay. Next week we're dragging you along, whether you like it or not."

The next week and the week after came, but Baruch stayed behind while all the boys went off. To his dismay, he found it difficult to fix his concentration and study. Instead, he kept imagining what the others were doing, where they'd go, which girls they'd meet from the girls' orthodox school.

Word reached Rabbi Blum that he'd been spending Saturday nights alone. At the conclusion of a tutoring session, the rabbi said, "I understand you don't go to Jerusalem on Saturday nights. It's good for you to have a break when you can relax and have fun. What do you do while the others are away?"

"I study in my room."

"That's what you want to do?"

"Yes," Baruch said, averting his face from the rabbi's gaze. The truth was he'd been too restless to study. He'd spent the time pacing his dorm room, looking out the window, or shuffling papers.

"I'm concerned. You look thin. You're growing and need to eat properly. I hope you're not doing anything foolish. There are always a few idealistic boys who enter a Yeshiva and take things to extremes. It says in the Torah that on *Yom Kippor*, 'Ye shall afflict your souls.' The Torah says exactly what is expected of you so that no one will mortify himself beyond the specified boundaries. If you carry things too far, you go against Jewish teachings."

"I'm sorry to cause you worry," Baruch mumbled.

"Whatever you're doing, stop doing it. Okay?"

Baruch nodded, relieved that Rabbi Blum had given him an order to renounce his

Musar practices. He was tired of acting as if every day was *Yom Kippor*.

"One more thing," Rabbi Blum said. "I apologize. I've been so distracted. I should have brought this up earlier. What will you do when you finish the Yeshiva program?"

"I'm going back to my mother."

"I thought you were. But if you happen to decide otherwise, I think you should be aware that Rabbi Tubol could create opportunities for you. There are several cities with Jewish communities in the United States where you could live, Los Angeles, Chicago, New York, and others. You've learned a lot these last two years. The director of the center where you volunteered told me that you're excellent dealing with children. One possibility is for you to teach at a Hebrew day school. You're smart and could do more. You could go to Yeshiva University in New York."

"I don't have a high school degree. It's probably too late to apply," Baruch said dejectedly.

"Rabbi Tubol's recommendation would suffice. He comes from a distinguished rabbinical family. Jews all around the world have heard of the Tubols. People are honored to do him a favor. He can help you. But he has to contact people and set things up. If you decide you want this, go speak with him. He'll get the wheels rolling."

"My mother expects me. She'll insist I come home."

Baruch rose, crossed the office, and began to step out.

"Talk to your mother about your future plans," Rabbi Blum called after him.

"All right," Baruch promised.

The next day Baruch phoned Lisa and said, "I'd like to talk about what I'm doing after the Yeshiva."

"It's not even February. You don't have to worry now."

He'd wanted her to say, 'But of course, you'll come back to me!' Whether or not he chose to go there, he needed to know her home was always open to him. "It doesn't hurt to talk about it in advance," he pleaded. "It's not that far away."

"Frankly, I'm too unsettled now. I'm going on another dig with Roger, soon."

"To Mexico again?"

"Uh-huh. This time, I'll be in Eastern Mexico on the Gulf. The point is I'll be away three months, maybe more. It makes no sense for me to pay rent during that time. I'm in the midst of giving up this flat and moving to Roger's place. Don't worry, when the time comes, I'll figure out something for you."

"You're giving up the flat?" Baruch said, finding it difficult to absorb the unexpected news. He felt queasy.

"Yes. There's no point..."

"It's my place too! You could have asked me before you decided to move," he cried angrily.

"You've been away for so long, it never occurred to me..."

"You didn't think about me at all. You might not even be in California when I leave Israel."

"What do you want me to do?"

"Don't move. Keep the flat."

"It's a waste of money."

"I'd have my old room when I came home."

"You're not being reasonable. I'm sure Roger wouldn't mind your staying with us."

"Where would I stay?"

"The couch in the living room."

An image rose in Baruch's mind of his sleeping on a lumpy couch while curious Lisa wandered over and poked into his *tefillin* bag. He saw her taking one of the boxes out, standing in front of a mirror and adjusting it to her head. A shadowy figure, Roger, someone not Jewish, stood in a doorway and observed with an amused smile.

"I need privacy," Baruch said.

"You'd manage. You know you would. We'd manage."

It was futile to argue. She wasn't going to keep the apartment for his sake. When a boyfriend was involved he, Baruch, no longer counted. A familiar misery descended on him, his boyhood horror of being locked out. "Sure. Roger's couch is great."

Lisa answered his sarcasm with, "I'm so glad you understand. For a moment, I thought you didn't. Here's Roger's phone number. That's where you can reach me, starting next week."

All these months at the Yeshiva, he'd withheld a question he longed to ask, not wanting to upset her. Now that she'd cast him out, he didn't care whether or not he hurt her. He had two parents! The long unasked inquiry tumbled out. "How can I reach my father?" His wanting to see Fritz was no longer a whim but a necessity.

There was a silence before Lisa stammered in an agitated voice, "I don't know where he is. Please, don't ask again. I have to go." The dial tone sounded. She'd hung up.

After a few moments, Baruch dialed the international operator. He gave the name Biederman and asked for his aunt and uncle's phone number. Receiving it, he dialed Vienna. A telephone rang in disconcerting couplets, different from the single rings on American phones. A woman picked up.

"Eva Beiderman?" he inquired.

The woman replied in a burst of German.

"Please, can you speak to me in English? I don't speak German," he said slowly.

"Yes, okay."

"Are you Eva?"

"Yes, I am."

"Aunt Eva, this is your nephew Karl."

It took her a few moments to grasp his identity. As soon as she did, he received a rapturous greeting. To Baruch's delight she said, "You must come and visit us. Your uncle and I would love to see you. Klaus and Freidrich will want to meet you too. You remember your cousins?"

"And my father. Could I see him?"

There was a pause, and then a confused, "Your father?"

"I...I'd like to see him."

"You don't know?"

"What?"

"Your mother didn't tell you? I don't know what to say. It would be better to talk face to face... Come visit us. I'll tell you then."

"I want to know now!"

"I suppose you have a right." Eva sighed. She proceeded to tell him about his father. When she was done, Baruch said 'goodbye' and put down the receiver in a daze.

Eva's words ratcheted about his head like sharp, rough rocks in a tumbler. He could barely breathe. He rose from his seat abruptly, banged his shin hard against the edge of the wooden desk. The pain made him gasp and hop about. His pants leg felt damp. Pulling the cuff up, he saw a jagged cut and blood dribbling down his shin. He limped down the hall to a bathroom where he washed the wound with stinging soap. Pink-tinged water circled down the sink drain. Round and round it went.

He looked about. The tiled walls and floor appeared to be solid, but they were soft and could crumble at any moment. The fifth commandment was "Honor thy Father and Mother." He couldn't honor Lisa. Not now. Not after what he'd heard tonight. His mouth and throat had a sour taste. He must spit out the fury choking him, twisting his intestines.

He rushed back to Rabbi Blum's office. His hands trembled, but he managed to dial his home. Yes, there were still a few days left before Lisa closed it down. He could still call it that.

"Why are you phoning…?" Lisa demanded, sounding ready to rebuff his questions again.

Interrupting her, he demanded fiercely. "Why did you lie to me?"

"What are you talking about?"

"Don't pretend you don't know. I called Aunt Eva!"

Lisa gasped, a long exhalation that sounded like she'd been kicked in the belly.

20

Albany, California 1972

Lisa dreamt Fritz phoned and told her that he was coming to California that very day. The vivid dream seemed like a prophecy. She woke tingling. Convinced it was true, she could barely keep from running to Karl's room to shake him awake and tell him. No, it was best to wait for Fritz's arrival to prove her right. If she told Karl, and his father didn't come, that would be cruel. But Fritz would come!

She wanted the flat looking its best. Energy surged through her, making her strong and light-footed. She was scrubbing the interior of the oven with Ajax and a Brillo pad when Karl pattered into the kitchen and asked for his breakfast. She gave him cold cereal.

As soon as he pushed his bowl away, she smiled and said, "Are you going over to see Phil?"

"Yeah."

"That's good. I need to straighten up." She helped Karl dress and shooed him out the door.

The radio in her bedroom was tuned to the classical station. A Bach Cello Suite carried to the kitchen. Humming along, Lisa mopped the floor. There was so much she hadn't noticed previously, dishes piled high in the sink, grime on the counters and stovetop, a cobweb trembling in a corner between ceiling and wall. All this must be repaired.

The phone rang. She rushed to the living room to pick up, certain it was Fritz, that he was calling as he had in her dream. "Hellooo," she crooned.

"Lisa, it's me!"

She recognized her mother's voice.

"How are you, Lisa?"

"I'm all right," Lisa said automatically.

"You...you sound a little strange."

"You do too," Lisa blurted. Her mother was usually more assertive.

"You better sit down, Lisa," Bernice said grimly.

Lisa understood her mother meant, 'Brace yourself.' "Okay," she said, although she didn't take a seat. Fritz was coming. If he walked in the next moment, she wanted to be on her feet, ready to drop the phone and leap into his arms.

"I don't know how to say this," Bernice said.

Her hemming and hawing was irritating. If only she'd spit out what she wanted to say, so she, Lisa, could return to cleaning the flat. Everything must shine for Fritz.

"I have terrible news."

Had her father had another stroke, Lisa wondered. Full of dread, she told herself he couldn't have died. Her dad had always been part of her life, would continue to be.

"I just spoke to a Connecticut highway patrolman."

"Was Dad in Connecticut?"

"Your father's fine."

The hard knot in Lisa's belly relaxed. What a fool she'd been to jump to conclusions.

"It's Fritz I'm calling about. He kept a letter you wrote in his wallet, a letter with my phone number."

"Fritz?" Lisa gasped. The hard knot was back. Slipping onto the couch, she listened to her mother's story about a car theft, crash and dead body. No matter what Bernice said, Lisa refused to believe Fritz was dead. Fritz...her Fritz was coming today.

Karl was over at Phil's. Soon, they'd be in the driveway washing the Ford. Karl would be the first to see Fritz. He'd race up the steps, burst into the house and joyously shout, 'Daddy's home!' Fritz, coming right behind Karl, would stand before her, alive and well!

"It's not Fritz. It's a case of mistaken identity," Lisa insisted. She wanted to get off the phone so she could shower, dress, brush her hair, and put on make-up.

"Listen to me. Your husband stole a car."

"Fritz isn't a thief."

"He was on drugs. My guess is he noticed a car with a key in the ignition. Next thing, he was driving it. Before long, he was involved in a high-speed chase. He crashed the car against a concrete wall."

"How do you know the dead man is Fritz?"

"I told you, they found his wallet."

"A thief might have robbed Fritz's wallet, then stole the car and crashed it. The highway patrol officer would have found the thief's dead body on the road."

"It was Fritz. I'm sorry," Bernice said.

"Does Dad know this story?"

"He knows."

"He'll say that I'm right, that there has to be more confirmation. Go ask him. He'll tell you."

"Stop it, Lisa... There is no question that it was Fritz. He had his passport with him with his photo."

"Put Dad on the phone," Lisa pleaded. Somehow, her father would tell her something different.

"I don't want your father upset. I'm trying to keep him out of this... you can count on me. I'll take care of things. What about Fritz's family? Who should I call?"

"Family?" Lisa murmured. "I never met Fritz's parents, only his sister and brother-in-law, Eva and Deitrich Biederman. They live in Vienna."

"I'll track down the sister. Whatever legal papers there are, I'll send on to you."

"Papers?"

"A death certificate, that sort of..."

"Oh no," Lisa cried, breathing hard. There was going to be a death certificate with Fritz's name. A death certificate made a death true. Oh God, her beloved was dead. If only she'd stayed at Fritz's side, he'd be alive. "I should never have left him!"

"Don't blame yourself. It doesn't help anybody."

"He wasn't himself. He changed at the commune, deteriorated. I was wrong to leave. I should have stayed to look after him. You've always looked after Dad..."

"I'm so glad you weren't with him in that car. You and Karl are alive. That's what matters."

"You don't understand," Lisa cried. "It matters to me whether Fritz is alive." She hung up. The phone rang again. She didn't answer.

The FM station was still on in the bedroom. This time Vivaldi's *The Four Seasons* was playing. Lisa curled up in a fetal position on the couch. Closing her eyes, she saw Fritz, the bright golden prince he was when she first met him. He kissed her lips. She shivered with happiness because he seemed alive.

Karl burst into the room. "Mommy, a big dog came in our yard."

Trying to conceal her confusion and grief, Lisa called, "Come here, you," and waved Karl closer. "Look how dusty you are." She sniffed his hair. It smelled sour. She'd have to give him a long overdue bath. "Did you play with the dog?"

"It ran away."

"Oh," she sighed, trying to keep back tears. Lisa was afraid to speak more, but after a few moments, she managed, "The dog will come back." She didn't have the heart to say otherwise, no less to tell Karl of a more profound loss.

21

Israel, 1984

Baruch told no one at the Yeshiva Fritz was dead, not wishing to receive condolences for a father he scarcely knew, and whose death occurred over a decade ago. Still, he marked down the date he'd learned about the death, January 28, 1984. From then on, he intended to consider that date the anniversary of his father's death and would light a *yortzeit* candle to remember him.

After over a decade of separation, there was no loving attachment to his father. Nevertheless, Baruch mourned Fritz. He was saddened that the opportunity to reach out to him no longer existed, that it hadn't for years. With the loss of his home in mind, he wondered whether he could have turned to his father for advice. He imagined Fritz alive, embracing him and saying, "You'll stay with me. We'll take care of each other."

As it was, he felt as if he were dangling above a pit with nowhere to go. He was furious with Lisa for lying to him, for giving up the flat he'd counted on being his future home. Rabbi Blum had suggested he go to Rabbi Tubol and put his future in his hands. But that wasn't acceptable to Baruch. He didn't want to be sent somewhere where everyone and everything was unfamiliar, somewhere he'd have to turn inside out once again, and take on yet another identity. Even moving in with Lisa and Roger seemed preferable to living among strangers.

Scarcely a week after Baruch had found out about his father's death, he learned to his astonishment that Rabbi Blum's father was sick. They were sitting side by side in the rabbi's office when Rabbi Blum told Baruch, "My dad has cancer. I might have to return to Detroit soon to help my mother care for him."

"No, you mustn't!" Baruch blurted. It was hard enough that they must part in August, let alone sooner.

"You're upset, Baruch. I am too. Let's try to be optimistic. The chemotherapy may work. My dad could rally. I might not have to go… Come, let's do our studying as usual."

A section from the bible about Joseph was on the desk. Baruch read it aloud. He felt vulnerable, upset. Why, Rabbi Blum might leave him at any moment. There might not be time to cast away his cowardice and tell Rabbi Blum the reason he'd come to Yeshiva. He needed to tell him before they separated for good.

Coming to the part where Joseph's brothers cast him in a pit, Baruch broke down and sobbed. He was Joseph. He'd been cast into jail and abandoned.

"What's wrong?" Rabbi Blum asked with concern.

"It makes me remember when I was in jail." The words he'd been holding back for so long had at last slipped out.

"Jail?"

"Rabbi Tubol didn't tell you?"

"No."

Baruch was impressed that the head of the Yeshiva hadn't spoken about the robbery and shooting to Rabbi Blum. Discretion—control over one's tongue—was admired at the Yeshiva. One wasn't supposed to even point at individuals when counting members of a group, as it might bring those persons bad luck.

"What did you do?" Rabbi Blum asked. When he got no answer, he said, "You don't have to tell me."

Baruch felt an overwhelming need to unburden himself. He must speak the truth before Rabbi Blum left! "I went to rob a house. The man who lived there came home. I shot him."

"Oh, no!" Rabbi Blum gasped. "How terrible. Did he die?"

"He lived. But I could have killed him. I did what a murderer does. That makes me a murderer, doesn't it? I've been honest like you wanted me to be. Now you know who I am. Do you hate me?"

Rabbi Blum placed his hand on one of Baruch's and squeezed it. "How can I judge you? I've made mistakes too. I know what it's like to feel responsible for a death, or in your case, a near death."

"Did you shoot someone?" Baruch asked with astonishment. They were brothers, twins, who'd sinned the same way. He stared at Rabbi Blum, and saw he was wrong. This mild, sad, subdued man who loved the violin had never held a gun.

"You don't have to pull a trigger to feel guilty. It's hard to know where responsibility begins and ends. The problem is guilt often gets out of hand. A disciplined person learns to subdue self-hatred before it becomes a sickness. Don't make yourself higher than *HaShem,* Baruch. God healed the man you shot. You're not a murderer."

"So you believe in God."

"In this case, yes."

"Thank you," Baruch said. Calm descended on him. He was filled with love towards Rabbi Blum for listening, for not hating him. If anything, they were closer than ever. This surprised and moved him. For the first time, he was willing to consider that *HaShem* had extended his arm and shielded him from becoming a murderer. Belief was trembling right before him. Yet, somehow, he couldn't seize it.

"I better go," he said and rose. He needed to be alone after his revelations.

At the office door, he stopped and considered apologizing for troubling Rabbi Blum while he was worried about his father. But he couldn't. He had to let him know the worst. An apology would be false. The rabbi told him to come back for another meeting the next evening. Baruch said he would.

In the courtyard, he sank down on a bench, heard a far-off jackal howl. He'd told his sins to his beloved teacher. He was grateful for Rabbi Blum's gentleness, as well as curious about what the rabbi had said about his own mistakes.

The next day Baruch walked into Talmud class, took his seat, glanced at Rabbi Blum, and looked away, shyly.

Rabbi Blum said the subject to be discussed was *Tshuvah*, an act of repentance usually performed around the Jewish New Year. People must apologize to those they've wronged. *Tshuvah* had to be performed in person. A letter or telephone call was too distant. You must stand before the individual you injured so he could look into your eyes and see your sincerity. It was like being naked. The apology must never be perfunctory. It must come out of self-searching and a desire to change. If you aren't forgiven, you were to go back to apologize again, and then a third time.

"*Tshuvah*," Rabbi Blum said, "is a way of transforming yourself. In the end, you became worthy of *HaShem*'s forgiveness. It is He who forgives, even if the wounded person refuses to do so."

At the end of class, an agitated Baruch rushed away. He was disappointed in Rabbi Blum. What he'd said to Rabbi Blum was confidential. He hadn't expected to hear it referred to in a class discussion. Even though he wasn't specifically named, he was resentful. All day, he planned on what he'd say when he met with the rabbi that evening.

"What's wrong?" Rabbi Blum said the moment Baruch walked into his office.

"Your lecture about *Tshuvah* was directed at me. What I told you was private," Baruch spat out.

"It is private. I thought everyone would benefit. There are others besides you who've done things they regret. I wanted to help them too."

"Oh," Baruch said, feeling foolish. Everyone else at the Yeshiva appeared to be on the highest ethical plain. It had never occurred to him that other students were beset by guilt. It was comforting to know there were a few exceptions to the general perfection. He wondered who they were.

Rabbi Blum sat patiently behind his desk. When Baruch didn't speak, he asked him to take a seat. In a subdued voice, he asked, "Are you going to make *Tshuvah* to the man you shot?

"I can't. He's in California. I'm here. You said 'in person.''

"It's not good to delay such things," Rabbi Blum mused.

"Even when my time here is over, I don't know where I'll be...I can't do it."

Rabbi Blum pushed his chair away from his desk. His forehead creased, he seemed to be thinking hard. "It's better for you to talk in person with him. But that's not possible. In this case, you should telephone."

"Talk to him?" Baruch gasped, remembering Sam Zeiger's cry of 'Shame!' in

Judge Thorn's courtroom. "How could I phone? I'll say, 'Hi, I'm the kid who shot you.' You know what will happen? He'll slam the receiver down. Then there will be two more times to apologize. So I'll phone back. He won't pick up, and if he does, it will only be to curse me out."

"And what if he were to let you speak your piece?"

"He won't." Sam Zeiger had wanted him sentenced harshly to the Youth Authority, not to have the privilege of attending a Yeshiva in Israel. Baruch didn't wish to crawl on his belly to someone who would never forgive him.

"What if he did?" Rabbi Blum persisted.

"Don't ask me to do this. Don't you see? I'm scared to do it. I'm too ashamed."

"Write a letter, then. Trust me. It will help."

The rabbi glanced out the window at the night sky, then back at Baruch. He looked tired and sad.

Sorry to worry him while he was upset about his father, Baruch quickly promised, "I'll write him tonight."

Jakob was already asleep when Baruch turned on his desk lamp and sat down to write his letter. Sam Zeiger's address had been read aloud in court. It took Baruch only an instant to remember Five Magnolia Lane, and jot it down on a pale blue airmail envelope. On a sheet of onionskin paper, he began to write. Every sentence slid further away from what he meant to say. 'I'm sorry' was poor compensation to someone you nearly killed.

As he set aside draft after draft, an imaginary Sam Zeiger looked over his shoulder, snorting, "How do you find the nerve to write to me after what you've done?" Baruch didn't have the nerve. He couldn't bear admitting his guilt to someone who hated him. He'd have preferred to beat himself with a belt, a punishment he'd almost inflicted when he was at his lowest ebb after he got out of jail. But he'd promised Rabbi Blum he'd write! He persevered.

On his sixth draft, he began to enter the spirit of *Tshuvah*. The words flowed almost faster than he could write them down. He was no longer addressing the red-faced Sam Zeiger he'd last seen in the courtroom.

Baruch strove to believe that Zeiger's twisted, angry features were only a mask, concealing a spark of holiness. This holiness would come alight when the letter arrived. The rabbis at the Yeshiva taught that enemy yearned to embrace enemy, that every effort to reconcile brought the Messiah closer. With all his being, Baruch hoped this was true.

February 6, 1984

"Dear Mr. Zeiger,

I'm a stranger, but you know me. I'm the boy who shot you while my buddy and I were robbing your house. I know I hurt you badly in a lot of ways, and I'm probably stirring up bad memories for you. When I saw you in court, I wanted to throw myself at your feet and ask your forgiveness. Instead, I'm doing it a year and a half later.

After my trial I went to Israel to a Yeshiva. I've led a strict, religious life. By teaching me high ethical standards, the rabbis have made me detest what I did. I'm so sorry that I broke into your house and shot you. My grandparents and my mother were hurt too. They'd expected me to behave decently. They wanted to be proud of me. I brought them shame.

I've tried to make up for what I've done by living a religious life. That is not enough. I'm still tortured by guilt. I realize that I can't make good on my own. I must reach out to you.

Humbly, I beg you to forgive me.

My name is Baruch now, not Karl."

Baruch sealed the letter in the envelope, stamped it and slipped it under his pillow. He'd mail it to Sam Zeiger tomorrow. Not wanting to take a chance that Jakob or a cleaner would come upon his discarded letter drafts, he carried them out to a gigantic dumpster at the rear of the cafeteria. Baruch opened it a crack, a space just wide enough to slip the drafts through. The reek of rotting food nauseated him. He let the heavy lid down carefully. Even so there was a metallic clang. He hurried off to the dorm and went to sleep.

Early the next morning, Baruch felt for the envelope under his pillow and slipped it into a notebook. Jakob was in the bathroom brushing his teeth. Baruch stamped and addressed two more envelopes and put those in his notebook too. While everyone else was filing into the cafeteria for breakfast, he went to the Yeshiva's main office. At the Xerox machine he made two copies of his letter, one for Lisa, the other for Grandpa Al and Grandma Bernice. He put those in the stamped and addressed envelopes he'd brought, intending to send them—his way of making additional *Tshuvah*. The original went to Sam Zeiger. All three envelopes were tossed into Shloime's makeshift cardboard mailbox.

For two weeks, Baruch checked the mail every day except on *shabbes*. He received no letter from Sam Zeiger, his grandparents, or Lisa. He dialed his mother's new phone number and, after she greeted him, inquired about his letter.

"Oh, that," she said. He tried to draw her out, but the only thing she said about it was, "Very interesting." All she wanted to talk about was her visit to a new Chinese restaurant with Roger.

Her flippancy about his apology hurt. But what did he expect? Lisa couldn't bear to speak of painful matters. 'The past is best-forgotten,' was her policy. The letter to his grandparents was returned four days after his phone conversation with Lisa. The stamp he'd affixed had fallen off. The letter had never left Israel. Stamped messages on the envelope told the sorry story of how it had been sent around the country. Shloime's criticisms of the Israeli mail system were true. Feeling discouraged, Baruch stashed the undelivered letter away in the back of a drawer.

That night, he wrote Sam Zeiger a second letter.

22

Albany, California, 1972

One morning in late August, Karl went over to Phil's at his usual time. Lisa accompanied him. Phil, she knew, was by himself. Joy had gone off to Kansas to visit her sister. Before leaving, she'd handed Lisa a note card with the phone number where she could be reached.

"I'm a bit uneasy about leaving Phil by himself," she'd confided. "He's so stubborn. He won't let me know if he gets sick. Please keep an eye on him."

Walking up the three steps to Phil's front porch, Lisa told herself, "Better late then never." She'd let three days pass without checking on Phil. Truth to be told, she'd come today with her own purpose. Lisa wanted to enlist Phil. He must help Karl accept the terrible news she was going to deliver later that day.

Too distraught to tell Karl when she'd first learned that Fritz was dead, she'd decided to wait until just after his sixth birthday. That occasion had passed last week. She still felt distraught. No end of her grieving was in sight. But she couldn't delay any longer. If she didn't tell Karl, someone else might. Also, he had a right to know that his father wasn't deliberately ignoring him. Forgiving herself in advance for a white lie, she planned on telling Karl that Fritz had been on the way to come live with them. That's when the car crash occurred. She'd take Phil aside this morning and tell him that too, so he'd know best how to console Karl in the coming days.

She knocked on Phil's door. Phil appeared. He greeted her and said to Karl, "Sorry buddy. You can't visit today. I've got a scratchy throat. I'll let you know when I'm better." He shut his door.

On the way home, Lisa considered phoning Joy. She decided 'a scratchy throat' wasn't significant. Why worry Joy? The poor woman worked hard and needed a vacation. Phil would recover in a couple of days. Lisa decided she'd wait until Phil was well before she told Karl about Fritz.

Phil didn't come out to wash his car that day or the next. Bird droppings splotched the Ford. Karl turned on the hose and washed the car on his own. Two mornings later, he picked a bouquet of sour grass and set the bouquet outside Phil's door. In the afternoon, his gift was still there. Lisa decided she'd better check on Phil.

With Karl at her side again, she knocked on Phil's door. No one answered. Karl grabbed his offering and ran after Lisa as she circled around to Phil's garden and unlatched the gate. The lawn was over-grown. Phil hadn't mown the grass like he usually did. Stepping onto the back porch with Karl, she pounded on the back door. Phil still didn't answer.

Lisa cried with alarm, "Please Phil, open up." She felt sorry she'd dismissed his sore throat, hadn't informed Joy.

A stubble-cheeked Phil opened the door a crack. "What ya' want?" he grumbled. He wore a faded terrycloth bathrobe. The robe hung loosely on him. With his false teeth out, his face looked crumpled and his bare gums showed. Usually, his hair was parted in the middle and slicked back with hair crème. But now it was uncombed. White showed at the hair roots.

"You look terrible," Lisa blurted.

Phil croaked, "I got one hell of a throat."

Karl handed him his bouquet. Phil scarcely looked at him.

"Can I get you anything? What can I do?" Lisa asked.

"Nothing. Just leave me alone."

Lisa stared at Phil and shook her head. "Joy left me her phone number. I'm going to call her. She'll take care of you."

"Don't go interfering and worrying her. I can manage fine on my own," Phil cried and slammed the door.

At home, Lisa made a cup of tea. Halfway through her cup, she drained the remaining tea in the sink, and made the long-distance call to Joy, who came home the next morning. Two days later Phil died. Karl was inconsolable. He barely ate. Nightmares about monsters tormented him. Lisa realized that the news of his father's death must wait.

As time went by, she knew she should tell Karl about Fritz, but she delayed. If he grieved so deeply for a neighbor, how would the news about his father affect him? She'd put off telling him until he was seven or eight; mature enough to not be devastated. At eight, he was having difficulties at school. She decided to wait until he was eleven. Eventually, it no longer seemed pressing to let him know about his father's death. Whatever Karl thought about Fritz, he kept to himself, the same as her.

Besides, coward that she was, she feared he might rebuke her for not telling him sooner.

23

Israel, 1984

Wanting to be done with the *Tshuvah* ritual, Baruch wrote a third letter to Sam Zeiger. He walked over to the *kibbutz* store to buy postage and to mail it, feeling certain there'd be no response. In this case, Lisa was right about burying the past. He must mail his letter, then make every effort to forget Sam Zeiger ever existed.

The *kibbutz's* policy was to rotate jobs, and Rhonda's turn to be storekeeper had come around again. She was standing in the doorway, dressed in a t-shirt and shorts, her red hair in braids. Remembering the last time they'd interacted, he wasn't surprised when she blocked the doorway and said, "Can't come in."

"Let me in," Baruch demanded. He wasn't in the mood to play, wanted to get this final letter to Sam Zeiger on its way.

"Make me," Rhonda said pertly.

"I need stamps." Baruch waved his envelope.

Rhonda snatched it out of his hand. "I need stamps too. Stamp my lips with a kiss," she crowed. She ran off. "Come on catch me." Cows lowed in the fields. Crows cawed and rose in a blazing blue sky.

"Give me back my letter," Baruch cried, breathless, furious. Yet when she let him catch her, and leaned up against him, he liked her pressing against him. He liked it even better when she flung her arms around his neck and drew his head down. Dry lips on dry lips, electric current zipping through Baruch. He was dizzy, could barely stand.

"Come, we'll mail your letter." The terse way Rhonda spoke told Baruch that the kiss was a joke she'd played on a Yeshiva boy, that she'd laugh about it later with her friends. Inside the store, she sold him stamps and tossed the letter to Sam Zeiger in a box for outgoing mail. It was if Mr. Zeiger had played a trick on him too. Baruch felt foolish, humiliated. Yet he came back the next day on the pretext that he needed a new razor, and the day after, to buy socks. Each time, Rhonda kissed him, harder and longer. By his fifth visit, Baruch saw her joke had boomeranged. Rhonda needed him. She took him for a walk, showed him a dilapidated cottage that stood alone in a field. There was nothing but a ripped mattress inside. She said they should meet there that night. Baruch agreed.

Back at the Yeshiva, he debated whether or not to go. An imaginary Phil weighed in with advice. "Don't get involved with this young lady. Just turn around and keep walking straight ahead."

The argument that swayed Baruch was, 'I'm not Karl any more.' He'd become someone who considered the repercussions of his behavior. This willing, crazy girl would tell people what they were doing. The story would get back to Rabbi Tubol who'd immediately expel him. He could still be sent to Y.A., even at this late date. The moon came up, and the time had come to meet Rhonda. Baruch yearned to go to the deserted cottage. His relief was great when the danger was over. Rhonda had to have tired of waiting for him and left. He was in his own world again, free, unfettered.

This private victory came a week in advance of Passover. The Yeshiva students were anticipating the holiday, Baruch along with them. New clothes were purchased in Jerusalem. There was talk about the special foods ordered by the kitchen staff, including strictly prepared matzos.

The day preceding the *Seder*, everyone labored to purge all corners of the Yeshiva of non-Passover foods. Counters, cabinets and kitchen appliances had to be scrubbed; the usual dishes, pots and pans, were put away; special ones for Passover were taken from a storage place; the dorm rooms were scoured for breadcrumbs, including inside drawers and closets. The purification rituals took on a personal meaning for Baruch. He was washing away his experiences with Rhonda.

Combing through his desk drawers as he cleaned, he came upon the copy of his first letter of apology to Sam Zeiger that he'd intended his grandparents to have. With little hope that they'd respond, he put it in a fresh envelope. Jakob sold him a stamp when he said he didn't want to go to the store. Baruch ran down to the office and threw the letter into Shloime's out-going box.

Students were too busy that night to sleep more than two or three hours. Weary, in an excited state of anticipation, no one was surprised when a boy had an attack of nerves. Baruch overheard a tearful phone call home, Leib saying to his parents, "I'll miss being at your *Seder*."

The next evening, the cafeteria was transformed. Small tables had been pushed together into two long rows joined by a head table for the rabbis. Vases of delicate desert flowers decorated the tables. The students and rabbis lined up for hand washing. Taking the pitcher and basin in turn, each poured a symbolic dribble over left and right hands, while reciting a prayer.

Baruch's turn came. He performed the ceremony carefully as if the goodness of it must last him the rest of his life. This Passover was the final one that he'd share with his friends before they dispersed all over the world. His future was uncertain. This would be their very last *Seder* altogether!

After the candles were lit, everyone took a seat. The tables were laden with platters of ritual foods—*matzo*, hard-boiled eggs, parsley, horseradish, bowls of *charoset*— chopped dates and nuts mixed with wine. There were carafes of red wine. *Haggadahs* were passed out, booklets with the step-by-step story of the events leading to the enslavement of the Jews—their misery and escape from Egypt; Moses' receiving the Torah at Mount Sinai.

Each student in turn read a paragraph. A brimming goblet of wine was set out for the Prophet Elijah. Elijah was an invisible angel who, at the proper moment when the door was opened, would step inside. During the *Haggadah* reading, everyone partook in the ritual foods and wine. The wine was sweet, like candy. It warmed Baruch's face, comforted him.

A meal of soup, salad, and roast chicken was served. The *matzo* made his mouth dry. He reached for the wine carafe and filled his glass again and again. By the end of the meal, his head was spinning.

Rabbi Tubol stood up. He was dressed in a *kittel*, a long, white robe. He droned,

"On Passover, in particular, we ask questions…"

"The famous four questions," Baruch tittered. His tongue felt numb.

"Shhh," Jakob whispered.

Baruch gazed at him with resentment. Jakob wasn't returning to a home where he might feel unwelcome. In Johannesburg, he'd plop into Mama and Papa's arms. "Darling *Eema* and *Abba*." "Darling Jakob." Soon he'd marry, and he and his wife would move to the same block as his parents, where his ancestors hovered protectively a foot or so above his roof. Or so Jakob believed.

As one rabbi after another rose and spoke, Baruch was too tipsy to focus on what they were saying. But he made every effort to concentrate when Rabbi Blum stood up.

Rabbi Blum said, "Passover is a celebration of freedom, not just from Egyptian slavery, but from ignorance and unenlightened behavior. The Passover story begins in turmoil, sorrow and slavery and ends in vibrant freedom and rejoicing because we have the Torah to guide our lives…"

Baruch's eyes filled with tears. There'd been no rejoicing for Moses. He hadn't been permitted to enter Israel with the Jews. He'd had nowhere to go, was homeless, shut out. Rabbi Tubol was staring at Baruch. Hurriedly, Baruch wiped his tears away with his paper napkin. He crumpled the napkin, pressed it with his fist.

The time had come to open the door for the Prophet Elijah. Each boy wanted to be chosen. Rabbi Tubol gave a majestic nod to Baruch. He was astonished to be so honored—and uncertain he could get to his feet and do it.

After a nudge from Jakob, Baruch forced himself up, hurtled clumsily to the door, and opened it a crack. It surprised him to hear Rabbi Tubol laughing and calling out, "Open the door wider, Baruch. He's a big man." Rabbi Tubol must like him. Otherwise why did he choose him? Why did he make a joke?

Baruch felt a slight breeze, as if someone was going past. He stumbled back to his seat, feeling proud. All around people were smiling. Love surged through him. The rabbis and students were his family. The Yeshiva was his home! His heart was brimming like the cup of wine waiting to quench the Prophet Elijah's thirst.

He stared with wonder as students slapped the tables and joyously belted out the traditional song, *Had Gadya*. It meant 'one only baby goat,' and was serious and silly at the same time. The insignificant goat was connected, as all things were, to everything high and low in creation. Whenever the baby goat was mentioned, everybody bleated.

To Baruch, the song meant there was hope. He too had his place. His was here at the Yeshiva. The students were going off soon, but after they left new ones would arrive. He'd find friends among them.

At the end of the *Seder*, everyone streamed out of the cafeteria to the courtyard. The stars and a bright moon hung overhead in the sky. It was late. The students went to the dorm, the rabbis to their residences. The cool night air was sobering to Baruch. He caught up with Rabbi Blum and asked, "Can I speak to you?"

Rabbi Blum nodded. "Come, let's sit down." He motioned to the stone bench. They sat in silence, waiting for the courtyard to clear.

Once they were alone, Baruch said, "I know what I want to do after I graduate. I want to stay here."

"In Israel?"

"Yes. Here."

Rabbi Blum's mouth fell open. "You mean *here*? Here at the Yeshiva?"

Baruch nodded.

"I know the Yeshiva feels like your home, but you'd limit yourself by staying. The courses would be the same. Not that there isn't always more material to explore, but you ought to move on to new challenges."

"Please... after another year, I'll be ready. Right now, there's nothing else I want to do. I'm used to this place. I know how to act. I feel safe. If I go, I'll...I'll mess up again."

"You won't mess up, Baruch. You've changed. You've become a fine, decent young man."

"Please, I want to stay here!"

"What happened to your plans to return to your mother?"

"She's moved in with her boyfriend. There's no place for me."

"I see," Rabbi Blum sighed. "You'll have talk to Rabbi Tubol about your staying on. Go see him after Passover."

On the way to see Rabbi Tubol the following week, Baruch recalled how tense he'd felt the first time he'd knocked at the principal's door. Over a year and a half later, he was still apprehensive. Eighty-two year old Rabbi Tubol had begun walking with a cane and using a magnifying glass to read. Despite his infirmities, the stern old man dominated every encounter with Baruch.

"*Shalom*. Have a seat," the rabbi said.

"*Shalom*, Rabbi Tubol," Baruch mumbled, cowering at the rabbi's gaze. He was used to Rabbi Blum, whom he loved as both a father and brother.

"Rabbi Blum told me that you don't care to go back to California."

"My mother isn't orthodox. It would be impossible for me to live a kosher life with her."

"Tell me about your father. Would he support your Jewish observance?"

"He died when I was five."

"I'm sorry. My father died when I was young too. It's a terrible loss. Are you in contact with his family?"

"They're Austrian."

"Austrian Jews, of course. So few survived." The rabbi shook his head sympathetically.

He knew the rabbi would disapprove of a mixed marriage—particularly to an Austrian! In Rabbi Wolfe's Holocaust class, Baruch had learned about the rampant anti-Semitism in Austria. He'd seen films showing jubilant Austrians waving flags with swastikas as they welcomed the invading Nazi army. They considered the Germans their liberators.

Rabbi Tubol, the scion of generations of learned, pious Jews, was known to believe in the significance of bloodlines as ardently as any Nazi. His belief was that even unknown ancestors influenced the family members who succeeded them. The possibility that Baruch might be descended from Nazis would horrify him.

"Not Jewish, Rabbi," Baruch said, reluctantly. He couldn't bring himself to lie. Not after he'd finally been honest with Rabbi Blum. To lie now seemed like a betrayal of that relationship.

There was a sudden pallor in Rabbi Tubol's wrinkled face. He licked his lips as if his mouth were dry. Baruch braced himself for an icy dismissal. The rabbi said, "There are many places you can lead a kosher life besides our Yeshiva."

Baruch took this to mean that as he was probably a descendent of Nazi, or Nazi sympathizer grandparents, he was no longer welcome. "Please, let me stay," he begged. "I don't expect another scholarship. I'd work in the kitchen or cleaning, or whatever's needed to cover my expenses. I'd try hard to be a good Jew. I need to stay here. I'm not asking for more than another year. Just…"

Rabbi Tubol held up his hand to stop Baruch's pleading, and asked, "When is your birthday?"

Baruch was encouraged. Perhaps there was hope. He said eagerly, "I'll be eighteen in August."

Rabbi Tubol shook his head. "It's not going to work. You'd be drafted once you turn eighteen."

"How can they draft me? I'm American."

"You were born here. That makes you a citizen. Do you want to join the army?"

"No!" Baruch stared at his hands. He didn't want to touch a gun ever again. "I don't want to be in the army."

"Then you can't remain in Israel. You could argue to the government that you're religious and want alternative service, but I don't think they'll grant you an exemption. The circumstances under which you came here would come out and work against you. So… where besides Israel would you like to go after you complete your Yeshiva studies? It must be a city with an observant Jewish community."

"I have to think about it," Baruch said dully. He wanted to remain here, assuming Rabbi Blum would be here too. His teacher's kindness and wisdom had transformed his life.

"When you decide, come see me."

Baruch stood up and said, "I'll probably be going back to California."

Rabbi Tubol began to say something, but Baruch was too upset to listen. "Thank you for your time, Rabbi." He fled from the office and raced upstairs to Rabbi Blum's. He hoped for sympathy and guidance.

The door to his advisor's office was partly open. Baruch stepped inside without knocking as he'd done many times before. He could barely believe his eyes. Rabbi Blum was stooped over his desk, sobbing.

"What's happened? What's wrong?"

Rabbi Blum looked up, his mouth twisted in a grimace. He tried to speak but couldn't. He took several deep breaths. Taking out his handkerchief, he used it to wipe his eyes and blow his nose. After he'd composed himself sufficiently to speak, he told Baruch, "My father...I just heard on the phone. We thought he had more time left. He died, suddenly."

Baruch sank into a seat and tried to absorb the news. He remembered how sorrowful he'd felt when he'd learned Fritz was dead. Rabbi Blum must feel worse. "I'm sorry," he said, wishing he could think of better words to comfort his friend.

"Tomorrow, I fly to Detroit for the funeral."

"You're...you're going away."

"I have to...the funeral...and afterwards, my mother may need me to stay a while."

"Do you think you'll be back before August?"

"I don't know. It depends on how she's managing."

For a while, neither spoke, then Baruch blurted, "Rabbi Tubol said I can't stay on another year."

Rabbi Blum's eyes darkened with sympathy. He said gently, "He can help you with other plans."

"This is goodbye for us, isn't it?"

"Probably."

Baruch had known their parting was inevitable, but had hoped that it wouldn't come so abruptly. If only they were brothers. If only they could travel to Detroit and mourn together, each for his own father. If only Rabbi Blum was his father. The perfect father! Baruch blurted, "I'm nothing without you."

"You're something. You're a real person on your own. *Emes,* the truth." The rabbi smiled, trying to coax a smile from Baruch.

Baruch didn't respond. He felt as if a river current was sweeping Rabbi Blum away.

"I've erred if I've made you dependent on me. It's time for you to move on. You have to find your way in the world. You'll manage. You've accomplished so much. You must be strong."

"Can I use your phone to call you in Detroit?" Baruch asked in a choked voice.

"Of course. You didn't need to ask."

Before they parted, the rabbi fumbled inside one of his desk drawers and said, "Here's my extra key. With everything uncertain, I better lock up this time."

The next day, when the rabbi was about to leave, Baruch stood a little apart from the students who thronged about their beloved teacher to say goodbye. Baruch was silent, full of regret for last night's outburst. To draw attention to his own needs—his anxiety about the future, his grief at their separation—had been selfish. Rabbi Blum wanted him to be stronger, more independent.

The students ran after the departing taxi, clamoring to their teacher: "Come back soon." "You're the greatest." "We'll miss you." They passed the *kibbutz's* orchards, black plastic covered fields, and cottages. The acacia in front of the store was blossoming. Baruch wondered whether Rhonda was inside. He hadn't visited the store since he'd stood her up for their date at the cottage.

The black taxi disappeared out of sight. Panting, sweating, covered with dust, the Yeshiva students started back. They talked about Rabbi Blum's generosity. Baruch focused on imagining his teacher's arrival in Detroit. Rabbi Blum would have to sit *shiva*, a week's mourning in which he wouldn't be able to bathe. Black cloths would cover all the mirrors in the house. He must wear slippers or socks instead of shoes; he must sit on a wooden crate instead of a cushioned seat. If Baruch wished to reach him, he wouldn't be able to call. The rabbi couldn't speak on the phone until the *shiva* was over.

The students passed through the Yeshiva's gate. It was lunchtime. A fishy smell floated down the hall outside the cafeteria. A few boys held their noses and complained that last night's catfish would be served again. Jostling each other, they squeezed through the doorway and went to stand in the buffet line. Baruch wasn't hungry. Alone in the hall, he leaned against a wall and struggled not to cry. He mustn't. Rabbi Blum wanted him to be strong.

He dragged up to the second floor and let himself into Rabbi Blum's office. The shade was drawn. The darkened room was soothing. Baruch sat at the rabbi's desk, opened a bottle of water, poured some into Rabbi Blum's mug and drank from it. Though it was a warm day, he put on the green cardigan that hung on the door hook. The rabbi had forgotten to pack it.

24

Albany, California, 1984

Dear Mom and Dad,

I know you've been angry with Karl for the robbery and shooting, and even angrier with me for raising him in a way that didn't prevent him from these criminal acts. Surely I, like almost all parents, wanted the best for him. I do not put 'good intentions' forward as an excuse for myself. The outcome shows that whatever I did do was fumbling and stupid.

My regret is that I didn't avail myself of your advice and help, that we weren't a team, all working together to raise Karl well. My belief is that it's not too late. Karl's nearly done with his time at the Yeshiva. He'll be eighteen, old enough to fly off on his own. But having been incarcerated, he seems fragile to me. Surely the transition from the regimentation of a Yeshiva to ordinary life will be difficult. I hope when he returns, we'll work together to give him support.

Let's put old battles behind us. I'd like us to be close. How can I blame you for this or that in my childhood, when I see that I've scarcely been the perfect parent? I suspect there is no such creature. Every virtue has a dark side, a lack, a black hole in space into which one can inadvertently stumble.

If we become closer, I believe Karl will draw near too. I confess that he's upset with me. He found out that there was something important that I wasn't open to him about. Honesty is a high wire tightrope that only the most courageous can walk. And here am I, fluttering, poor in balance, but trying my best after a terrible mishap. Please, please, be on either side of me, holding my hands so I won't fall again. Please, please, do the same for Karl.

Love,

Lisa

25

Israel, 1984

An unexpected letter appeared in Baruch's mailbox cubby three days after Rabbi Blum departed. When the rabbi was able to speak on the phone, Baruch would tell him about the note he'd received from Grandpa Al and Grandma Bernice, their response to the copy of the letter he'd written to Mr. Zeiger. His grandparents' note was in the spirit of *tshuvah*. They said, "You've matured. The Yeshiva is a good experience. We're proud of you. It takes a man to apologize..." The message was, 'we forgive you,' and more than that. He was so proud—they said he was a man. He read and reread the letter with relief and happiness. When Rabbi Blum had explained the concept of *tshuvah*, he'd declared that *HaShem* forgave the repentant. His grandparents' letter showed Baruch that he needed forgiveness from flesh and blood people.

The rest of the week, he checked and rechecked his mail cubby, reaching inside with a trembling hand, hoping against hope that there'd be an envelope with the return address of Magnolia Lane.

On one of his visits to the main office, instead of checking for mail, he approached

Shloime and asked, "When's Rabbi Tubol free to see me?"

"I'll ask." Shloime slipped into his boss' office, returned shortly, and said, "Go on in, Baruch. He has a few moments."

Baruch knocked on Rabbi Tubol's door.

"Come in," the rabbi called, greeting him with a warm smile. "I was about to go looking for you so we could talk. You see *HaShem* wishes to spare an old man trouble. He brought you to me." He offered Baruch the padded chair not the hard one, told him to take a mint from a bowl he kept on his desk. "You've made up your mind?" he asked.

"Yes."

"Where do you want to go?"

The letter from his grandparents was in Baruch's pocket, giving him courage. "New York," he said.

"Good. That's all I wanted to know. I'll make phone calls and see if I can find work for you there. Drop by my office tomorrow night."

"But don't you need more time?" Baruch objected. He doubted a good position for him could be found so quickly. He had no skills, no high school diploma, or job experience, and he had a criminal history.

"I'll move heaven and earth," Rabbi Tubol promised as he picked up his telephone receiver and waved him off.

Baruch stepped out of the rabbi's office and went to the wall of wooden mail cubbies. Once again, there was nothing from Sam Zeiger. Baruch shuddered. Zeiger's silence seemed to announce a greater rejection: No one wanted, or would ever want him—not even his grandparents. After all, they'd only written him a letter in response to the one he'd sent. The reality of his presence might be harder to accept.

At their meeting the following evening—to Baruch's astonishment—a smiling Rabbi Tubol said, "I have a proposal for you. This is what you can do: You can be a live-in aide at a residence in Brooklyn. Religious services are held on the premises. You can count on everything being strictly kosher. It's run by Hasidic Jews."

"What exactly would I be expected to do?" Baruch asked uneasily. He was dismayed. He didn't want to live in a Hasidic enclave where he'd be expected to dress in the black Hasidic suit and hat and wear a beard and side locks. Ordinary, non-religious people would stare at him as if he were a freak. Must he take the position? At the Yeshiva, students weren't forced to follow a rabbis' advice, but they were taught to comply out of respect. Rabbi Tubol was not only the head of the school, but a scholar and related to distinguished rabbis. His guidance was an honor.

"You'd work with patients suffering from cerebral palsy, retardation, and other disabilities. Your job would be to bathe the patients, help them to dress, make beds. Many of them are incontinent. You'd have to change diapers. I won't deceive you. That might be the main part of the job."

It sounded depressing, especially the part about changing adult diapers. Of course, someone must do it. Baruch was ashamed to reveal his revulsion for the humble tasks that Rabbi Tubol had described. "May I think about it?" he asked. He needed to consult with Rabbi Blum. The week's *shiva* was over. Some of the restrictions had been lifted. Rabbi Blum could talk on the phone again.

"Come back in a day or two."

Baruch left Rabbi Tubol and raced upstairs. In the hallway, his stride slowed. With each step he thought of reasons he shouldn't phone Rabbi Blum. Their relationship had changed. The rabbi was no longer his advisor. That position now belonged to Rabbi

Tubol. The following semester, Rabbi Blum would have new students. Baruch couldn't burden him as before. Besides, he didn't wish to put the rabbi in the painful position of becoming an adversary to his boss.

Using the rabbi's key, Baruch let himself into the room. Everything—the desk where they used to study together, the dusty bookcases—reminded him of the last time they were here together when the rabbi was weeping at the news of his father's death. The rabbi's week of sitting *shiva* might be over, but his sorrow wasn't. It would be wrong to burden him. Jews were supposed to visit mourners, and departing, take a portion of the grief away. You weren't supposed to add to the bereaved person's worries.

Yet Baruch had to talk to someone. Since their heated conversation two months ago, he'd called Lisa only three times. During each of these calls, he'd inquired how she was, told her that he was well, then got off the phone as quickly as he could. He dialed her number. This time he wanted a more extended conversation.

Lisa picked up. Recognizing his voice, she greeted him warmly. "How are you?" That was Lisa, never a grudge-keeper.

"Fine. How's Roger?"

Neither of them mentioned the January call when Baruch had told her he knew his father was dead. Fritz was once more a forbidden topic.

Attempting a casual tone, Baruch said, "The head of the Yeshiva wants me to go to New York after I graduate and work at a home for disabled people."

"Wait! I thought you were coming to California?"

"I don't know where I'm going."

"You haven't consulted me. You don't need me," Lisa said in a petulant voice.

Baruch had thought she'd be relieved not to be responsible for him. Her hurt tone was unexpected. "I haven't decided for sure...I want to tell you about..."

Interrupting him, she asked, "What about college?"

"I never graduated from high school," Baruch spat out. All he wanted to talk about was the aide's job.

Lisa brightened. "You could pass the equivalency test. There are colleges that accept students without a high school diploma when there are exceptional circumstances."

Using one of Rabbi Blum's pens and a scrap of paper, Baruch doodled a hangman's post with a rope and a dangling stick figure. Lisa was far more optimistic about his chances than he was.

"They'd want to know why I dropped out of high school. They'll find out I've been in jail. If the head of the Yeshiva wanted to help me get into a place like Yeshiva University, it would be different. But he wants me to work at the home."

"What kind of work?"

"I'd be washing and feeding patients. I'd be changing adult diapers."

"Diapers," Lisa laughed. "No, definitely not. Absolutely, don't take it! Promise me, you won't!"

Baruch was grateful that she understood his distaste for the job. With a resigned sigh, he said, "I ought to be willing to help others who are less advantaged."

"I'd never take a job like that!"

"I know you wouldn't, Mom." He couldn't help but smile at the thought of her devoting herself to such work. Her philosophy had always been: enjoy the moment and move on. She never appeared bogged down by questions of right or wrong. A part of him wished he were more like her. If he were, it would be easier to refuse the aide's job.

Assuming a playful tone, Lisa said, "Well, that's settled. You must come home!"

How amazing that she felt he must! He was flattered, glad that she continued to press him to return. But as she spoke, he realized he no more wanted to live with her than go to a Hasidic residence. At Roger's flat, they'd be in close quarters where she'd witness his religious duties. She'd examine his prayer book, prayer shawl, phylacteries, *tzitzis* and skullcap. Each object had become part of him, as personal as a part of his body. His values, how he thought and the person he was, had changed. He couldn't return to live with her.

Gently, he said, "I'm sorry, Mom. It would be hard for me to keep kosher at Roger's."

"I understand," she said, huskily. "But do you have to take that aide's job? Isn't there anything else you could do?"

"I suppose I could ask Rabbi Tubol to find me something else." Until now, he hadn't considered the possibility. Yet his mother's support gave him courage. So did the thought that Rabbi Blum would encourage him to inquire about other possibilities. He'd always urged Baruch to speak up.

"Would that be in New York too?" Lisa said.

"New York has an observant Jewish community."

"You'll be near your grandparents," she said in a wistful tone. "They always wanted to raise you."

Attempting to soften his rejection, he said, "You come to New York. You'll see them too. We could have a family reunion."

They said goodbye, and Baruch headed back to the dorm. His room was dark. Jakob had gone to bed early. Baruch tiptoed to his desk. Once he flipped it on, his gooseneck lamp dropped a small cone of light on the desktop. Baruch carefully slid open the drawer in which he kept a stack of paper and took a fresh sheet. He wrote—

April 5, 1984

Dear Rabbi Tubol,

Thank you for helping me. But after much thought about the aide's job, I feel I'd rather not take it. Are there other positions available in New York City? I'd be grateful if you'd let me know.

Respectfully,

Baruch

The next morning, Baruch carried his letter about until he found a moment between classes to go to the main office. He feared his rejection of the proposed job might anger Rabbi Tubol, and he'd come up with a worse offer. Even so, he knew he must speak up. It wasn't necessary to have Rabbi Blum at his side to know that's what he'd advise him to do. Baruch walked up to Shloime's desk and waited for his attention.

Peering over the rim of a folder he'd been immersed in reading, Shloime asked, "*Nu*? What can I do for you?"

"I have a letter for Rabbi Tubol."

"Leave it with me."

After a moment's hesitation, Baruch handed it over.

Two days later Rabbi Tubol sent Shloime to summon Baruch to his office. The moment Baruch was seated across from him, the rabbi said, "I read your note. You said you don't like the aide's job."

Baruch stopped breathing. He felt as if he were in Judge Thorn's court waiting for his sentence.

"I've found a place for you with Rabbi Linderman's Hasidic group in New York City. Rabbi Linderman said he'd welcome you to his community, and will get you a job as an apprentice in the diamond trade. What is more, he will send money for your plane ticket."

"Why are both the jobs you've offered with Hasidim? Am I supposed to be a Hasid?"

"Do you object?"

"I want to follow what I've learned here at the Yeshiva..."

The rabbi interrupted and said calmly, "I've been teaching for a long time. Boys I've known have joined the Hasidim and found a satisfying life for themselves. When you came to us, here, everything about the Yeshiva was strange to you. Now, you wish you didn't have to leave. Take a chance. Spend time with the Hasidim in New York. Trust me, it's right for you. You'll live in a moral atmosphere that will help you to act righteously. Here you found friends, good friends like Jakob and Eli. With the Hasidim you'll discover more than friends. You'll have a family who will help you for the rest of your life. Spend time living with the Hasidim. If after a year you're dissatisfied, contact me. I'll do everything in my power to help you to fit in elsewhere."

Baruch gathered his courage and said, "I'm sorry you went to so much trouble. I won't do it."

"Tell me why."

"All of the *haredi* think and act alike, and do exactly what their rabbi says. Rabbi Blum taught me to think for myself!"

"Ah, Rabbi Blum. I wish he'd taught you more," Rabbi Tubol said, tapping his arthritic fingers together. Prominent veins crisscrossed the backs of his large hands. "I wish he'd taught that stereotypes of the Hasidim aren't accurate. There's great variety, many differences between groups."

Forgetting his manners, Baruch cried indignantly, "Why me? Why should I become a Hasid? You're not a Hasid. Nobody else at the Yeshiva is a Hasid. You're not treating any other student like me!"

"None of the others have your background," Rabbi Tubol said. His eyes narrowed into a fierce, burning gaze, emphasized by his thick white eyebrows.

"What do you have against me? Is this because I committed a crime?" Baruch cried.

"That…as well as other things. I'm recommending what I judge best, 'a fence around a fence.' Special precautions must be taken for you. You must be in a strict Jewish environment. In a more worldly setting, in a less strict setting, you'll lose the qualities you acquired here. I'm trying to help you."

Baruch hung his head. Rabbi Tubol believed the rigors of Hasidic life were necessary to cleanse him of his sins—and perhaps to cleanse him of his ancestors too, the ones who were Austrian and may have been Nazis.

"Don't lose hope." Rabbi Tubol's was voice gentle this time. "We will find what's best for you. Come to see me in a week's time. We'll talk again." Rising with difficulty, he placed out-stretched hands over Baruch's head and blessed him as Baruch had learned a father blesses his child on the Sabbath.

In deference to Rabbi Tubol, Baruch retrieved the pamphlet about Hasidism that had been languishing unread in his bottom desk drawer for over a year and a half. It was printed on cheap paper and poorly bound. Baruch took care as he turned the pages. He read that the Polish Gerer wore high crowned hats with rounded peaks, not at all like the Satmer's short flat hats; that the Lubovitcher didn't have the long sideburns called *peyes*; that Lubovitcher considered it their mission to be *shaliach*, messengers for their *Rebbi*, and went about trying to persuade non-observant Jews to practice their religion. Each sect reached towards God in a special way—song, dance, story telling, poverty, or on the contrary, through riches.

As a Hasid, Baruch learned, he'd be forbidden to watch television or movies, listen to radio or read secular newspapers. Contact, even casual contact with outsiders, was, in general, discouraged. Hasidim didn't ride on the subway or buses. Two years ago, Baruch was in jail. He didn't want to accept another type of confinement. The pamphlet convinced him more than ever that Hasidic life meant isolation. He feared a closing of his mind.

Meeting with Rabbi Tubol the following week, he took his seat and announced, "I thought about what you said. I don't think I can fit in with the Hasidim."

"Spend a *shabbes* with a Hasidic family in Jerusalem. Get to know them."

"I don't speak Yiddish."

"You don't have to for a short visit... Once you're in New York, it won't take you long to learn. You learned Hebrew. Yiddish is similar."

"The *haredi* in Jerusalem throw rocks at cars driving into *Mea Shearim* on the *shabbes.*"

"In Israel. Not in New York, as far as I know."

"I'm an outsider. They won't like me."

"In time, they'll accept you... Make an effort. Remember, 'a fence around a fence.'"

Baruch looked away, his face hot. He resented the pressure the old man exerted on him with his reiteration of 'a fence around a fence.'

"We'll talk again," Rabbi Tubol said. "Come to me in two weeks."

"What's the point of talking about it any more?" Baruch blurted.

"In a month you'll have had time to absorb what I've told you." Once again, the rabbi struggled to his feet and blessed Baruch.

When they met again, it was mid-May. There was a small fan on Rabbi Tubol's desk. Summer came early to Israel. The room was hot, the window open to allow a flow of air. From the courtyard came students' carefree cries. They knew what they were doing after graduation. Baruch's situation was different. He felt like flotsam with nowhere to land.

After an hour of arguing with Rabbi Tubol, he felt worn down. The Yeshiva head had decades of experience in Talmudic discourse. He was an expert debater, and stubborn.

"You're Baruch now," he said. "I don't want you to lose this identity." Baruch shrank inwardly. The rabbi had touched on his own fears. The rabbi stood up and blessed him, a signal their meeting was over. "We'll meet again in two weeks and talk about this some more," he said.

That evening Baruch lay awake in bed, his mind racing with soap bubble schemes that burst the moment he conceived them. Should he ask Aunt Eva for help? He barely knew her. Should he call his grandparents and beg them to let him move in with them? Would he get along with Grandpa Al and Grandma Bernice? Lisa hadn't. When he was ten, Lisa and her father had a fight. Lisa stopped taking Baruch to New York to see them.

Baruch didn't know what they'd expect from him, only that their standards were high, and that they were secular Jews who didn't keep kosher.

He tossed and turned in bed. Needing to escape the whirl of his thoughts, he called softly to Jakob, "Are you up?"

From the adjacent bed, Jakob said sleepily, "What is it?"

"Nothing." The room was silent. Baruch blurted, "I met with Rabbi Tubol today."

"What about?"

Baruch longed to confide that the rabbi was trying to force him to become a Hasid, but hesitated knowing Jakob would ask why. It had been hard enough telling Rabbi Blum about his criminal past. "Nothing," he said again.

"When a student meets with Rabbi Tubol, it's about something."

"He wanted to know whether I'd heard from Rabbi Blum," Baruch said, offering a lesser secret, hoping it would satisfy.

"Have you?"

"I got a post card from him two days ago." On the card, Rabbi Blum had scrawled, "Feel free to phone." Baruch had been tempted, but was proud that he hadn't. There were so many reasons not to call, including Rabbi Blum's warning that Baruch was too reliant on their relationship. Hard as it was for him, Baruch was trying to manage on his own.

"He's doing all right?"

Baruch's "Yes" ended the conversation with Jakob.

Lying in the darkness, he imagined he heard Phil's voice—"You don't need no phone to talk with me. So why'd ya need a phone to talk with that rabbi fella? And he ain't even dead. Just close your eyes so ya can concentrate, and you'll hear what he has to say."

Baruch closed his eyes, and posed his question, 'What should I do?' The words "Don't accede to a lifestyle you don't wish!" rose in his mind. Rabbi Blum would have said exactly that in person! Baruch felt strengthened in his resolve to resist Rabbi Tubol's demands.

They began to meet every other week, usually for only five minutes or less. Their struggle continued unabated through June and into July. During these brief encounters in which nothing new was said, Baruch stared at the office window and saw the desert become more and more parched. Sweat pasted his clothes to his skin. He felt as ineffectual as the small desktop fan. His efforts to sway Rabbi Tubol were futile. But he'd become as stubborn as his adversary. His resistance began to anger the old man. Sometimes, passing his wayward student in the halls, Rabbi Tubol barely nodded. He was obviously offended that a boy at his Yeshiva wouldn't submit to him.

Meanwhile, to Lisa's credit, she sent Baruch a check that would cover the cost of his airfare to California. Baruch didn't wish to consider returning to her an option. Yet perhaps he must. Each passing day brought him closer to the conclusion of his two years in Israel with no other plan for the future.

In mid-July, the Yeshiva students began to buy souvenir gifts to take home with them. On a Saturday night, Baruch tagged along to Jerusalem with a dozen of them. To his dismay, they went to shop in *Mea Shearim,* the religious section. He waited outside. Looking in through the shop window, he saw his friends buying copper Passover plates, *challah* covers embroidered in gold thread, silver spice boxes for the *havdallah* ceremony that marked the end of the *shabbes.*

Haredi thronged the cobbled streets, the men in black coats, knee-high pants and white stockings; the women in long skirts, their hair covered by scarves. Baruch couldn't bear to look at the way the women humbly followed a few feet behind their husbands. A *Rebbi* had arranged these couples' marriages. When Baruch married, he hoped he'd make his own choice, as would his future bride.

Two days later when he met with Rabbi Tubol, Baruch told him as much.

"The Hasidim are too extreme. They control everything, even the most personal matters," Baruch said.

The rabbi said, "Yes, they're extreme. Do you know why?"

Baruch shook his head. He was surprised and pleased that the rabbi had agreed with something he'd said.

"They think that control is necessary, that otherwise Judaism will be diluted and eventually disappear. Many of these people survived the camps. They believe their pious observance honors the relatives lost in the gas chambers. For a while, there was a trend among some Hasidim to dress in the modern way. But during the years following the war, they resumed dressing like their ancestors from Poland. They chose to become living memorials."

After leaving the rabbi, Baruch thought about what Rabbi Tubol had told him about the Hasidim grieving for a lost world and their taking on the sacred mission of preserving the Jewish traditions. Finally, Rabbi Tubol had made a crack in his resistance. The Hasids had a purpose he could embrace! That night, he was unable to sleep. Through his dorm room window he saw a star-studded sky and a bright moon. Throwing on his clothes, he rushed to the courtyard, and paced up and down. He sank down on the stone bench. The hard seat reminded Baruch of Rabbi Blum's *shiva*.

'Think for yourself' was Rabbi Blum's motto. Baruch had fought to honor this teaching. By now he was too tired and anxious to go on fighting. Despite their struggle,

Baruch had always believed that Rabbi Tubol wanted what he saw as best for his students. Shivering in the night air, Baruch resolved to go talk to him in a day or two, and say, "I agree to anything you say."

His submission would be a first step to accepting the leadership of the Hasid community.

The next morning, a long white envelope appeared in Baruch's mailbox. He didn't have on his glasses. Squinting, he saw his name above the Yeshiva's address. It was printed in block letters, the way an elementary school teacher might write for children who had not yet learnt script. There was no return address. With difficulty, Baruch made out a 'California' postmark. His heart hammered away. He guessed he'd received a note from Sam Zeiger. His first class was soon. He hurried to the dorm and left the unopened letter in the desk drawer where he kept mail from Lisa. All day, he delayed opening his letter but thought of nothing else.

That evening, Baruch remained at his desk after Jakob went to bed. He waited until he heard his roommate breathing regularly, then opened the envelope. Inside he found a piece of lined yellow paper, ripped from a pad. The neat printed signature at the bottom of the page read, 'Sam Zeiger.' Slouching in his desk chair, Baruch read the long-awaited letter.

"It was a shock to hear from you. I almost ripped up your letter. You, who hurt me physically and psychologically, want me to be generous to you. Can you imagine what it's like to find a couple of jerks robbing your home? Since the night you shot me, I haven't felt safe. I sleep at most one or two hours before I wake and start listening for footsteps. I needed pain pills because of the injury you inflicted. I became addicted to them. My former wife decided to stop my daughter's visits. She thought I was a poor influence. After that, I hated you more than ever, and kept hating you even after I kicked my drug habit and was allowed contact with my child again.

You wrote asking me to forgive you. My first reaction: Never! You might have put on a prayer shawl and skullcap, but that didn't mean you weren't still the punk who shot me. After your 'time' in Israel, I supposed you'd come back and take over where you left off, ripping off houses and shooting people. I figured, why should I bother writing back? Why should I lift as much as my pinky finger for you? Probably your rabbi dictated the letter you wrote and ordered you to send it.

All I wanted was to forget you and what you did to me. That's not how things worked out. Your letter nagged me. A voice in my head kept whispering, 'What if no one forced him to write and say he was sorry? What if the letter is a true apology?' My entire life I've tried to be a fair man. In spite of myself, I had to give you the benefit of the doubt.

I now believe you've changed and are trying to lead a decent life. I forgive you. There, I've written it. Maybe it will help us both."

Trembling, Baruch held the letter for a while before setting it carefully into a drawer. He turned off the desk lamp, undressed and prepared for bed in the darkness. Stretching out on his back, he let his head sink into his pillow. A long-held knot in his chest was loosening. He felt stronger, almost whole. Through the window across the room, he saw a black sky lit by a full moon. His room looked different. The cracks in the walls and ceiling made a fascinating map-like design.

He had doubted that Sam Zeiger and he could honestly address each other. But he'd apologized. His act of contrition and regret had created powerful electricity between them. Sam Zeiger forgave him. 'Sleep well,' Baruch told Mr. Zeiger in his thoughts. 'Don't be afraid any longer. It's over. You're safe." The same, he felt, was true for himself. He went to sleep, knowing he no longer had to accede to Rabbi Tubol's plan for him to join a Hasidic community. He wasn't going to work in the diamond district.

The following evening, he climbed the stairs to Rabbi Blum's office to phone his grandparents to ask for their help. It felt as if Sam Zeiger accompanied him, confirming, as Baruch climbed each step, that he was a good person. He knew now that no one achieved virtue on his own through fasting and other deprivations. A single individual couldn't heal anger and hurt. If not for Rabbi Blum, he would never have written to the man he shot. If not for that letter, Sam Zeiger wouldn't have responded. Goodness depended on connecting with others.

He must dare to, must risk seeking his grandparents help. He dialed their number. His grandfather answered the phone. "It's Karl," Baruch said.

"In your letter you said you call yourself Baruch."

"You remembered," Baruch said gratefully.

There was an awkward silence. They hadn't spoken in over two years. His grandfather's voice sounded like a stranger's.

"Why are you calling?"

"I want to come to New York," Baruch forced himself to say.

Grandpa Al demanded stiffly, "What are your plans exactly?"

This was the question Baruch had asked himself all day. He was prepared with an answer. "I'll take any job I can find. I'll also work on completing my high school equivalency certificate. Then I'll take college courses."

"To what purpose?"

"Grandpa, last winter, I did some volunteer work with boys who'd been in trouble. I enjoyed helping them." After a pause, he ventured. "I think I'd like to have some kind of counselor job." His heart beat hard. He expected his grandfather to dismiss his plan.

"You mean you'd study psychology?"

"Yes," Baruch said. He hadn't thought of 'psychology,' but out of the blue, one of his goals now had a name.

"Good plan," his grandfather said. Al called to Grandma Bernice, "Baruch wants to come to live in New York and study psychology."

"Will he live with us?" Baruch heard Grandma Bernice say.

"Get on the other phone and ask him yourself."

She did.

Baruch said, "I'll come if you'll have me."

"Will you keep kosher?"

"Yes."

There was a silence. He interpreted it as meaning his grandparents were reluctant to take him. Aside from his criminal history—they'd said they forgave him in their letter—kosher was fuss and bother. Unobservant Jews like his grandparents might not be sympathetic. Yet he must be kosher. It was a way to hold fast to being Baruch.

"You could kosher a corner of my kitchen," his grandmother said.

Baruch could tell she was struggling not to cry. He was amazed. She wanted him! Happiness flooded him.

"New York has many kosher restaurants. Why, there's a kosher restaurant right down the block," Grandpa Al said with enthusiasm.

In a short while, everything was settled. Baruch would live with them.

On Tuesday, the following day, Baruch set out for Rabbi Tubol's office. The Yeshiva Head had tried to help him. Baruch needed to tell him his new plans. Not that all apprehension about living on Park Avenue had disappeared. The arrangement might not last long. But he knew now that he was a deserving person. That made him optimistic, even confident that he'd be able to ultimately achieve his goals. Mr. Zeiger had conferred these gifts on him.

Entering Rabbi Tubol's office, he sat down in the chair where he'd often felt exposed and tormented. "Rabbi," Baruch said, "I want to study psychology. I want to work with boys who are in trouble. I liked doing that when I was a volunteer at the center in Jerusalem."

"To the Hasidim, their rabbi is their psychologist."

"I'm not going to become a Hasid!" Baruch said. He regretted the sharpness in his voice, but knew it was necessary. Rabbi Tubol must understand that he refused to become a Hasid. No one would force him.

"You have some other plans?"

"Yes. I've talked to my grandparents. I'm going to live with them."

Rabbi Tubol stared at him. After a while, he gave a nod of understanding. "Perhaps you could be a psychologist in another Jewish community."

"I don't want to work only with Jewish boys, but with any boy who could use my help."

"I see...will you keep your Jewish commitment?"

"I'll try hard."

"I can't change your mind."

"No."

"So be it."

The old rabbi stood but not to bless him. This time, he extended his arm so they could shake hands.

On the last week of term, there was an informal graduation ceremony. The students received certificates of completion at the Yeshiva. There was a party with cake, candy, and fruit juice. Afterwards, Baruch went to his dorm room to pack. He emptied drawers, dove under his bed to retrieve his slippers, reached up to the top of his closet to look for forgotten belongings. Jakob did the same. The two boys talked as they worked.

Jakob said. "Write me when you're settled, and I'll write back. I think of you as a friend for life."

"You've always stood by me. I'll never forget you."

Both boys had flights booked for the following morning. Their cab drove into the Yeshiva's courtyard where they waited with their bags on the concrete paving. The driver hoisted their two big suitcases into the trunk, along with Baruch's backpack. He had trouble fitting in Jakob's duffel too, and ended up putting it on the front seat beside him.

Baruch sat in the back next to his friend, staring out the windows at what he was leaving behind, the desert, distant hills and jagged mountains. At the Ben Gurion Airport, Baruch and Jakob stepped out of the car and retrieved their luggage. The taxi pulled away. People burdened by suitcases rushed past while the boys ignored them and embraced wordlessly. Two years before, they'd 'come up' to Israel. Now, they were 'going down,' one to South Africa, the other to New York.

Settling into his airplane seat an hour later, Baruch couldn't help but think back to that day, two years ago, when he'd left San Francisco for Israel. His mother had taken him to the airport. He'd only had time to scan her last letter which had come the day before. Taking it from his pants' pocket, he read it again.

26

Albany, California, 1984

Dearest,

You went off to Israel, and in the process you became someone else...not Karl, but Baruch. The letter you wrote Mr. Zeiger told me as much. You've become someone who perhaps judges me as harshly as you judge yourself. After your Aunt Eva told you about your father, weeks went by without your phoning. Then you phoned as if nothing had happened. But ever after, I felt there was a difference between us.

You asked Mr. Zeiger for forgiveness. Are you able to forgive me? I'm sorry that I was unable to tell you your father was dead. My intention was to protect you. You were only five. The news would have hurt you.

I see that I was wrong not to tell you later when you were older. By error, I left to chance how you found out about his death. Aunt Eva gave her interpretation of things she knew nothing about. You said she told you we shouldn't have gone to 'the drug commune.'

Don't you recall, Karl? You were content there. You loved being in the country. Do you remember the beautiful snowy woods? Yes, your aunt is right that your father took drugs while he was there. He was an idealistic person who wanted to make the world a better place. The opportunity to experiment with LSD was important to him. He said the experiences he had with LSD were the most profound of his life. He said that they shaped and helped him as an artist. His belief was that ultimately LSD would be the means to create peace between people.

Even now, it's difficult for me to talk to you about him. I've never accepted that he's dead. He lives on in my imagination. To me he's a hero, a man who despises the cruel ways people act to each other. He's clever, impulsive and out-spoken. You have many of his qualities. Now that your voice has deepened, it sounds exactly like his. The last time you phoned, I was shocked. For a moment, I thought it was Fritz. He was always full of surprises.

As soon as I can, I'm going to visit you in New York. I don't want a schism in our relationship when we see each other, not about your father…and not about other issues that might have arisen because of what you've been taught at the Yeshiva. So, I'm going to try to catch thoughts and feelings of mine that are as light as butterfly wings, and put them into words. I hope what I write to you will help you understand and keep you from being a harsh critic.

Here's the person I am. I try not to interfere with other people, not to suffer and worry, not to preach or take sides. I want to exist in this world as it is. I don't use the word sin, and I don't judge. When I accept the world's reality, I achieve vitality and happiness. To me guilt is neurotic. I don't rebel. I mind my own business and attempt to live naturally like an animal whose need is to fulfill her needs. Why is there so much judgment against sex? It's a natural activity. During sex, we are most present in our bodies. Why doesn't everyone understand this?

When you live with your grandparents, I hope you don't absorb their prejudices towards me. I'm sure you'll discover that my parents resent the fact that I don't work. They see me as a dilettante, flitting from one enthusiasm to another. They are right in a way, because I don't want to be a slave to any discipline. I choose to have the leisure to dream and create. I don't want to be dogged, but spontaneous. I choose to live joyfully. The tiny prison of routines isn't for me.

I don't pretend to be a member of a profession. It would be easier to put on the 'coat' of a specific job. I could tell others, "I'm a doctor...an accountant." The uniform would conceal my real identity. No one—including me—would have to look at who I actually was inside the coat. But there's no pin on my shirt saying I'm part of a larger group. I'm Lisa, and that is who I want to be, how I want to be. I find Henry David Thoreau a kindred spirit. He avoided work whenever possible. His desire was to go into nature to enjoy each moment, and to develop his own individuality.

At the commune and later here in California, I've tried to give you the freedom to develop and make your own choices. My parents criticize me. They say that I didn't discipline you. Your grandfather hurt me by saying, "You let your attention stray from your child." My reply is that by living my own independent life, I have given you a role model for yours.

So Karl-Baruch, you are free now. No judge is ordering you to do anything any more. What does freedom mean for you? Have the rabbis remade you in their image? I hope you'll find your own way. But whatever you'll choose to become I will accept with the hope that you will be as tolerant of the choices I make for my own life.

Please, remember that I am always—

Your loving mother,

Lisa

*   *   *

Made in the USA
San Bernardino, CA
17 August 2014